Rhunken Chronicles: Tongass

by Mark F. Mahoney

© Copyright 2020 Mark F. Mahoney

ISBN 978-1-64663-102-5

Published by

köehlerbooks™

210 60th Street
Virginia Beach, VA 23451
800–435–4811
www.koehlerbooks.com

Dedicated to

My brother Jim, friends Donna and Marcia, thanks for your help.

My wife Rochelle, thanks for everything.

My granddaughter, Colleen, for showing me true strength.

RHUNKEN CHRONICLES: TONGASS

MARK F. MAHONEY

VIRGINIA BEACH
CAPE CHARLES

CHAPTER 1

ON ONE FINE, SUNNY day.

Low tide was exposing the large bed of mussels clinging to anything not moving on the shoreline, and he couldn't help crushing some of them when stepping out of the raft and dragging it out of the water. The cold water seeped through a hole in his left boot, reminding him again to buy a new pair of boots. Xtratufs really didn't require breaking in like a regular set of leather hunting boots, so that wasn't the reason. He just found shopping a pain in the ass.

Unloading his gear from the raft took one trip. Then he made his way back out, stood the raft on its side and lifted it with his shoulder, carrying it instead of dragging it well above the high tide line. He tied the mooring line to a young spruce. His boat he had left anchored in the small bay. He never liked leaving the C-Dory unmanned, but he'd set the ground tackle with a full 7:1 scope.

In addition to his gray wool socks and heavy black canvas pants and jacket, he carried his old Ruger rifle, chambered-in .338 Winchester Magnum with a dinged wooden stock. A custom five-inch Smith and Wesson model 500 in its specially made bandoleer holster was strapped across his chest. Lastly, he bent over and carefully retrieved a small, wooden box wrapped in an old bath towel, secured with silver duct tape.

He knew the clothing and weapons were overkill for the task at hand, but he liked being prepared when roaming this land alone, especially this far from any kind of help. If you knew and respected this land it could provide just about everything you need. Nevertheless, become impertinent, take one miss-step, or even just get unlucky and this land will eat you.

He wasn't planning on pushing it this trip. He was just here to find a secluded spot for the box he carried with a view of the Tongass, so anything else was a bonus.

Brad Michaels had never set foot on this island before, though he'd drifted by it many times while fishing and never gave it much thought. If it had a name, he didn't know what it was. With over a thousand islands in the Alexander Archipelago, it was impossible to know all the names. His map didn't include names for the vast majority of them.

Brad had heard people say, "No one hunts there. There are no bears or deer on that island." It was one of the larger islands, well forested except for a rocky hilltop clear of trees. A small creek supported a run of chum and pink salmon, which would help with the hunting part of the trip. The fish spawning in such a small creek wasn't out of the ordinary. Chums and pinks will spawn in a cup of water if you leave it out too long. Despite what the self-proclaimed experts said, the fish run would make the island attractive to bears. Brad had learned quickly that if people didn't hunt there, the odds were the "dumb animals" had figured that out long ago.

Sure enough, within the first hour of his arrival he found sign of a big brown bear. Both new and old scat told him the old bruin had been here awhile and was set in his ways. So Brad set out on his quest, keeping an eye out for a good spot for an afternoon ambush.

This was Brad's favorite part, trying to pattern and then outsmart his quarry. The hunt itself.

A well-worn bear path made crossing the small marshy valley easier than it would have been if he was forced to cut his own way through the waist-high grass and willows. A small stream snaked slowly through the large wilting leaves of skunk cabbage and salmonberry bushes that were turning yellow. When crossing the crystal clear creek he could see and smell scores of dead and dying salmon that were hung up on snags and rocks or partially eaten on the gravel banks. There were also a few late running chums and pink salmon doing their best to spawn before they die. And while he couldn't see them, there would most likely be fat Dolly Varden swirling behind the salmon catching the eggs that didn't settle in the gravel, and who knows, maybe a sea run Cutthroat trout or two. He'd have to check this out with a fly rod later next spring when the Dollys and Cuts return to intercept the smolt trying to make their way to the sea.

After crossing the valley and climbing the far side ridge, he settled down on an outcropping of lichen-covered granite. That would also give his forty-year-old legs a rest. He carefully sat the box on the rock next to him and took in the slight warmth caused by the special appearance of the late morning sun peeking through a hole in the heavily overcast sky. Inhaling deeply, taking in the smells of wet grass and trees carried on the cool, clean air, he was thankful for the breeze carrying the smell of the hundreds of spawned-out salmon carcasses the other way.

Looking down the valley he'd just come up, he drank in the view of the surrounding hills, the light deepening the contrast between the grey-green peaks with their highlights of an early termination dust and the grassy meadow surrounded by hemlock, spruce and alder just starting to put on their fall colors. The little valley ended at the shore of the rocky ocean inlet that held his boat. His gaze widened across the wind-blown strait to the mainland mountains with their glaciers of ice and snow with its flowing white surface broken by dark moraines and crystal blue crevasses.

Brad had read many writers try to describe how beautiful this landscape was. Some had enough skill in the use of the English language to come close to giving the "feel" of a view like this, but he knew someone had to physically be there to truly experience its beauty. No, it's more than just beautiful. It's Alaska.

Looking over his left shoulder and then up to the north face of the hilltop, then back down the valley and nodded, "I think it might be the place."

Movement. Brad was snapped out of his musing. Yet as quickly as Brad's gaze shifted to the spot . . . nothing.

To minimize being detected, Brad froze, moving nothing except his eyes. After a few minutes, he slowly brought his binoculars to his eyes and started dissecting the area. Nothing. Lowering the optics and shifting his focus to just above the location to maximize the use of his eyes rod photoreceptors thereby increasing the chance of detecting any further movement, he sat and waited. His hands were in position on his rifle with the scope covers off and his thumb on the safety. Brad could feel the adrenaline, the addictive rush that keeps hunters coming back.

Continuous surveillance revealed nothing. But he trusted his first assessment that "something" had moved, and that it was only a matter of time before it moved again. Patience was a skill that came with age.

An hour passed. His ass was going to sleep and his lower back was starting to complain. Nothing.

He watched the light in the silent valley fade as sun goes behind the clouds, glimpsing in his periphery a bald eagle soaring down the valley, silent and majestic. His thoughts drifted back to the many times he and his wife watched them from the deck of their home that overlooked Tee Harbor. It's been almost two years since her passing, and he's now at more of a loss of how to feel than ever. His reflections make him more uncomfortable than the cold rock, so he decides it's about time to move, slowly removing his pack and putting the box inside. "She'll understand," he thought to himself.

Shifting his gaze down slightly, Brad studied the terrain, looking for a route that would provide the best chance for a successful stalk. It doesn't take long and he found a path that should work. It should allow a silent approach at the same time allowing him to keep the location of interest in view at all times. Just as he was raising his butt off of the rock he saw it move again, but it was gone just as fast. Now there was no doubt in his mind.

Brad continued to rise slowly, glancing down to locate where to place his feet and then only moving when looking at the target. Brad began to close the distance. He saw stirring again, and this time whatever it was, it flowed deeper into the woods. Its movements were slow and smooth. If one didn't know what to look for, the eye would not be attracted to the location. The ghost slowly disappears into the woods. Brad marked the location and sped up his pursuit, knowing that tracking would be the next method required, unless it could be spotted again through the thick underbrush.

The thought crossed his mind that he was still unsure exactly what he was pursuing. Having tags for both black and brown bear as well as deer meant he wasn't wasting his time.

Quickly Brad slung the .338 over his shoulder, checked the wind and moved silently through the damp grass to the location of the last known spot. He found no tracks, no scat, nothing. Nothing! Unbelievable. Unwilling to second-guess his senses, he started widening his search, looking for anything.

Twenty yards away a rock caught his gaze; it was mostly obscured by the brush. At first he didn't know why, but he knew something was not right. Slowly he raised the 10x50's to his eyes and adjusted the focus. The gray stone for some reason seemed out of place.

It moved! With lighting speed, Brad let the binoculars drop into its strap and he automatically grabbed his revolver. The .50 caliber would be better at this distance. His eyes stayed trained on the moving rock. In the time it took to draw the Smith & Wesson and raise it to the firing position, the rock seemed to sprout legs and rush deeper into the trees. The rock transformed into a huge silver bear, but it was too fast. It headed up the valley and out of sight before Brad could shoot.

"Holy shit!" was the thought that went through his mind as he put away the revolver, unslung the rifle, and told himself to calm down. His heart rate was jumping through the roof.

Still not sure what happened—how was he not able to tell a bear from a rock?—he told himself, "Hell, I must be getting old."

The trail was easy to follow through the heavy, wet undergrowth covering the ground. No clear tracks, but the heavy bear had disturbed the moisture on the plants and left depressions in the moss and organic matter on the forest floor. It was an obvious trail and Brad made good progress.

The trail led to a slight rise overlooking an older part of the forest where the canopy blocked the sun, allowing the floor to remain relatively open. And there it was. About fifty yards away, with its attention focused on something to the left. But this bear was brown, almost black. Brad was sure it was the same bear due to the size, and the trail led straight to it. The Ruger came to his shoulder, his eye lined the cross hairs on the bear's shoulder, finger on the trigger, but something wasn't right. Its shape was off; the legs were a little too long. And the "hair," well, it was not hair.

Brad's hesitation allowed the bear to stand up on its hind legs and then change into—the only thing that came to mind was Big Foot. It had a large, lightly haired flat face. Brad lowered his weapon and just stood there as it started to walk away, continuing up the draw, its color changed again. All the time the bear-thing was focused on some unseen object off to its left, moving as silently as smoke until it was out of sight again.

Brad's mind was reeling. "Should I shoot it, follow it, or run?" Shaking the questions from his mind, he headed off at a trot toward a rocky outcropping where he should be able to get a second look. Hopefully he would have a little time to dig out the camera from his pack.

All thoughts of wet feet, sore knees and aching back were gone as he climbed the rock point, cussing under his breath when he slipped on the moss, falling on his side, but keeping his rifle from hitting the ground. Brad got up and checked to make sure nothing had fallen loose, and then continued the pursuit. Just before coming to the peak of the first ridge, Brad stopped and slowly eased his head over the edge, bringing a good-sized open saddle into view.

Once again, a movement caught his eye and it brought a small smile to his face. There it was again, heading through the pass. As he raised the camera to take the shot that should supply the proof his story would require, the Big Foot thing lay down between two old fallen tree trunks partially covered in green moss. And to Brad's utter amazement, Big Foot changed into a third tree trunk. The colors and texture were identical, and with its arms laid against its side, it was indistinguishable from the other dead trees. He never got his brain to move his finger to take a single photo.

Brad's eyes caught the shadow of movement of something on his right, close. His quick reflexes had him ducking before fear could register. His right hand darted for the grip of his sidearm while turning to face what was on him. But as fast as he was, Brad's world was enveloped in stars when he was hit on the left side of his head. His knees buckled and he fought to remain standing. His vision narrowed to the blurry patch of ground at his feet. He could see his rifle lying on the moss, not sure how it got there. A rush of pain behind left eye was so intense he was forced to close his eyes and try not to pass out.

Brad realized he hadn't fallen to the ground but he—he was moving. Something was wrong; he couldn't quite focus on any one thought. The pain slowly released its grip, allowing Brad to open his eyes. He was being carried. Both of his arms were pinned to his sides. Brad was unable to move. Struggling, he tried to reach his revolver but couldn't. A brief attempt at fighting to get free just solidified his fears that he was stuck. His mind started to clear and now he could see he was being carried back the way he'd come.

Unable to do anything else, Brad turned his head to get a look at his captor. But what he saw didn't make sense; a massive gray creature was carrying him. He was still dazed, so he figured he must be hallucinating. What he could see was an almost flat, featureless face. Its legs were the size of Brad's waist, and its arms were long in comparison to its body, but still larger than Brad's legs, and it smelled like wet earth or tundra. The thing also had picked up his Ruger and was bringing it along.

As his head cleared, they came to a stop. Brad saw a shadowy figure wearing a faded military uniform with no insignias, carrying an old bolt-action rifle with iron sights, slipped noisily by Brad up the trail. Brad caught glimpses of the man from time to time as he forged into the pass, but he paid no attention to Brad. The unknown man was headed toward the bear-tree thing. Brad was amazed at the stealth the man exhibited before slipping completely out of sight.

The report of a large-caliber weapon startled Brad, but he noticed the creature holding him did not flinch. It seemed to be expecting it, because it quickly turned that way. Brad was carried deeper into the woods towards the location of the shot. The "thing" carrying him possessed unbelievable strength and thwarted all Brad's attempts to escape with no apparent effort. After this totally humiliating experience, the creature stopped and set him down unharmed in front of a sixty-something, almost nerdy, but obviously competent man in well-worn woodland camouflage.

"Good afternoon," said the old man with a knowing smile.

Brad backed a short distance away from the creature, straightening up and checking his gear, unsure why, but happy, to still have his weapons. He was also glad to be set free. The man introduced himself as Bob and offered Brad a firm handshake. Looking around, he found a seat on a log.

"You okay?" Bob asked, Brad nodded as he glanced back at the creature, sitting as still as a rock. Bob answered his unasked question. "They're called Rhunken, and they've probably been around these parts longer than we humans have."

A question flickered in Brad's mind, but he was too overwhelmed to respond.

Bob took off his small day pack, opened it and retrieved his water bottle. "As I said, my name is Bob, Bob Strom. My official title is Population Control Officer, or PCO for short. Me and Old Scout here just happened to be on this island today for a little control job. When we found our target, you were already on it. Now, I'll let you know right now, that alone impressed the shit out of me. But when you started to track it, well, I had to step in and stop it."

"Stop what?" Brad asked.

"It from killing you, that's what." Brad was about to say, "I don't think so," but Bob added. "Well, I'm not going to say you didn't have a chance, but the only way you saw it once it turned brown is because it'd seen us and was on the run. I've been working with these things for many years, and in my opinion, you had a good chance of becoming a smear."

Bob went on to explain that these creatures removed potential hazards by grating them on a rough granite rock until every bone and ounce of flesh was turned to nothing but a red smear. "Mother Nature takes it from there. In a few days, sometimes sooner, there's no trace."

Brad looked over to the large Rhunken sitting mostly hidden in the cover of the large leaves of a devil's club bush, totally oblivious to its large thorns. It looked alert, even tense, with its head up, slowly scanning. Even the shape of its head looked different, longer somehow. Without looking away Brad asked, "You said, 'one of your targets.' Are there more out there?"

Bob had shifted his focus to his left, so Brad's gaze followed his to a previously unnoticed mass, no more than fifteen feet away. It looked like a gray leather rock. On closer inspection it was similar to the Rhunken, but it was obviously dead. It was smaller and had what looked like undeveloped wings.

Bob noticed Brad's keen focus. "You're very observant. Yes, there might be another one. This one was young, reckless. By its actions I expected an older one as well, possibly wounded."

Brad could see Bob wanted to ask him something else, but wasn't quite sure if he should. Brad stood up and put his daypack over his shoulder. He grabbed his rifle by the barrel with his left hand but kept the butt on the ground. Nodding at Scout, he said to Bob, "I sure I'm not supposed to talk about this. I won't. Even if I wanted to, no one would believe it."

Scout's head jerked to its left, and his eyes focused on something behind Brad. Brad knew something was wrong and he spun around, dropping the rifle and reaching for the 500 with his right hand as he knelt on his right knee in one quick motion. A large black Rhunken broke through the berry bush, twelve feet away, and charged him. Its mouth was open in a grimace, showing a row of yellow-edged, brown teeth. The Smith & Wesson cleared the holster, and Brad's left hand gripped his right as he brought the gun up, pulling the trigger through its smooth double action. Instinct, not sights, brought the muzzle on the target as the handgun roared. Less than a half second later another blast from Bob's 30.06 added to the ear-splitting noise.

The black Rhunken took both rounds to its chest, killing it instantly, but the momentum carried it forward. It smashed into Brad, knocking him to the ground, the dead Rhunken lying on top of him.

Brad struggled to push the dead beast off. "Holy shit" was all he could say.

Bob laughed as he helped pull the dead Rhunken off. "There he is. That was a little more exciting than I hoped for, but you look okay."

Brad climbed to his feet, still gripping the 500 in his hand. He looked down and could see the Rhunken's color was already fading to gray. Looking over to Scout, he could see a change in its posture; it was definitely more relaxed. Brad watched it as it moved over and picked up the smaller Rhunken and carried it off.

Bob worked the bolt on his rifle, chambering a new round, and leaned it against the log he'd been sitting on. He looked at the .50 caliber in Brad's hand. "You're pretty good with that thing."

Brad looked at the hand cannon and nodded, then put it back in the holster with slightly shaky hands.

Bob rolled the new Rhunken over and examined it. Brad could see the festering wound on its hip.

"Is that why this thing attacked us?" Brad asked.

"It may be part of it. But the story behind these two is a little more complicated. And I'm afraid I can't get into it."

Bob pulled out a small notebook and wrote some notes. On a separate page he wrote a number, ripped out the page and handed it to Brad.

"What's this?" Brad asked.

Bob looked off and up the hill. "There's a spot on the north side of the peak for that box of yours. I'm sure you'll find a spot with a beautiful vista, and what I can only imagine, would have an epic view of the northern lights. And I'd like for you to think about what would happen if that Rhunken had come across someone without your skills and reflexes. I'd like for you to come to work for us."

CHAPTER 2

Fifteen months later

WATCHING THE HELICOPTER DISAPPEAR over the ridge and the following silence was a little more disturbing than Ilene expected. It shouldn't have been. This wasn't the first remote-field trip she and her friends had been on, and it was early in the year, when most of the bears were still in their dens. But it was the group's first trip to Alaska. Admiralty Island had the claim of having the largest population of grizzlies anywhere. The Tlingit name for the island was Kootznoowoo, which translated to "Fortress of the Bears."

Of course, this was exactly why they had come, to observe hibernating bears emerging from their dens, and document as much as possible about the den itself. They hoped to gather as much data as possible and clear the area before the spring hunting season started. They had made a similar trip to Yellowstone last year with little success, so they were hoping for better luck with a different group of animals.

This place felt different, though, larger, even overpowering. She shuddered as a chill ran up her spine.

Camp had gone up smoothly. There wasn't a lot of snow left at this altitude, and it was still cold enough to keep most of the bugs down. The site was next to Hasselborg Lake trail in a small opening in the forest. The wilted ferns and grass lying flat and rotting on the ground, along with the dried stocks of cow parsnip, moss-covered rocks and the mostly frozen lake made the location look dead, but she knew that soon new shoots would emerge and rapidly cover the valley with a lush bed three to four feet high.

Of course, there was halfhearted joking from David about the tent-mate setup. "Boys will be boys," thought Ilene as she and Debra moved their gear into their tent. Ilene knew the sleeping arrangements wouldn't change what was going to happen between Debra and David, but she didn't want to listen to it, much less share a tent with Billy. Billy was an okay guy and a good woodsman, but he was just a friend and she wanted to keep it that way.

The first day was always long and tiring. That made relaxing by the evening campfire even better. Ilene and Debra sat close to the flames trying to keep the chill away; this was aided with cups of hot cocoa mixed with shots of peppermint schnapps. David and Billy were out with flashlights looking for more of the elusive dry firewood for the morning fire; the sun had fallen quickly and caught them a little off guard. But it was clear with no wind, and the stars were just amazing. It had been awhile since she'd seen the Milky Way so vividly.

Ilene was thinking of how much more wild the wilderness felt here, a completely different feeling than Yellowstone and Yosemite, somehow more intense, much more, almost to the point of being uncomfortable.

"Feels like we're being watched," Debra said, jerking Ilene from her musing.

"You too, I thought it was just me." Ilene involuntarily shuddered.

"Maybe we should have let Dave bring his gun," Debra said timidly.

"The gun thing again. I thought that was settled."

"Well, it is. Even if we needed one, we don't have one."

"Thank God. Now let it rest." Now Ilene was a little pissed. She never knew a gun to settle anything.

The tension was broken when the men loudly announced their return by dragging a small but completely intact dead tree over to the wood pile. They held up their arms in triumph and made grunting sounds like cavemen, then laughed as they joined the ladies by the fire.

"Well, we have wood now, and you've frightened away every living creature within a mile," Ilene said, mostly to herself.

The next morning the girls were awakened by the breaking of branches. At first they weren't sure what was happing, until Billy started cussing about something. Leaving the warmth of their sleeping bags, they quickly got dressed and left their tent to assist their wounded fire builder, eager to get the warming fire going as quickly as possible.

The sun wouldn't officially rise for about another hour, and the forecast promised a mostly clear morning. An early start wasn't required, as they had no real time schedule, but it was the first day and everyone was anxious to get started. The lake was brightly lit by the moon even though it was only half full. At six o'clock, they had plenty of light to work by.

A breakfast that consisted of coffee and instant oatmeal mixed with dried fruit was cooked and consumed, daypacks were filled, cameras and spotting scopes were checked. David put on a LED headlamp to study a topographical map spread on the ground.

"There's not a lot of snow this year, but there should still be sufficient amounts high on the north-facing slopes for the dens. So I suggest we split up into two teams and hit these two south-facing slopes. We should be able to find good observation points to watch the north sides of these mountains here," David said as he pointed to the map.

David looked up and saw Billy looking off to the south.

"Billy, did you get that?"

"Yeah, I got it," Billy replied but not changing his point of focus.

Ilene looked in the same general direction. "What are you looking at?"

"Nothing, I guess. I could have sworn there was a rock next to that tree when we got here, but now it's gone," replied Billy as he shrugged his shoulders, while looking back to the map.

Debra and David went back to planning their routes and setting a rendezvous point, but Ilene looked again at the tree Billy had pointed out, trying to remember the rock but couldn't. Ilene had trekked in the woods with Billy enough to know that even if he was an immature brat sometimes, he did have a knack for wilderness observation, and she had learned to trust him.

Ilene was already starting to worry about this trip. Something was wrong and she could feel it. But she shook it off and decided to ignore it. She rejoined the group in the planning and the programming of the GPS with the waypoints.

The sun was starting to turn the sky a light blue, proving it to be a mostly clear day with just a few clouds. The sun wouldn't clear the ridge for an hour or so, but it was light enough to start. The frozen ground and grass made extremely loud crunching noises as they headed north to the first GPS waypoint, which was also going to be the split and rendezvous site. Ilene's mood improved once they were on the move. It made everyone else's mood that much better.

They had been on the trail for a little more than an hour when the sun broke over the ridge. The group stopped to soak up the sun's rays and look back to enjoy the view. Billy took a picture of Hasselborg Lake set in the frosty valley with a veil of mist rising from the small open water areas of the lake. He'd hoped to catch their camp in the shot, but they still hadn't gained enough elevation and it was still blocked by a hill. As they stood looking south, they felt a chilling breeze hit the back of their necks. Ilene looked north: the sky was still clear with no clouds in sight. But she knew a small front was coming. She wasn't too worried; the forecast said it would pass quickly, leaving only an inch or so. A little fresh snow would help in locating bears, since it would wipe out the old sign. That would save them from chasing dead-end trails.

At ten o'clock the group arrived at the rally waypoint. Ilene announced, "It took us about two and a half hours to get here from camp. Sundown is 4:15, so we need to be back here at 1:15. That'll give us an extra half an hour on the way out."

"That means we only have three hours and change out here. We won't even make it to our lookout points," complained David.

"Well, we'll adjust the plans for tomorrow," Billy said. He adjusted his pack, turned and led Ilene off to the east.

Debra glanced over to David, the look in his eyes said they would only be going far enough to find a comfortable place, out of sight. She grinned back at him and grabbed his hand, and they headed north.

After a half hour David and Debra found what they were looking for, even though they hadn't gone very far. The relatively dry bed of spruce needles out of the wind and slightly off the trail would do just fine. David started digging out a military poncho and poncho liner from his pack. Debra helped him by grabbing him from behind, reaching around and working her hands down through the layers of clothes to lay her cold hand on a very warm part. The coldness of her hands did nothing to stop his arousal, but they did slow his progress of laying out the poncho. As soon as it was spread over the bed of needles, he pulled her around to face him and started to work on her jacket zipper. Debra was quicker than he was and had his jacket open and pants undone. She was freeing him from his layers of restriction when David finally lifted her polypro just over her bare breasts. He moved his mouth from her lips to her nipples. His hands fumbled with the buttons of her insulated pants. Debra finally decided he was taking too long and she pushed him away, removing her boots and pants, and then climbing under the poncho liner. David watched her, never even thinking of the open spaces surrounding them. In a hurry, his pants just down to his knees, boots still on, he climbed under the liner.

The chilled air was forgotten. Sharing breath and body heat, they moved deeper into their private world. Pleasure was both given and taken.

Debra's eyes were closed when she heard a sickening thud. David's upper body was thrown off her to the right, though his lower body strangely remained still in place. Her eyes jerked open and hot liquid splattered on her face and chest. Her eyes focused on her breasts and saw them covered in dark red spots, but the horror still didn't register. She looked over at David and found him unmoving, his hair matted and wet.

Debra's mind was still unable to comprehend what was happening. She started to rise up on her elbows when movement close by caused her to change her focus from David to something standing over her and her lover. An odd arm raised a rock over her head, and she watched as if it were happening on TV, mentally disconnected from the event. As the arm and rock came down, clarity arrived in a rush. Debra's eyes opened wide in terror. She gasped, taking in a breath to scream. The breath was never fully drawn.

An hour into their hike, Billy stopped and waited for Ilene to catch up. He was in much better shape than the rest of the crew. While he didn't care what the other two thought, he did care what Ilene thought. He didn't want Ilene to think she was slowing him down, so he checked his GPS, then the map, as well as the clouds starting to build to the north, and she caught up.

"I figure we won't make our primary lookout point in time, but we can get to this rocky point quick enough." Billy pointed to a spot on the map only a short distance from their current location. Then he added, "Which should give us a pretty good view of this ridge, and we'll actually have a little more time than I hoped for to look for animals."

Ilene studied the map for a few seconds, then compared the corresponding terrain and nodded her head in agreement.

When they reached the new lookout, the two had a spectacular view of the valley and facing mountainside. They were also greeted with a light breeze and the first few flakes of the forecasted snowfall.

They found an acceptable spot and started setting up their

scopes and cameras. A large boulder blocked the chilling wind, and the ground was flat and clear. Billy announced, "Better than just acceptable, it's actually a great location."

As Billy started to scan the opposite slope, Ilene set out taking GPS readings of their location and logging it in her book along with notes concerning date, time, weather, reason for changing location, etc.

"I've got one," Billy said.

Ilene dropped her journal, sliding up to her spotting scope. "Where?"

Billy kept looking through his scope and guided her to the bear, using landmarks.

The large lumbering boar was located by Ilene, and she could see it had just emerged from its den. Its tracks were easily followed back to a hole in the snow, near the ridge top just under a cornice. Elated, she started documenting the sighting.

"First specimen, Alaskan brown bear, boar, eight to eight and a half feet," she said aloud to give Billy a chance to make corrections or additions to her estimation data. He made none; they were about right, but he really didn't care about the numbers.

Billy let Ilene continue with bear number one, gathering all the data she could: location, color and the like. He was searching for more.

Billy's watch started to beep, letting them know that time was up and they needed to start heading back. Ilene kept watching the first bear with a slight groan, not wanting to give it up. Billy stopped the unfruitful search for the second and started to load their gear. That's when he noticed how much it had snowed, there was a good two inches on the ground and it was starting to come down heavier.

"I think we'd better get a move on. I don't like this weather," he said, trying to spur Ilene into action.

It worked. Ilene looked around in amazement, as if she'd just been beamed here from a different location.

"Holy shit, I guess so. Think we'll be okay?"

"Yeah, as long as the others are at the rendezvous point on time. But put your Crampons on just to be sure." They dug them out of their packs, slipped them over their boots and packed up their gear.

Billy looked at his watch as they left. "Good. Right on schedule."

Billy led the way, but he was constantly checking on her. But the hike back to the rendezvous point wasn't as bad as he had thought it might be. The snowfall had increased until visibility was less than half a mile, obscuring the valley and mountains around them. The GPS gave them confidence but wasn't really needed as the trail was easy to follow and the grippers helped with the traction on the icy spots. The soft snow made a slight crunching noise as they worked their way down the trail. Other than the sound of their footsteps and the nylon cloth of their outfits rubbing as they walked, it was quiet. When they stopped, it was dead quiet.

He could see by the undisturbed snow that they were the first to arrive. He wasn't surprised.

"We're a little early, I guess. Do you want me to build a fire and heat some water for cocoa or instant coffee?" Billy asked.

"Think we have time?"

Billy took that as a yes and started gathering kindling and small twigs. Ilene started to clear a spot in the snow with her feet.

A half hour later, they were sipping hot cocoa from their titanium mugs next to the small fire. Billy looked at his watch. "They're officially fifteen minutes late," he announced.

"Surprise, surprise," Ilene said, causing Billy to smile.

An hour later, the snowfall had let up and he could see the worry in her eyes. He, on the other hand, was getting more pissed off. He knew they were just goofing off.

Billy got up to stretch and said, "I'll walk up the trail a bit and see if I can spot them."

Ilene shrugged, "If you want." Then she added, "Don't go too far. We should leave soon."

Billy left his pack but took his GPS and binoculars and headed up the trail. None of their tracks from earlier were visible due to the new snow.

He walked only about fifteen minutes before stopping at the crest of a rise, yelling out their names. Nothing.

Something caught his eye. In a group of fallen trees less than a hundred yards away was a light gray or brown figure. There was nothing remarkable about the color or shape, and normally he would have ignored it. But there wasn't any snow on it. He raised his binoculars and adjusted the focus. Billy could clearly see the object, but couldn't really identify it. "The trunk of a lightning struck tree maybe?" he thought. Whatever it was, it looked out of place.

Billy glanced at his watch: almost three. "Shit," he said, knowing that even if they left now, it'd be dark before they got back to camp.

Deciding to head back to Ilene, he looked one more time at the "tree" before turning around.

It had jumped off the fallen tree it was on and started to move through the underbrush.

Billy froze. He had no idea what this was. He couldn't get a good look at it, but it was almost ape-like. It gave him a really bad feeling. He knew it was dangerous. He watched it walk to the trees to its right, angling toward him.

Billy thought it was a good time to walk back to Ilene. Or maybe running was a better idea. As he turned to leave, he saw another one, fifty or so yards from the first. That was enough. Billy bolted down the trail.

He glanced over his shoulder multiple times but saw nothing following, and after a few minutes he stopped running. "Calm down," he told himself.

Breaking into the small clearing where their fire was still brightly burning, Billy could see Ilene's disgusted look.

"Didn't find them?"

"No, but I saw something else."

She caught the distress in his voice. "Are they okay?" Her eyes now had a worried look.

"I don't know," he said, then paused to catch his breath. "There is something out there. Something I've never seen before."

"Are we going back to camp?" Ilene was now frightened.

"I think we should stay here. We already have a fire going. I've got an emergency shelter. It's not much, but we'll be okay." Then Billy added, "Besides, David and Debra are still out there, so I think we should stay here."

Ilene nodded her head in agreement, and together they gathered as much wood as they could without straying too far from the fire.

In the next hour they built their emergency camp and increased the size of the fire, then waited as light failed.

As the darkness closed around them, the snow and wind stopped and the temperature fell. Ilene could feel the moisture around her eyes lightly freeze, telling her the temperature had dropped into the low teens. Nothing could be heard but the occasional pop of the fire.

She stared at the fire, watching it dance, trying to tell herself the others were fine. But she knew something was wrong. Something bad had happened. She felt her tears and her fear building. Looking up she saw Billy staring into the night. Following his gaze to the edge of the light cast by the flames, all she could see was the shadows moving in the trees as the flames danced. Her thoughts moved from the others, to the "things" he'd seen.

Ilene was caught completely off-guard when Billy dove toward the fire and reached for a burning piece of wood. He brought it up as if he was going to hit something. But his swing never went forward. Billy was hit by a large animal that seemingly came from the sky. Both Billy and the creature flew backward. Ilene tried to get out of the way, but she was too slow and was knocked down, sliding through the snow, dazed. She could hear Billy scream out for her to run. Still not understanding what was happening, she rose on her knees and turned to look.

Ilene watched as the thing, which was not quite as big as Billy, crouched on top, pinning him to the ground. It had wings! Her attention was ripped from the creature as Billy yelled at her once again. Whatever he said did not register. Her mind was reeling.

Billy's arm was badly broken, his face was covered in blood, and Ilene knew she had to help him. She found Billy's spotting scope lying near her. In desperation she picked it up and threw it. Her aim was off and the scope hit Billy's leg.

The impact from something forced the air from her lungs as it drove her to the ground. Ilene's eyes flashed stars, and then blackness engulfed her. . .

Ilene came to her senses slightly. She could feel the weight of something on her, and it was hard to breathe. Her eyes came into focus. The fire had burned down to a bed of red coals, but they still gave off enough light to see Billy. He was looking at her, and he opened his mouth to say something but only a gurgling noise came out. Ilene watched as his eyes changed. They went into a blank stare, then glazed over.

"A dream, just a dream," she thought. The tugging on her abdomen turned her attention from Billy. She could see it sitting on her. Its back to her face. More tugging.

She couldn't move her legs.

"It's so hard to breathe," she tried to say, but couldn't.

"It's a dream, over soon, just a dream," she told herself again.

She could move her right arm. So she lifted it and tried to push the thing off her. She tried to tell it to get off, but as she tried to say the words, only a wet, wheezing sound and bubble of blood came from her mouth. The blood bubble popped and splattered in her eyes, causing her to blink.

The creature turned to look at her.

Its long face was covered in blood, the skintight on its jaws, its black teeth exposed. Its face started to fold in and the skin on the jaws slackened, its face widening as the eyes shifted from the side of its head to the front. They focused on her.

As Ilene looked at the small campfire reflecting in the black eyes, she lost focus a little, her vision started to change. Blackness started at the edges, and she blinked, trying to comprehend what was happening.

"Just a dream."

Her vision was now like looking through a tunnel.

The tunnel was closing. She turned her head to find Billy, but it was black.

"Dream. Just a. . . "

CHAPTER 3

SITTING IN AN OFFICE is not what Brad wanted to do with his weekend, especially the head office in Seattle. This meeting, he was told, "required his presence." He had procrastinated until the very last day to make his flight arrangements, hoping that all the seats would be taken. But luck was not with him, and all the reservations for the required flights, rental cars and hotel rooms fell nicely into place.

Any trip "into town" was normally something most Alaskans looked forward too, Brad not so much. This trip was to attend the scheduled quarterly all-hands meeting and training sessions, that in reality normally only happened maybe twice a year. They actually weren't that bad, and Brad would have enjoyed them if they weren't held in a city. As city travel goes, it could have been much worse. His hotel and the office were close to the airport and there were a couple of bars within walking distance, so he didn't have to deal with any real traffic.

Overall, Brad was very pleased with the Wilderness Control Council and its management. It had only about a hundred employees total, with half focusing on research and the rest population control. Management seemed to have their shit together, which surprised him because of his past experiences with government organizations. Most of the Ph.D.'s calling the shots understood his job and wanted to have little to do with him, Bob or any of the Control Officers, for that matter. That was fine by Brad.

In the last year and a half with the WCC, he had worked primarily with Bob in the field, mostly Alaska, learning the ropes as a PCO. Bob had become a good friend, and his skills as an outdoorsman continuously amazed him. At the same time, Bob was more impressed with Brad than anyone he'd ever met, and Bob passed on great reviews to his superiors.

Bob was talking to the receptionist when Brad walked in, and by the way she was smiling, he was probably flirting with her. But Bob broke off and met him halfway.

"Damn good to see you again," Bob said, giving Brad a firm handshake.

Bob stepped back and gave him an exaggerated looking over. "Look at this: you even dressed for the occasion."

Brad was wearing his going to town outfit: clean Wranglers, cowboy boots, collared shirt, all black, and a gray sport coat, with no tie. If it was a marrying or burying, he would have added a bolo. He shrugged and said, "It's as good as it gets, I'm afraid."

Bob had a suit and tie on, and he actually looked as comfortable in it as he did with his old camouflage when he was in the bush.

Bob slapped him on the shoulder with a smile. "I wouldn't expect anything else."

Brad and Bob followed a group into the small auditorium. Its sloped seats would accommodate two hundred people. Going by experience with past meetings, Brad doubted it would be a quarter full. He also saw the usual small social groups sitting apart, so it was easy to spot the group of PCO's off to the side. Bob nodded to them as they passed, but he led him to the front row. Brad would have preferred a seat in the back, but he took this seat and kept his mouth shut. Looking around, he could see that the auditorium was well kept and up to date. The audiovisual equipment looked first-rate, and every seat had AC power and a LAN connection. No Wi-Fi was available for security reasons.

The lights dimmed slightly and everyone quieted down. A tall, thin man confidently approached the podium. Brad recognized the facilitator for the event. He was the host of a television show that hunted down mysterious monsters and legends. Bob saw the question in his eyes and leaned over and whispered, "The WCC sponsors his TV show. It's better if we control the media, as much as possible, anyway."

Much to Brad's dismay, he discovered that the main reason he was seated in the front row was the announcement that he had been promoted to journeyman PCO status a full six months early. With the round of applause he did his best to smile when he became the focus of everyone's attention, shaking a couple of hands of nearby people. The news was fine, but he would have preferred learning of it over a beer.

This good news announcement was tempered by a second announcement that Bob would be retiring later in the year. This came as a shock, as Bob hadn't given him the slightest hint.

Bob leaned over and whispered to Brad, "I probably should have told you earlier."

Brad nodded, "No problem, I understand."

But he knew it would have been a hard thing for Bob to tell him, so he let it drop.

The meeting continued with the week's training schedule. Most of it went in one ear and out the other, until the announcement that this year's annual picnic would be held in Jackson Hole. This was greeted with a cheer from the crowd.

On the way to lunch, Brad and Bob were congratulated by a few members of the staff, many of which Brad had never even heard of. Bob tried to introduce most of them, but he was soon overwhelmed and gave up, and he went to find a cup of coffee, leaving Brad to fend for himself. While talking to Jamison Parker, an older man in the biology department, he found himself distracted by a redhead nearby, an attractive, athletic woman in her mid-thirties facing slightly away, talking to another woman. He couldn't keep his eyes off her. The color of her greenish pantsuit and jacket wasn't a normal shade, so it probably had some fancy name, but it complemented her hair perfectly and the suit cut accentuated her slim figure and enhanced the view from behind. Parker noticed Brad's eyes on the young lady and knowingly smiled. He touched her on the shoulder to get her attention.

Jamison said, "Erica, may I introduce you to Brad Michaels. Brad, this is Erica Hunt."

Erica smiled and stuck out her hand. Brad took it and found a surprisingly firm handshake. She looked him in the eye and said, "It's good to finally meet you, and congratulations on your promotion. But I must admit I wasn't there for that part of the meeting."

It had been a long time since Brad had butterflies when meeting someone, and he couldn't believe he felt this way. He said "It's my pleasure, and thank you. I don't remember seeing you around here."

Jamison jumped in, "Well, I'm not surprised. You two are at opposite sides of the compound. . . "

He wasn't listening too much of anything the old geezer was saying about her. He did catch that she was a junior veterinarian/biologist and that she had been on the job less than a year. He lost track of the conversation again when she smiled and bit her lip. "Shit, this is all I need," Brad thought. Hell, he'd been out of the dating game for more than twenty years, having married just after high school and staying with her until she passed away just before he started working for the WCC.

Somewhere along the line Parker started to tell Erica about Brad: " . . . Alaska and Brad was promoted to journeyman PCO."

Erica's expression changed to disbelief, then to anger. Bob had come back with his newly acquired cup of coffee. He had been back long enough to get the general gist of conversation and catch Erica's shift. He inadvertently let out a little laugh that drew Brad's attention.

Bob held up his hands and said, "Sorry, I couldn't help myself. I didn't mean anything by it."

Brad looked at Bob, confused, and when he turned back to Erica, she was gone.

The older biologist, Parker, said, "I'm sorry, Erica has a lecture to give, so . . ." Without finishing his sentence he departed, looking uneasy.

Bob looked like he was about to laugh, and this further confused Brad. "What the hell just happened?"

With that Bob did burst out laughing, and he put an arm around Brad and walked him over to get some coffee.

"She hates PCO's. Well, she did until she met you anyway," Bob said, finally composing himself.

This stopped Brad in his tracks. "What does that mean? And why does she hate PCOs?"

"Well, I've only met her once before myself, and it was as cold an introduction as I've ever had. Later, it was explained to me that Miss Hunt adamantly disagrees with the whole Population Correction policy, and she focuses her resentment of the policy on the PCO's. So I guess you shouldn't take it personally."

Brad looked back to the spot she had been standing, the image of her ass still fresh in his mind.

"But it's obvious she likes you," Bob added with a smile.

"Likes me? You're full of shit. She took off like a rabbit."

Brad was slightly embarrassed by his initial attraction. But if she was so high and mighty, her quick departure was for the better.

They caught up with Parker at the refreshment table that was set up for the conference. Brad looked at the muffins, doughnuts, fruit and assorted drinks and decided to get just a cup of coffee. As he poured his cup, he remembered he needed to stop by the sporting goods store on his way back to the hotel and pick up a couple thousand primers.

Bob looked at Parker, who was also at the table making a cup of tea, and asked with a wink, "When is Erica giving her lecture?"

Brad shook his head and said, "Look, I'm not going to chase

someone that doesn't want to get caught. Plus, my dad always said, 'Don't date women in the office.'"

Parker understood the look of mischief in Bob's eyes, because he laughed and said, "This way, young man," and off they went back to the main auditorium.

The sign outside had changed and now said, "Rhunken Basics, Lecturer Erica Hunt."

Brad wasn't going to back down from their unspoken challenge, so he led the way to center front and found three open seats. Both Bob and Parker were smiling like schoolboys.

Erica entered from the back and walked up to the podium, checking the sound and projection systems with the skill and confidence of someone that had done it a hundred times. As she stepped up to the microphone, she spotted Brad in the front row. A look of horror flashed in her eyes, but it only lasted for a second before she gathered her composure.

Bob leaned over and said, "She handled that better than I thought she would."

Brad just smiled and nodded, thinking to himself, "Yeah, she did. My wife would have just flipped me off."

Bob had a questioning look.

Brad smiled, "It was a term of endearment in our house."

Erica's lecture started with the lights dimming and the projector illuminating the movie-theater-sized screen behind her dimly lit podium. It showed a map of North America.

"Rhunken, while it's hard to determine, are thought to be a separate clade of the subclass Coleoids. In layman's terms, its closest living relative is speculated to be the octopus and cuttlefish. They are highly intelligent omnivorous creatures inhabiting several remote locations of the world. Their actual total numbers are unknown, but the range is thought to be five to seven thousand worldwide. Populations are kept low naturally by the Rhunken themselves. The females stop bearing young when their numbers reach the carrying capacity of the local ecosystem. In some areas, we keep the population to an even lower number. For example, in the US/Canadian region a joint group of controllers oversee and manage their numbers and ranges. The controllers also remove unwanted offspring called Tacks. I'll cover more on those later."

The screen behind Erica started to change with images keeping up with each topic.

"Rhunken can communicate using clicks and tones, some at frequencies humans can't hear. But primarily they use body language, as do humans, and they are far better at reading the subtle gestures and facial expressions, theirs as well as ours. They also have the ability to manipulate the excretions of scent glands and the release of pheromones. The discovery of this capability is relatively new. We're just starting to study it, but we know that they are able to change their scent. It has been reported through PCO eyewitness encounters that Rhunken may use this scent control to lure prey within striking range. This scent adaptation also makes it all but impossible to track them this way." Erica glanced at Bob. "Some of our more experienced field operators even believe that this is their primary form of communication. We have learned they associate scents with individual humans, and we've used these 'call scents' to contact them."

She glanced down at her notes. "They even have a limited form of writing, mostly one or two symbols consisting of lines of different sizes, angles and slight bends. They use these to mark a location, or as a short message for Rhunken that might follow. We are in the process of cataloging these, but we're still in the infancy stage."

Brad thought, "Maybe these desk jockeys are doing something." He was surprised how thorough and up to date the information was. They must actually read our reports. So far he actually knew all of it except the octopus part.

"Some of the Controllers can converse with the more patient Rhunken to a limited extent. But it seems they can understand us with little difficulty if they wish. It's been long standing debate as to how much they actually do understand. Some think they understand most of our words. Others think that because they read our body language better than we can, they understand much, much more than we say.

"It is because of this communication we have with the Rhunken that we are able to set up treaties of sorts. We set aside tracts of land to be left as wilderness, like certain national parks and refuges. Have you ever wondered why some parks and refuges exist? These treaties also include an agreement that the Rhunken themselves contribute to the implementation of the population control and culling policies."

Brad thought that last sentence sounded like something Bob would say, but she looked a lot better saying it. She had obviously spoken in front of a crowd before; she stood straight with not too much hand motion, plus she didn't hide behind the podium, but did so without walking around too much and she had good eye contact with the audience.

"There are two known types of Rhunken. The most common type: males reach an average eight feet in height and weigh four hundred pounds. Females are a foot shorter and a hundred pounds less. They have a flexible modified cartilage skeletal structure. They also have an undeveloped and unusable set of wings behind and slightly below their arms. Most of these wings are damaged and heal over as they mature, and on some will completely disappear.

"The modified cartilage cells used in its skeletal system are quite unique. Simply put, it is more like a system of interlocking cells floating in liquid. When the liquid is between the cells, the 'bone' is extremely flexible, but once the liquid is withdrawn, the cells interlock and the 'bone' becomes ridged and remarkably strong. The transition of flexible to ridged skeletal structure happens constantly. They can control it mentally, but it also appears to be subconscious most of the time. They have opposing thumbs, with the four finger claws closely resembling normal seal claws, but the thumb claw is large, more talon shaped, even though the thumb itself is slightly underdeveloped, almost like a dewclaw."

Erica took a drink from a plastic water bottle and glanced up and made eye contact with Brad, she quickly shifted her focus away, continuing her presentation without seeing Brad's grin.

"By manipulating their flexible skeleton they are able to mimic other objects or other animals to a certain degree. Their skulls have a suture, or hinge using the same Sharpey's fibers as our skulls do, that runs vertically in the center of their faces that allows the shape of the skull to change from flat-faced to a long face. This not only manipulates their appearance, it also allows their vision to go from more binocular, like a predator's, to a wider field of view of about three hundred degrees, similar to most prey animals. We have observed that in order to feed, they normally have their skull elongated in a prey-like arrangement."

Bob leaned over and whispered, "She's pretty good."

Brad just nodded.

"What I think is one of their strangest features is that they are covered with a special form of chromatophore and iridophore cells that reflect light in many different colors and are even capable of changing the texture of their skin, enabling the Rhunken to blend into their background almost perfectly. Another adaptation they have is the ability to restrict blood flow to their skin—not unlike the walrus, only to a much greater extent. This allows them to conserve body heat as well as all but eliminate a heat signature. But when the blood is restricted, it limits their ability to control color and texture changes. Both male and female are actually lightly haired, but the skin texture can be changed to resemble hair. When Rhunken age they, like us, get old and lose some of their flexibility. For them, it also affects their morphic abilities, both color and shape shifting. Very old ones are limited to merely gray colors. A side effect is that the old Rhunken's skin is very dense, enough so it can stop small-caliber bullets. Thus the name for the old one, Stone Rhunken."

The large screen changed to a close-up of a dead Rhunken mouth, showing its jagged, plate-like "teeth." The image caused some in the audience to gasp. Erica smiled; she had expected this, so she waited for a few seconds before she continued.

"Nasty-looking, aren't they? The Rhunken's teeth are a chitin/calcium carbonate composite. They're more like beaks than like our teeth, and as these show, they can range in color from light yellow to black. Throughout the mouth, the 'teeth,' for lack of a better term, do change shape to accommodate the eating process."

Erica had walked over to stage left almost in front of Brad; she looked at him, this time holding his gaze. She could tell he was following her, not that she expected him not to be, he gave her an almost indiscernible nod of approval, and she allowed herself a small smile before continuing.

"Now for the second type of Rhunken. Sometimes called Thacken, Tacks is what they are normally called. They are quite rare, but can show up in any colony and at any time. Some biologists say they exist because of a rogue gene from a lost time. The specialists state that it happens at a rate of about 1 in 17,000, which is about the same rate that albinism occurs in the human population. They are not expected to weigh over a hundred pounds. They are completely fertile, so it's thought that if left to breed with other Tacks, they could create a new subspecies. The Tacks are born with fully developed, leathery wings, and in the limited number of specimens we've studied, they all have an unexplained bend in the ulnas of the wing near the carpal joints. The large pectoral muscles are divided into two parts, with about two-thirds supporting the arms and one-third the wings. Using aeronautical modeling and calculations, it's believed that even smaller Tacks would still not be able to fly. The other known difference is that they have a more drastic skull shift. It appears they can shift from flat-faced to an elongated shape that gives them a field of view better than 320 degrees.

"It's assumed they would still have all color and shape-changing capabilities as the common type. As you can tell, not much is known of this variety of Rhunken because of the strict but unexplained culling policy."

When she finished, she asked for any questions. Brad tried hard to think of one that would make him sound smart. He couldn't, so he kept his mouth shut. She had impressed the hell out of him. Her book knowledge was as good as it gets, but she obviously lacked any experience. But she was smart, and that was even more attractive than her nice ass.

"Have you seen one yet?" asked a man in the back.

A little embarrassed, Erica quickly glanced at Brad and then replied, "No, just pictures and tissue samples."

A small man with a program in his hand asked, "It says they mimic things in their environment and that they appear sometime as a Bigfoot type of creature. Does this mean there is such a thing as Bigfoot"?

"I don't know. That's an interesting observation, though."

Then a woman in the audience asked, "What do the Rhunken think about the culling"?

Before Erica could answer, Bob stood up. "May I answer this?"

Erica said, "Yes of course. This is Bob Strom, our most senior PCO."

Bob turned around to face the small audience. "I want you to remember that these creatures, no matter how smart or unique they are, they are not human. They don't think like you or I. They don't have feelings of right or wrong, good or evil. Try to control your anthropomorphic tendencies toward these beings. It will do nothing but get you in trouble. And remember, we are not culling for their protection. We do it for ours."

Bob's answer must have made everyone rethink their questions because none followed, and soon after, everyone started filing out. Bob and Brad hung back waiting for Erica. As she approached, she thanked Bob and, never even looking at Brad, quickly made her way out of the room.

Brad watched her walk by and out of sight, without saying a word. Bob let out a big laugh and slapped Brad on the back. "Enough science. There's an ale house just down the street. Let's go get a drink, I need a Crown."

CHAPTER 4

THE NEXT MORNING BOB drove Brad to the airport.

Brad said, "I was worried they might assign me to a different area, once my training was complete."

"They wouldn't have, even if I hadn't retired. Your knowledge of the area is far too valuable."

Brad nodded. "May be so, but I really hate to see you go."

"I'm sure I'll miss it some. But, it's time. And I'll still be around for a while."

Anyway, it was only going to be a couple of months or so until they'd get together again in Jackson Hole, so they'd catch up then.

Bob's mood turned darker after he dropped Brad off, but it had nothing to do with Brad or his retirement. It had to do with his next meeting.

Bob drove back to the WCC without thinking about the drive, his mind going over what needed to be done. Stopping by his office, he grabbed his leather day planner that held his notes before walking up the stairs to Jim Starkey's office.

Jim Starkey, the director of the WCC, had held the position for about fifteen years. He was well respected, firm, but he treated everyone fairly. Bob had liked him instantly when they'd met. Jim's unpretentious and to-the-point attitude spilled over into his office décor: warm, dark wood and lots of books with a slight nautical theme.

"Good morning, Bob. He's waiting for you," said Jim's secretary as he walked past her.

Bob replied, "Good morning Renee."

"Bob" was Jim's greeting, and he waited for Bob to shut the door and sit down. Jim pushed a button on his phone and after a beep, said, "Renee, hold my calls."

He settled back in his chair and folded his hands. "You didn't sound happy when you requested this meeting. Hell, you never request a meeting, you just walk in. So, what's up?"

"It's about Jeff Moore's Tack lair."

Jim nodded. "Figured as much. Your reports on that have been minimal and the content is vague at best."

Bob had a good reason for his secrecy. "As you know, I've been working on this for a little over a year, and that was the evaluation period I gave myself. I've learned quite a bit, and with Jeff's notes, we'll be able to rewrite a good portion of the Tack handbook, but it's now to the point that I think it's dangerous. We need to completely eradicate the lair."

Jim didn't seem surprised. "Your reports stated you've already culled two Tacks. How many more are there?"

Bob said, "Six. The two I killed were the oldest and most troublesome. I'd hoped it would settle the rest down, but it didn't, it made things worse."

"Eight Tacks? Jesus, how did Jeff get so many? That's more than twice as many as any of the other training lairs. The most I've ever heard of was three."

Bob said, "The answer was in Jeff's notes, the ones I didn't include when we sent them to that asshole Dr. Clark. While the rest of the project trainers followed their, as they called it KET or Key Environmental Trigger, Jeff took it one step further. It was a stroke of genius, and it got him killed."

"Who else knows of Jeff's modified KET?"

"No one. Well, Jeff had a report almost ready to present his findings and hypothesis, but he was killed before he released it, so as far as I know it's just me," Bob said.

Jim took a deep breath, thinking for a moment, then said, "Let's keep it that way for now."

Jim walked over to a side table where he kept a water pitcher, and poured two glasses of water. Bob knew this was more about Jim needing time to think than being thirsty, so he waited patiently for Jim to hand him a glass.

Jim finally said, "I don't have the resources for this. If you could do it yourself, or if you could do it with just Brad's help, you wouldn't be here. So that tells me it's going to take a larger team to get it done."

"Not just larger, but trained as well."

Jim nodded, "Well, I think we need to give this back to the idiots that created it, and let them deal with it, if that's OK with you?"

Bob smiled. "Actually, that's what I was thinking. I know they've had to destroy lairs in the past, so they must have a team, and it will have at least some experience. Most important, we won't be the ones getting killed if something goes wrong."

Jim nodded, making a decision. "You up for a phone call to Dr. Clark and see what he says?"

"Sure, let's do it."

Jim searched his computer, then dialed the number. He left the phone in speaker mode and Bob heard four rings before it was answered: "Dr. Clark."

"This is Jim Starkey and I've got you on speaker with Bob Strom. How are you today?"

A sharp voice replied, "I'm well, thank you for asking. Can I help you with something?"

Jim said, "As a matter of fact, there is something you can help us with. The Tack training colony that was abandoned when Jeff Moore died has become a problem."

The pause on the other end of the phone was shorter than he figured it would be, and the answer was not at all what Bob expected. "It's not a problem, and we'll take care of it."

Bob and Jim looked at each other and Jim silently mouthed, "What does he know?"

Bob shrugged. "I don't know."

Jim said, "Dr. Clark, I appreciate the quick response. Do you need any more details or help from us on this end?"

Dr. Clark replied, "No, I'm sure we can handle whatever comes up."

Bob added, "We'll have the area PCO, Brad Michaels, stop by at the end of the operation to help assess the results and any clean-up efforts."

Dr. Clark's tone changed slightly. "That won't be necessary. As I said, we will handle it. All of it."

Jim said, "I insist. Brad will be a great help, and other than Bob, no one knows more about the area."

This time Dr. Clark's voice was stern. "I don't think that would be wise. My men are well trained and can handle any situation, and I wouldn't be able to vouch for Mr. Michael's safety. He could easily be hit in the crossfire or have an accident. So I won't be responsible for him."

Bob smiled and replied, "Oh, I wouldn't worry about that. If bullets start flying, my money would be on Brad."

Dr. Clark said, "Very well. When we're finished, we'll contact you and you can send a representative to verify that the operation is complete." Then he added, "Mr. Starkey, I'll have the team lead email you with the details before we start." Then he hung-up without waiting for a response.

Jim looked at Bob. "That was too easy. What's he know?"

Bob shook his head. "I don't think he knows anything. He just wants to get his hands on the colony. I think it may have something to do with the email that came out a couple months ago that said the Russians had some success in their training program. My sources say it's a bunch of bullshit and the initial report will be retracted within the next two months."

Jim said, "I'm almost sure that's all it is, but just in case he does know more, you'd better fill me in on Jeff's KET."

Bob sat back in his chair and said, "The standard version of the Key Environmental Trigger is to focus on older and smaller colonies, since they were found to have a higher Tack birth rate. The factor was thought to be that the colony was subject to higher environmental stress. Jeff's hypothesis was that the increase in the Tack birth rate was a response to a collapsing colony. He basically proved it by being a complete asshole. He found a healthy colony and killed all the young females, setting up a terminal colony. And sure enough, the four older females produced Tack twins, two batches a year apart."

Jim looked shocked. "Holy shit, that's unbelievable. What a dick."

Bob continued, "He goes on to surmise that Tacks are a sort of colony defensive adaptation, attacking anything they think is a threat. This would explain their extreme aggressiveness. Jeff didn't stop there. He also suggests the Tacks could recolonize in different locations faster if they were able to fly, explaining the wings."

Jim sat in silence for a while, staring at nothing, thoughtfully rubbing his chin. "It does make a great deal of sense. And if Dr. Clark knows anything at all about this, he's going to want to know more."

Bob said, "It's got to be wiped out."

"Absolutely, but like you said, we should let them—no, make them—do it. You'll need to bring Brad up to speed on this."

Bob nodded. "I agree. I'll get with him at or just after Jackson Hole, but either way, I plan to do a face to face and absolutely no written documentation. And I think we should use this information to modify our culling procedures in regards to young females. Actually, our culling hypostasis needs to be reassessed."

Jim nodded in agreement, but he was already lost in thought.

CHAPTER 5

THE HEAVYSET MAN, MADE to look even larger with his insulated clothing, sat in the leather seat and looked out of the window. The view was breathtaking, but he didn't see it. He was thinking about the call from Jim Starkey, weighing its possibilities and problems. This trip had been arranged before the call, but now it took on a secondary purpose. He needed to assemble a team with experience. One he could trust.

As soon as he stepped through the door of the Agusta Executive helicopter, Dr. Clark was hit with the cold. New York had its cold spells, but nothing like this. The air hurt his sinuses when he inhaled. Though not a lot of snow on the ground, he could see winter was still in control here. Ice still held fast to the shore of Lake Baikal, even more so in this part of the Barguzinsky Gulf. Yet working at this time of year was a necessity to reduce the chance of an eco tourist screwing up the dog and pony show.

He was to meet the local Russian PCO and Brian Robbins, a member of his group that arrived three days earlier. The Russian was the first to report success in the training of a pair of Tacks, so Dr. Clark wanted to see the progress firsthand, and find out where his loyalties lie. He had been advised that this was the closest point to the colony that he could get using motorized transportation. The rest he'd have to hike. He was assured that it wouldn't be far or strenuous. So Glinka it was.

Glinka was a burnt-out resort of some kind, with only the caretaker's lodge remaining. It was thirty or so kilometers by air from the town where they spent the night. He couldn't pronounce the name of the town or hotel, and he didn't care enough to learn how. The hotel was barely adequate, made less so by the owner's cat and parrot. The only upside was the food, which was surprisingly good.

While this was not his first trip to Russia, it was to this part of the country, and he had only visited it in the summer months before. While it was beautiful, it wasn't his cup of tea. "Give me the Manhattan skyline anytime," he thought. Plus, it reminded him of Alaska, and he hated Alaska.

Brian met him before the blades stopped turning, Dr. Clark handing him his small day pack. But Dr. Clark could see by the look on Brian's face something was wrong.

Dr. Clark asked, "What's wrong?"

"There was an incident yesterday evening," Brain responded.

Dr. Clark waited for the rest without asking.

Brian paused when he saw another man get off the helicopter. In stature he wasn't remarkable, he was of average height and weight, but in good shape, mid-thirties, and with short graying hair. But he was intense. It was the look in his eyes that made that difference. If Brian had to guess, he'd say the man was ex-military. The man looked around, assessing the area without a word. Then all three walked toward the small caretaker's cabin.

Brian continued, "Maxim went up to the lair yesterday and he was attacked by the Tacks. He had to shoot one of them, but made it back here last night."

Dr. Clark glanced around. "Where is he now?"

"He went back up this morning to make contact with the other Tack and get it under control for your arrival."

Brian looked at the other man, then back to Dr. Clark, "I didn't know there would be another person with you."

Dr. Clark ignored his comment. "Do you know how to get to the Lair?"

Brian looked unsure but answered, "I have a GPS with a route, but I've never been there. Maxim has a satellite phone on him if we get lost."

Dr. Clark looked at the other man. "What do you think, Jack?"

"We're here, so I think we need to try, but I'd feel better with a weapon."

Brian had a solution for that. "There's a shotgun in the caretaker's cabin, and Maxim has an AK-47 with him."

Jack started for the cabin and was followed by the others. "Let's look at the shotgun. But I'd feel better with the Kalashnikov."

The old caretaker came out of the cabin just before they arrived. He looked the part, bent over with age, fur hat and cigarette. He sized up the two newcomers but didn't say anything.

Brian said something in Russian to the old man. Brian stepped around him and went inside the cabin. He reappeared with the shotgun and a box of shells.

Jack took the side-by-side, double-barrel shotgun. It was a well-used Baikal. He opened it and removed the two shells and inspected them: new Winchester double X magnum 00 Buck. Jack opened the box and took out a handful and slipped them into his jacket pocket.

Jack nodded to Dr. Clark. "Ready."

"OK, let's go."

Brian led the way around the cabin to the start of the main hiking trail leading into the Zabaikalsky National Park. Brian looked up from his GPS and said over his shoulder as they started, "We'll follow this for seven-tenths of a mile, then make our way up an unmarked trail."

Maxim stood over the spot where he'd killed the Tack yesterday. It was gone, just as he expected. He kept himself calm: body relaxed, confident and with the AK slung over his shoulder. The last thing he wanted was to create more tension. Reaching into his left breast pocket of his jacket, he pulled out a small plastic bag with three candy orange slices on a string. He tied the string around his neck and stood still, allowing the call scent to carry and give the Tack time to present itself.

While he was waiting, his mind went back to yesterday evening's training that had gone wrong. The basic drills of "come" and "move" went fine. He had been able to send the Tacks to different spots and return. He still had no luck having them retrieve objects or attack on command. So yesterday he'd brought a piece of fresh bear hide, thinking it might inspire the Tacks to show more interest in the training.

Showing an interest would be an understatement. As soon as he removed the hide from the bag and the Tacks caught its scent, they both reacted. Their faces flattened, brown and yellow plate teeth were bared, and their eyes became focused. Their color turned almost black, the skin becoming hard and roughly textured. Full attack mode.

Maxim must have shown fear because they came at him. He threw the hide as hard as he could. One of the Tacks turned toward it, but the other still came at him. He'd shot the Tack before thinking. He was now sure the creature would have killed him, so in hindsight it was the only thing he could have done.

After talking to Brian, they decided he needed to try to salvage what he could, and contact the last Tack. So he'd left early to assess the Tack's attitude before the program director showed up.

The strong scent of candy oranges snapped him from his musing. Maxim didn't see anything, so he waited for the Tack to emerge as it normally would. It didn't, even though the scent remained strong. So it hadn't moved. "It must be nervous," Maxim guessed. He moved toward the smell, with as much ease as he could muster, keeping his hand away from the AK. About five paces into the tree line the scent became very strong, and he saw what looked like mucus spread on a tree. Touching the slime, then bringing it to his nose, he sniffed, candied orange. He'd been lured.

His hand reached for the AK. Grabbing the fore grip, he was starting to unsling the firearm. But he was hit on the right side by the Tack, its movement a black blur. Maxim spun to his left, deflecting the main force of the blow, but it still knocked him to his left knee. A searing pain in his right side and abdomen caused him to buckle over slightly, but he finally brought the AK to bear and fired at the fleeing Tack. Two bullets of the four-round burst hit the Tack in the back, spinning it around. It went down, but quickly regained its feet and charged. From the hip Maxim fired the AK-47 in a clean three-round burst, all three finding their mark, folding the Tack over, and it slid to a stop at his feet.

Keeping the AK pointed at the dead Tack, whose color was already turning gray, Maxim stood up. A rush of cold hit his stomach. Looking down, he saw his intestines lying on his boots, steaming in the cold air.

"I've got to get back" he said aloud. Bending over, he put the rifle down and scooped up his guts. They didn't want to cooperate, but after a couple tries he had them contained and started back.

After two steps he turned back looking at the AK, He couldn't focus. He went back and picked it up, losing control of some of his load. Struggling to keep his thoughts straight he looked at the trail. He had to get back.

Maxim was stopped when the rest of his load was pulled from his arms. Turning back, he saw his intestines strung out behind him. They'd caught in a bush. Maxim wasn't sure what to do, he needed help. "Bob would know," he said and fished the satellite phone from his pants cargo pocket.

The sound of automatic gunfire stopped them in their tracks: a burst of four, then another of three.

Jack said to no one in particular, "AK-47."

Dr. Clark looked at Brian. "Well, let's go see."

Brian looked sick, but nodded and continued up the slight rise.

The trail was wide and clear, making it as easy as walking down a sidewalk, so it didn't take much time to reach the unmarked turnoff. And while the first fifty meters was hard to follow, the trail became clearer and they made good time.

Brian said, "It's only about a quarter of a mile farther."

Jack nodded and took the lead.

Jack soon came to a sudden stop. The shotgun butt came to his shoulder, muzzle down in a low ready position. On the side of the trail a man was sitting with his back to a tree, an AK-47 lying on the ground next to him. The man was looking at him, and at first Jack thought he might be dead because he was so pale, but he blinked as they approached. A small puff of steam came from a gap in his abdomen every time he took a shallow breath. In Maxim's bloody right hand he held a satellite phone, and in his left he held most of his intestines. The rest were strung out up the trail. They were covered in dirt and debris and appeared to be partially frozen.

Jack knew he was dying, more from hypothermia than from the blood loss. Kneeling next to Maxim, he asked, "The Tack?"

Maxim shook his head. "Dead."

Brian came up to help but backed off when he saw Maxim's condition. But Maxim held up the phone to Brian. "It's for you."

Brian wouldn't come close enough to take the phone, so Jack took it. The screen was lit, and said it was connected. He handed it to Brian.

Brian held it to his ear. "Hello?"

After a pause, "Is this Brian Robbins?"

"Yes, it is."

"I just wanted to make sure I had the name right. I've spent the last half an hour talking with a good friend as he is dying. I also understand you have Dr. Clark with you?"

Brian looked at Dr. Clark, and the unknown voice said, "Give him the phone."

Brian handed the phone to him.

"This is Dr. Clark."

"Good. I just want you to know, you just killed a good man with your bullshit experiment. I'm going to do everything in my power to terminate it and if possible put you in prison."

The line went dead before Dr. Clark could say anything.

Brian was watching, and when Dr. Clark turned off the phone he said, "Do you know who that was?"

Dr. Clark nodded and said without seeming concerned, "Bob Strom."

Maxim's eyes were glazed over and the little puffs of steam had stopped. Without checking, Jack knew he was dead. He picked up the AK, checked it, and said, "I'll locate the dead Tack."

Jack guessed that neither Dr. Clark or Brian wanted to stay with the body, so they followed him up the trail. He saw that Brian had picked up the shotgun. He wasn't sure if that was a good thing or a bad thing, so he didn't say anything.

Jack spotted the empties first. The 7.63x39 rounds stood out on the trail even though they were the olive drab steel cases bought in bulk. The cases were on the right side of the path, telling him that Maxim had been firing up the trail, so Jack continued on. He didn't have to go far; a large pool of blood was spread across the trail, not ten yards away from where the cases were. Jack knelt and could see where the Tack had laid and the blood pooled around its body and coagulated. But the dead Tack was gone.

Dr. Clark spotted the blood and asked, "Did it get away?"

Jack shook his head. "No, it was dead for quite a while before something took it."

Brian put in, "I understand that Rhunken take their dead. The PCO's can sometimes track them, but only sometimes. These things are like ghosts if they want to be."

Jack prided himself on being a world-class tracker, so he looked for sign. After fifteen minutes he found one possible print, and even that was a guess, and then nothing. Whatever took the body just vanished.

Dr. Clark finally said, "I've seen enough. Obviously, this guy didn't know shit, so he deserved what he got and if he was a friend of Strom's, he couldn't be trusted. So no loss. Let's head back. Brian, you get to deal with the body."

Jack hated to admit he couldn't find any sign of the Rhunken, so he was happy for the excuse that he was being called off the search. He quickly passed the other two men and led the way back to the helicopter.

CHAPTER 6

BRAD HAD ENJOYED HIS first two months as the official Alaskan region PCO, even though nothing had really changed in the last year and a half since he started his new job, other than his title. He had met with the FAA Alaska district manager for a few days in Anchorage, they had a few teleconferences and set some ground rules, but overall the transfer went smoothly.

Once back in Juneau, he moved into his new office and set up his computer with a secure LAN to the WCC main office. He had been relocated to a back office in the FAA maintenance compound with a cover of "Airport Projects Coordinator." The position was created specifically for him, and the rumor was that Brad had stepped on the wrong person's toes and was going to be kept out of sight until retirement.

This was not even questioned by the local FAA employees because they'd seen this happen before. With this reassignment the local FAA folks knew he wasn't working for the local shop, so they pretty much left him alone. Some were afraid that if they asked too many questions, they'd be asked to help Brad in his job, thus more work. Brad actually loved this. His true friends at work were still his friends, and now he didn't have to deal with the others.

A week after his trip to Seattle, Brad decided to take a short contact trip. Checking the weather, he found a forecast of rain with a light mix of snow—"snain" to the locals—but the winds were down and the seas only two to three feet. And on a Wednesday, he shouldn't have to dodge too many people.

Morning broke with a little fog to go along with the snain. The ducks didn't seem to mind, but Brad decided that another cup of coffee was a good idea, and that waiting a bit for the tide to come in meant he wouldn't have to carry his raft so far down the rocky beach.

The wait was worth it. The weather and fog cleared a bit, and the tide cut the portage in half. Brad rowed the short distance to his buoyed boat. He circled around the boat, checking it from the water, and found everything in good shape, then boarded and started with the systems check. Once complete, and the motor warming up, he moved the fishing rods to the holders on the RADAR arch, thus clearing the cabin. He turned on the marine radio and selected the weather broadcast channel and listened for any changes as he untied the mooring lines. The radio report covering the local area forecast had changed—it had improved a bit.

Brad's departure time from Tee Harbor was logged as 6:30. Brad put the boat in gear and eased his twenty-five-foot C-Dory out of the harbor. The boat cut easily through the clear, calm water. Just outside the harbor, Brad saw the Alaska Marine Highway System ferry *Taku* heading north up Favorite Channel on its way to Haines and Skagway. Turning south, Brad pushed the throttle forward until the C-Dory was on plane, and then backed it off until the tac read 3600 RPM as he headed around Douglas Island and past the Taku Inlet to Sweetheart Creek. The leisurely seventy-mile trip took about four hours. He even had a brief escort by a small pod of eight to ten killer whales.

Arriving at his destination just north of the creek, Brad set double anchors to help combat any winds that came up. He removed the raft from its storage place atop the cabin, dropped it in the water and attached the small kicker motor to the transom. Then he tossed in his backpack and checked that everything was secure before he jumped into the raft and proceeded to shore.

Brad carried the raft up the beach, pausing once to look at a fresh set of brown bear tracks; they were heading away from his destination, so he continued above the high tide line and tied it off to a tree just to be sure. He grabbed his gear and headed up the hill. The short hike past the three waterfalls to the long-established meeting site near Sweetheart Lake was just long enough to warm the muscles after the long boat ride and cool, damp weather. He spent some time looking around for any hint of recent activity, but he found none. Satisfied, he decided to set up a spike camp near the lake's outlet, thinking that if he got bored waiting, he might try his luck at catching some of the cutthroats he knew resided in the lake.

Contact took less time then he thought it would, so he was slightly startled when he saw the Rhunken standing just inside the tree line, still as stone. Even though it was right out in the open, it was still hard to see, as the long shadows of the trees broke up its outline. Darkness was falling.

It must have been close and identified his boat, like a dog identifies its owner's car. Rhunken had hearing roughly equivalent to dogs in sensitivity, Bob had said, but it was believed to have a greater frequency range.

Brad smiled as the Rhunken moved toward him, constantly amazed at their stealth. It didn't make a sound as it squatted on its heels on the edge of a salmonberry bush, hidden in the shadows cast by the small campfire. Brad sat on his folding stool closer to the flames. If anyone happened by, it would look as if one man was cooking dinner.

Brad recognized this Rhunken, having dealt with him on a couple of visits to this area when he was in training with Bob. It was able to understand him with little difficulty and he was learning to read him better with every interaction. Scout was the name Bob called this one, even though he tried not to name them. Scout just came around so much it was hard not to put a handle on him.

This visit was just that: keeping the lines of communication open and to gather any information he could. Brad could see by his relaxed posture and movements that Scout was at ease with him being there. That worried Brad a little, since this was his first time here without Bob. And the blank stare to his question about any human contact told him there'd been none of any consequence.

This location was of particular concern because of a hydroelectric facility that was in the planning stages for this lake. It also held one of the larger Rhunken colonies. The colony would probably move, but the WCC's position was to wait and see.

Brad spent the rest of the night fixing dinner and drinking the three beers he brought. Scout just sat and watched from a short distance. Bob had stressed that this "doing nothing" was very important in establishing a good bond. The longer the Rhunken hung around, the stronger the bond was. The Rhunken did eye the bananas he brought, something Brad almost never did. It was supposed to be bad luck to have them on a fishing boat, but he wasn't planning on fishing. So he offered the fruit to Scout, who quickly devoured both of them. They liked bananas; he'd have to remember that.

Movement off to his left caught his attention, and an adult female came out into the clearing. She had an infant with her, probably no more than two months old. It clung to its mother's back with its tiny hands and feet; they were the exact same color.

Scout paid them no mind. He just sat on his haunches and scanned the area.

Another Rhunken came out just behind the female, a juvenile, ten to twelve years old. It was about half the size of the female and still on the skinny side. Brad assumed it must be an older offspring of the female. The juvenile watched Brad with interest for the first few minutes, but shifted its focus to the infant when it climbed off its mother. It looked very thin, even anorexic, but Brad had learned that was normal. It was wobbly on all fours, because its cartilage structure wasn't developed enough to stand upright. The little guy's face was flat, as it focused intently on everything. Brad was amazed to see its colors shifting with almost every step.

The female started to selectively feed on moss and lichen off nearby logs and rocks, looking totally oblivious, but Brad knew better. The infant had almost reached Scout when the juvenile came up and knocked it over with the back of his hand. Scout's face flattened out, focusing on the juvenile. He grabbed him and pinned him to the ground, holding him there.

Brad smiled, thinking, "Kids will be kids."

The little one regained his wobbly composure and made its way back to mom, still constantly changing colors. It didn't look any worse for the wear.

After a few minutes Scout let the troublemaker up, and it sheepishly made its way back into the bush, out of sight.

Scout was back to his vigil as the infant climbed back on mom's back and went to sleep. And after a while she wandered out of sight as she fed.

Brad realized all this happened without a sound.

It was good to see the female had been so at ease with him, especially this far from the lair. Ignoring him was a good sign. If Rhunken hid, they didn't know or trust the human at all. If they kept an obvious eye on him, it meant they didn't fully trust him. Of course the young ones were always curious and it wasn't unusual for them to approach a PCO. If the mother wasn't comfortable, she'd have stopped the infant. As for the adolescent troublemaker, it was probably an older sibling, but not necessarily, because at its age they became more of the colony's child, raised and taught by the group. Scout, on the other hand, hung around more than normal Rhunken, and it wasn't because he didn't trust him. Bob figured he just liked people.

Around midnight, Brad made a bed of spruce needles under a large spruce bough, wrapped up in his military poncho and poncho liner to guard against the light drizzle, and fell asleep.

At first light Brad was up and gathering his gear for the return trip. He had expected the Rhunken to leave during the night, as they always had during his previous encounters. So he was truly shocked when he saw Scout still sitting at the edge of the clearing, still looking at ease. Brad wasn't sure if he should leave or spend more time. But he needed to get back, so he finished packing and said good-bye. The disinterest of the Rhunken, who continued to pick and eat old blueberries, told him it was okay, but it didn't feel right. Something was off, whatever it was. It didn't feel an imminent threat or Scout would show it. Rhunken didn't know how to explain "possible" issues, so Brad would just have to be watchful on his way out.

Brad was thinking the visit went better than he'd hoped as the C-Dory cut through the early morning mist. Bob would be anxious to read his report, No, he wouldn't want to read it, he wanted to hear it. Plus, It would be good to see the old coot again. The old percolating coffee pot was on the stove and was almost finished brewing, filling the cabin with its mouth-watering aroma as well as removing the morning chill from the air. The seas had calmed to a slight ripple, the skies opened and the stunning clear blue of the morning sky graced him on the ride back to Juneau.

CHAPTER 7

OVER THE LAST TWO months she kept randomly intruding into his thoughts. He had been doing a better job lately of keeping Erica out of his mind, but now that he was getting ready to go back to Seattle, that was a different story. He'd gotten a haircut the day before, and Terri at the bar had noticed and told him he needed to get some nicer shirts. He hadn't thought about that, quickly dismissing the idea, but he did iron his shirts. Well, some of them anyway.

On the morning of his flight he felt a little more anxious than normal and blamed it on hunger, so he stopped off at the mini mart for a quick breakfast sandwich. He figured he'd need something to hold him over until lunch anyway. But it didn't help much with the nerves.

"New shirts. What a load of crap," he said to himself.

The flight went without a hitch, smooth and on-time, and Bob was waiting at the ale house bar, just as planned, with half of a beer sitting in front of him.

"I'd better get one of those," Brad said as he walked up to the bar and shook Bob's hand.

"Welcome back. You know I asked if she wanted to come with me to pick you up, but she said she was busy," Bob said with a grin.

"Who?" Brad replied.

"Who, my ass. Did you get a haircut?" Bob said, and then laughed.

"I can tell this is going to be a long weekend."

After two ambers and a prime rib sandwich, the two headed for the office. On the way Brad filled Bob in on his visit with Scout. Bob was amazed about the Rhunken staying while Brad slept. He thought for a minute, then said:

"The only thing I can think is that it's really comfortable with you, or that there may have been a bear or something else in the area that could have caused you some trouble. But who really knows what they're thinking?"

Brad could tell that Bob missed the field already. "Still planning to retire?"

"Yeah, I think so. It's time. I think I need to try fishing in a warmer climate. Then, if I don't like it, I plan on coming back here and bothering you," Bob said with half a smile.

"Well, you know you're welcome anytime. But you have to cook."

Bob nodded, but he looked like his mind was elsewhere, and he made his way through the traffic on autopilot. The volume of traffic didn't seem to bother Bob, but it did Brad, reminding him once again, why he lived in a small town.

At the office, everyone was excited about the upcoming trip to Jackson Hole. Most were already wearing cowboy outfits or Hawaiian shirts with stupid-looking hats.

Bob nodded at one of the biologists in white shorts and a pink shirt. Trying not to laugh, he said, "There you go. Now we know what kind of outfit you need."

"Not on your life. Don't they know it's not that warm in Jackson Hole?" Brad said, smiling at the spectacle before them.

When they walked into Jim Starkey's office, they found Erica standing in front of his desk. Brad stopped short of entering the room. Her being there surprised him. She had turned her head to the door opening, looked at Bob momentarily, then shifted to Brad, making eye contact. Brad blinked first, and looked down, feeling a little awkward. That knot in his gut was back.

Bob hadn't knocked, as usual, so he quickly apologized and

started to back out, but Jim shouted, "No, no, hold on, Bob. Do you have Brad out there with you? Come on in and bring him with you."

Brad walked in and headed across the large office, thankful for the pause to gather himself. "Ms. Hunt," he said as he approached. Erica kept her head down, looking apprehensive about something.

"What's up, boss?" Brad said as he walked past Erica and sat down in one of the three empty overstuffed leather chairs, while Bob took another one. Erica looked around and then took the last empty seat.

"We just received a call of a human contact event in your area, Brad. I was going to delay your response and let you attend the Jackson Hole shindig, but it looks like there're maybe deaths involved."

"Deaths? As in plural?" Bob said, startled, beating Brad to the question.

"That's the report. We don't know how many for sure, and it's in an area that's never had Rhunken activity reported before."

"Where?" Brad asked.

"A relatively well-used area on Admiralty Island is the location of the camp, and the casualties remains were found north of the campsite. As I understand, no one saw the Rhunken, but the reporting official, a Fish and Game guy, Jim Straighter, found a smear. And their preliminary tests show multiple blood types."

Bob said in his most authoritative voice, "Brad and I will head up there tonight and investigate."

Jim shook his head. "I knew you were going to say that, Bob, but we've got a fully qualified PCO assigned to the area."

He raised his hand to stop both Bob and Brad from interrupting. "I know what you're going to say, so just hold off. Yes, Brad will need help on this. That is exactly why Miss Hunt is here. Anyway, this is only a fact-gathering trip. If we need to respond with a control event, I might let Bob go as an advisor, but I still haven't made up my mind on that yet."

Both Brad and Bob started to complain, but Jim just stopped them with a look. "I know Erica doesn't have field experience, and I know she's not familiar with Alaska. Hell, I know everything you're going to say, and I've thought it through twice."

Jim sat back and let what he said sink in before continuing. "This is a tough event to be someone's first time out, but Brad is the best PCO we've got, now that Bob's riding a desk, so I know Erica will be in good hands."

Brad smiled but didn't look at her. "The last place she wants to be," he thought.

Jim looked at Erica. "Plus, she's junior in her shop, so it fell to her when the others didn't want to do it. That's what I was explaining to her when you walked in."

Brad could see that she wasn't happy about this assignment. "Well, Erica, it could be worse. You could have been stuck with both of us."

Bob shrugged his shoulders and looked at Brad. "Well, I still think you should buy those white shorts and the pink shirt."

As the two of them chuckled, Jim stood up and told them to get the hell out of his office.

Brad led the way with Bob behind him saying. "Boy, what I wouldn't pay to be a fly on the wall for this event. In truth, I would like to be in on this one, though. This may not be the best time to break in a newbie."

Brad nodded. "You might be right, but she's got her shit together when it comes to her knowledge. She just needs some experience to go along with it."

Erica had been trailing behind, but she caught up to them. "What? Am I missing something?"

"No, no. I was just saying how sorry I was that I can't go along, is all," Bob said with a smile.

Brad stopped and turned back while Erica was talking to Bob, and she ran right into him and almost fell over backward. But Brad caught her, sparing her further embarrassment. She weighed almost nothing, but he was impressed how firm she was and how quickly she regained her balance. Her hair smelled like lavender.

"You okay?" Brad said, still holding her.

She was stunned, but she managed to make a joke. "For someone who just ran into a brick wall?" She glanced momentarily into his eyes. "I can't believe how solid you are," she said, giving his chest a trial pat.

They both stood there longer than was necessary, but then she backed away. "I'm fine, thank you," she said. And she started to walk off.

"Erica, we need to get together and come up with a plan for this thing."

"Not now. How about an hour from now, in my office?" she said as she turned and left without waiting for an answer.

Brad watched her go, conflicted; coming to Juneau was too close to home. For a moment he thought of his wife. Most people thought enough time had passed, and he'd thought so too, and in fact he had dated a few times, but somehow this was different. He wasn't ready.

He decided on keeping the relationship just professional and the sick feeling instantly subsided. So he knew he'd have to stay focused on that track. He also knew staying on that track wasn't going to be easy because of the dangerous bumps and curves.

CHAPTER 8

BRAD AND ERICA'S FLIGHT to Juneau went well, mostly since they sat in different parts of the plane. Somehow Brad got upgraded to first class without even asking. And while this annoyed Erica, she was too excited by this adventure for it to truly dampen her mood, even when she saw Brad's reaction to her coat. He had told her she'd need a good one, so she had stopped by the mall and got a nice one that was on sale. "What?" she'd asked him. But he just shrugged.

The flight was blessed with a rare clear day for Southeast Alaska, and the starboard side window seat showed her Alaska at its best. She was in awe of the scenery: glaciers, fjords, mountains still topped with snow, lakes and the sea looked like mirrors reflecting the crystal blue sky as they surrounded the countless tree-covered islands of the inside passage, all of it visible at the same time.

Erica got up during the flight and broke the rule of using the lavatory in your section of the cabin. She didn't need to use it, she was just going to check on Brad and give him a dirty look or something. But he was sleeping next to an empty bottle of beer.

Arriving at the Juneau airport, Brad walked over to the FAA Flight Service Station to retrieve his truck, while Erica walked around and explored the art and stuffed bears in the quaint, and smallest, airport terminal she'd ever been in. After a few minutes Brad showed back up and they retrieved their luggage and headed out to the parking lot.

After a short drive, Brad dropped Erica off to get settled in at a local bed and breakfast, and then he made a quick stop at his office to check his messages and emails, since the office was basically just across the street from the B&B. The "quick" stop took an hour and change, so when he was done, his belly said it was time to get something to eat.

Looking out the window, Brad's mind started to go through the reasons for and against asking Erica to join him for dinner. She had been a little standoffish; for no reason that was apparent to him. "Damn, this shouldn't be so hard. We're both professionals, it's her first night in town, and she doesn't know anybody. Hell, if it were Bob, we'd run out to the pub for a beer and some pizza."

Against his better judgment he called Erica to ask if she'd like to go out for an early dinner, maybe pizza and a beer.

"Pizza and beer? I don't think so. Good night." Click, was her answer.

Brad was not really surprised. He looked at the phone, hung it up and made a stop at his favorite and, as it just so happened, last watering hole on the way home.

Brad picked up Erica outside the B&B just before eleven. She ran around the truck holding her arms tightly around her torso, trying to stay warm in her little jacket. It was much cooler this morning with a light mist falling.

"Didn't you bring a raincoat?" Brad asked.

"No, I don't own one and I don't want to get my new leather coat wet," she replied with disdain.

Brad shook his head, turned up the heat, and kept his mouth shut.

They met Jim Straighter at a local mom and pop restaurant for lunch. But they were unable to talk about "work" due to the local people being locals, and listening in on almost everything. The meal and small talk about local Juneau news was enjoyable enough. Well, other than when Erica wasn't able to get the salad she wanted, being it was lunch and that item was only available for dinner. Its limited availability was commonly known to locals, but not explained on the menu. Brad smiled inwardly, happy to be home.

Brad suggested they take a drive "out the road." He explained to Erica that the local term meant the area north of Auke Bay on the Glacier Highway. The nice thing about heading this way, there could be little to no cell phone coverage. So no interruptions.

Brad kept glancing over at Erica. She was mesmerized by the scenery. They had just begun their drive when they passed by a giant glacier. Brad didn't even notice it, but he could tell she thought it was stunning. Every turn brought a new breathtaking vista, he realized when he thought about it.

Just after they passed the Tee Harbor cutoff, Jim finally started to talk.

"On April 1, a group of four researchers chartered a helicopter and flew to Hasselborg Lake on Admiralty Island for a remote early season bear viewing trip. The report is, they were looking to catch bears emerging from their dens, and if possible, study the actual dens. They were to radio for a pickup when they were ready to return. They left no drop-dead date for retrieval.

"Friends reported them missing on the 3rd of May. We put together a SAR team and went into the area, not expecting to find much due to the time of year. But as you can see, this is a light snow year and we found their camp on the lake shore on the first pass. As soon as we landed next to the camp, we knew the story was not going to have a happy ending. The camp had been disrupted by bears and/or some other critters, but even that had been some time ago.

"There was no sign to indicate that anyone had died in the area, so we unleashed the dog and let her go at it. Well, to make a long story short, a couple days later after finding nothing, we widened our search for the second time and the dog hit on something. She started to whine and licks this big rock; she didn't want to give it up, even after some scolding. That's when I took a closer look."

Jim stopped there and it was obvious he was trying to find a way to explain what he saw. He didn't want to go there.

Erica put her hand on his arm and said, "That's all right. You don't have to describe it."

Brad immediately responded, "Yes, he does," and he made no effort to dodge the daggers shooting from Erica eyes.

Jim nodded and started again. "As I got closer to the dog, she turned and looked at me. I noticed the blood on her tongue. She'd found a big patch of still partially frozen blood and gore. The biggest bone fragment was not quite three millimeters; we also found some hair in the mess. By the different colored hairs it appeared to be from multiple people. But there wasn't enough left of anything for four people. We assumed predators had been at them. I'm getting ahead of myself. Anyway, we sent off the samples with one of the team members, and the rest of us continued the search for evidence for five more days before we were called in."

"We found nothing else at the site with the remains. No clothing, cameras or any other equipment. Nothing. So, we were thinking foul play. But we found no evidence of anyone else, and then there was some high-dollar equipment at the camp that hadn't been touched. So we're at a loss."

After a pause to gather his composure, Jim continued. "Once we got back to town, we were informed that the lab had identified all four of the missing-persons blood types in the samples, and now we're waiting for test results on DNA. But we're sure it's them. It was determined by the coroner that, based on the types of organ tissue in the samples, no one survived. So the decision was made to call the recovery team in for now."

Brad looked over at Erica, expecting her to reply, but she just waited for Jim.

"Well, I looked for any other events with the same M.O. and after typing in the data I had, the computer came up with your number, just your number. So that's about it for me, unless you have any questions."

"Not at this time, but we have your report and your number, so if we need anything else we'll call," Brad said, hoping this would end the conversation.

It didn't.

It never did.

Brad was turning around at the Eagle River turnoff, heading back to town, when Jim asked, "So what did this?"

Brad thought through the canned statements he was supposed to use. But knowing Jim's background, he knew the bullshit flag would go up instantly if he used any of them. So he decided to tell the truth, sort of.

"We're, or at least I'm, not completely sure. There are too many missing pieces. We'll get with your coroner and maybe even fly to the site if what we need isn't here. Then we'll let you know. I don't like to speculate."

This seemed to satisfy Jim. Brad was correct in his assumption that Jim just wanted this event to go away, and now he was going to be able to redirect the multitude of inquiries he'd been receiving lately to someone else.

When they crested the hill approaching Cohen Road, cell phone reception returned, as announced by Erica's cell phone ringing. Brad could tell it was not good news by the look on her face. After a few minutes of mostly listening, Erica hung up and looked out the window, but not at the scenery this time. "The WCC's chartered flight went down, killing everyone onboard. We've been directed to head back."

"Did they give a reason why we need to go back?"

"No, they didn't. They said to report back at once." She said with a bite.

After dropping Jim off at his truck, they drove back to the B&B. Brad called Alaska Airlines and secured Erica a seat on the late afternoon flight back to Seattle, while she checked out of her room. He drove over to the airport and pulled up to the passenger drop off area.

"Aren't you coming with me?" Erica asked.

"I'm not going home like you are. I don't have a return ticket, I need to pack and make some other arrangements before I leave. Plus, I wouldn't have enough time to drive home, get my bags and still catch the flight, even if they were packed. I'll catch the flight out in the morning."

"Maybe I should wait until the morning also," Erica said.

Brad could see she was upset, but she was holding it together. She didn't want to go. He knew she didn't want to deal with the problems that losing a good portion of the workforce would bring. He didn't know but she probably had lost some friends in the accident as well.

"Go on home. It's been a long day. You'll sleep better in your own bed," he said, adding, "If you don't want to go in alone, wait until I get there. You can pick me up at the airport as an excuse for going in late."

"I'll be okay. I guess I'm just tired," she said, gathering herself, and giving Brad a half smile. "Just get there as soon as you can."

Brad smiled back and then touched her lightly on the arm. "See you tomorrow."

Then he turned and walked away.

CHAPTER 9

BRAD WALKED THROUGH THE entrance of the headquarters building at 10:45 am with a box under his arm, but it was a day later then he'd planned. He couldn't get a seat on the morning flight the first day, so he scheduled one on for the next morning.

The normally busy building was eerily quiet, with a completely different feel. The receptionist was new, young and cute wearing a neat light gray pant suit. With a fake smile, she asked if she could help him as he walked up.

Holding out his ID, "I'm Brad Michaels, I'm h—"

"Oh yes, you're expected," the young blonde interrupted. "The CEO asked for you to go directly to his office. The others are already there waiting. Room 301."

"CEO?"

"Oh, that's the title the new director prefers. His name is Scott Clark, Dr. Scott Clark."

"Doctor?"

"Yes," she said with annoyance in her voice, and pointed to the elevators.

Brad thanked her with a mocking bow and smile, and then took the stairs to the third floor.

On the way up Brad recognized only one other person, a grumpy old bean counter he had to deal with once when he had a pay problem. Brad nodded and said "Hi," but received only a scowl in return. "Good to see some things are the same," Brad thought to himself. But he stopped the old man anyway. "Excuse me. Have you heard anything about the accident?"

The old guy stopped, looking perturbed, "Yeah, they gave us a briefing yesterday morning and said that the cause is still unknown and everyone on board was killed. A list is posted at the front desk. Looks like we lost around half of our workforce, most of them from here."

"Who's this Dr. Clark?"

"He's Jim Starkey's replacement. He showed up on the afternoon of the crash."

"That was fast. Thanks," Brad said.

The old man nodded and continued on his way.

As he walked up to the bosses' old office Brad noticed the CEO's secretary, or more politically correct, "Personal Assistant," had new furniture and a nice new brass name plaque was on Dr. Clark's door. All in less than three days. It was amazing how fast some things get done in the government while others take forever.

Brad knew agencies didn't grieve and they needed to continue doing business, but somehow it struck him as disrespectful to make such sweeping changes so quickly. It put him in a bad mood. He knew he was being unfair, but he could only hope this would go smoothly.

"Mr. Michaels?" asked yet another nice-looking blonde.

After Brad nodded, she called the CEO to announce his arrival. She asked him to have a seat and wait.

Brad walked around instead, looking at the new art hanging on the walls. Some of it still had tape from the packaging here and there. It looked expensive, but honestly Brad wouldn't know. The art review only took a minute, so he found the only magazine that remotely interested him, a *Yachting* magazine, and sat down in a new overstuffed leather chair.

After ten minutes the personal assistant's line buzzed and she said, "You may go in."

Brad got up, then decided to leave the box with the PA, then headed back to the leather chair and replaced the magazine. He took his time; it was maybe only an extra two minutes the CEO would have to wait before entering the double doors, but even without ever meeting him, Brad was sure his new boss would notice it.

A large, heavy-set man sat behind a new, very large mahogany desk looking at notes or something in a file folder in front of him. He didn't look up as Brad entered but just said, "Please shut the door."

Three others were sitting in the chairs facing, which Brad assumed, was the CEO. One, he didn't know. A middle-aged, forty-year-old man, but he looked to be in good shape, a biologist he'd seen before but hadn't met, and Erica. She was looking down at her hands, not wanting to make eye contact. They all remained quiet. He looked around the newly decorated room, wondering what it cost, not only the furniture, but the speed with which it had been done. He reminded himself not to prejudge. But it wasn't working.

Brad sat down in the chair next to Erica and waited for the CEO to acknowledge his presence. Right on the front edge of the desk, blocking much of his view, was an arched glass certificate of award acknowledging Dr. Clark's ten years of service with the Department of Homeland Security.

Brad waited and smiled, thinking to himself. "Tit for Tat." He could smell Erica's perfume. It struck him as strange, he's never notice her wearing it before. He wondered what the occasion was.

"We've been going over your file, Mr. Michaels," the large man said without looking up.

"Mr. Clark, I presume?" Brad asked.

That got his attention. His eyes snapped up but his head stayed still. "Doctor!"

"Then Dr. Clark, I presume?"

"Who else would I be?"

"Sorry, just making sure."

The CEO continued, "As I was saying, we've been going over your file and there seems to be some things missing."

Brad said nothing, just waited. But he thought, "This is not going well."

Dr. Clark finally said, "Your file doesn't contain a copy of your degree," then added after a pause, "Or for that matter, even mentions what school you attended or what you majored in."

"That's easy, I don't have a degree. But I think you already knew that," Brad said coolly.

"Sorry, just making sure," Dr. Clark said in a mocking tone.

"Anything else?" Brad asked.

"Yes, it seems that you did not complete the full two years as a trainee before you were advanced to a PCO."

Again Brad said nothing.

"Can you explain this?" the Dr. asked

"It should all be there. Training completed, hours in the field, time in contact, all meet or exceed requirements. And the recommendations of my mentor as well as the director." Then Brad added, "If it's not there, I have copies."

Dr. Clark studied the file for a few seconds, and then said. "Well, from what I see, you didn't warrant the position."

Brad was sure this was said to get a rise out of him. So he just let it slide and showed no emotion.

"I think—" started Erica, but was quickly cut off by the CEO.

"Your input has already been noted, Miss Hunt."

Brad gave her a small smile and a wink when she looked at him. She was backing him.

Erica quickly looked away, but Brad caught a glimpse of her faint smile.

Just that little exchange with Erica made a world of difference in Brad's mood. Sitting back in his chair, he took a deep breath and relaxed.

The CEO closed Brad's file and looked out the window of his office, then started to talk to everyone, Brad assumed.

"The Board appointed me, so I must assume they want me to

lead this agency. If my assumption is correct, then I will lead it to the best of my ability."

The CEO turned and looked toward them, but not really at them, then continued.

"I think a change of direction is required. We are given an opportunity to advance in the light of this minor setback."

Brad almost jumped across the desk, but he was able to keep his calm and he thought, "Minor setback. Almost the entire agency work force killed in an aircraft accident. Minor?" Ten years ago, he would have been headed for jail for beating the shit out of the guy.

"I intend to bring this agency out of the dark ages and up to speed with today's world. Streamline costs by using updated computer systems and programs and contract personnel where possible, doing away with the good old boy way of business by requiring proper education for all employees. And lastly, we need to change our way of thinking to a less is more approach."

By looking at the faces of the others in the room, Brad knew they'd heard this before. So, this was for his benefit. Why? Feeling this was a setup, he decided to keep his mouth shut. Something he'd only recently learned to do, and still failed at occasionally.

There was an awkward minute or two of silence before the CEO smugly looked at Brad and said, "Well, are you on board?"

"Yep, setup," Brad thought.

"Well, I work here and you're the boss, so I'll do my best," Brad said, trying to buy some time.

"That's not really an answer," pressed the CEO.

The others looked more nervous than he did. Well, except the first guy, the one he didn't know, he seemed to be almost enjoying it.

Brad finally said, "Without the actual details of your proposed changes, it's hard to give proper feedback. But I assure you, I'll work with everyone here to give any changes the best chance at success."

"There's a load of bullshit for you," Brad added mentally.

"Lack of a formal education puts you at a disadvantage," said the

CEO, and then sighed tiredly. "We need an infusion of new blood. I see that you were transferred here from the FAA. I don't think it will be a problem sending you back. You'll be on administrative leave until it's arranged."

Brad wasn't mad. He didn't know why, he should have been, but he wasn't, at least not yet. He just said, "Is there anything else?"

Everyone looked at him in disbelief.

Then the CEO said with a little unease in his voice, "No. That'll be all."

Brad got up to leave and caught Erica eyeing him. He gave her a sly smile and another wink, and then walked out, leaving the door open. As he passed the PA, he told her to give Erica the box he'd left there earlier.

Brad grabbed his coat and decided that he needed a beer. The closer he got to the bar the more the event started to get under his skin. He was trying to tell himself it was for the best; after all he really didn't want to work for the son-of-a-bitch. He reminded himself, he still had a good job with the FAA that he liked well enough and still lived in Alaska. So it was a good thing, Right? Bullshit, it still pissed him off. The guy was an asshole.

Halfway through the second beer, Brad was jerked from his internal musings by the smell of Erica's perfume. Looking through the mirror behind the bar, he saw her standing a few feet behind him, holding a new raincoat in her arms.

"Have you had lunch yet?" Brad asked without turning.

"No," she said as she sat on the stool next to him.

"They have good fish and chips here, or would you rather go someplace else?"

"I'm sorry about that," Erica said. She seemed more congenial, Brad wasn't sure if she didn't like to see people bullied, or if the loss of their co-workers had built a bond of sorts.

"What's that?"

"You know, up in Dr. Clark's office."

"Oh, that. Don't worry about it. I've got a good job and I still live in Alaska."

"It was bullshit, you don't deserve that," she stated.

Brad smiled at her through the mirror, causing her to blush. "She doesn't like bullies" he thought.

"What about you? Are you going to be able to work with these guys?"

"I've got to. I don't have another job to fall back on."

Erica stopped talking as the bartender came up and asked if she wanted anything.

She looked at Brad's almost empty beer. "I'll have one of those."

"Make it two, Mike," Brad said.

"Two ambers coming up," Mike said and retrieved two fresh mugs from the freezer and walked to the tap.

The two sat silently until their beer arrived, and they both ordered the fish and chips.

Once Mike was gone again, Erica continued, "He said he wanted you out from the start. I tried to say something, but he just got mad. I was afraid I'd lose my job."

"You didn't have to do that. But I really appreciate it. Thanks." Brad was looking at his beer and could feel Erica's eyes on him, making him a little self-conscious. He didn't like others fighting his battles for him. But he wouldn't tell her that.

"Before I forget, thanks for the jacket," Erica said as she looked down at the Marmot Skyline.

"How'd you know where to find me?"

"I saw you and Bob come in here once. It's also the closest bar."

"I'm going to miss him," Brad said, realizing this was the first time he'd allowed himself to talk about Bob.

Erica put her hand on his arm, her touch sending electricity through him. Looking over at her, he didn't see pity or sorrow in her eyes; he saw a question. Possibilities raced through his mind; after all he doesn't work with her anymore, the knot in his gut reappeared.

But it wasn't quite the same. He was at a loss, he wanted to ask her something, but he had no idea what. He started to get mad at himself for his insecurities. She must have seen his conflict because she smiled and her eyes told him, "I understand, I can wait."

Their food arrived, saving them from the tense moment, yet at the same time, they were both a little disappointed.

Erica broke the silence, "I might see you again anyway. I think I'm still on that Juneau investigation. So I should be going there again."

But with that came a new thought, something that really bothered him. He wouldn't be working with her anymore, so he wouldn't be there to protect her if something went wrong. And after today's meeting, that was the only way things were headed.

Brad reached for his wallet and retrieved a business card and wrote on the back, and handed it to her.

"What's this?"

"Not an option anymore. Please trust me on this." was his reply.

Erica looked at the card of a Seattle–based firearms instructor, with Brad's note on the back. "Priority. Brad Michaels." He could see the worry grow in her eyes as she read the card, but when she saw how serious he was, she but put it in her pocket without a word.

CHAPTER 10

ON ONE OF THE countless uninhabited small islands of southeast Alaska's Alexander Archipelago, eight-year-old Millie Odem ran back to the beach, trying to stay away from her younger brother. She was mad at him, again. Bobby had thrown moss at her while she was having a picnic with her doll Lucy. She knew it would be hard to hide from him. The island wasn't that big and the small grove of trees where they were camping was too well known by the whole family to hide there.

She came to a halt on the rocky shore and didn't see a good place to hide, except for their boat. The outgoing tide had left it high and dry on the beach. Millie decided that would have to do, and she covered the distance as fast as she could across the slippery rocks and wet sand, holding Lucy and the play dishes wrapped in a small blanket.

She tossed her load over the side and climbed on board the eighteen-foot StarCraft, hid under the canvas cover, then looked out the plastic windows to see if that brat of a brother was following her. She didn't see him. Good, she thought, and once again she laid out the make-believe feast.

Lucy had just started to drink her make-believe tea when Millie heard her mother calling to her, announcing that it was 9:30 and after her bedtime. Millie knew it was late, but the sun was still out and it wasn't raining, so she didn't answer or head back like she knew she should and went back to playing. Just a little longer, she thought.

Charlie Odem had seen his daughter go into the boat, so he wasn't worried about her, and he told his wife, Jean. He was enjoying his wine, homemade tapenade on pilot bread and the peace and quiet of the view offered by one of his favorite camping places. He just didn't want to be the bad guy right now.

"The sun will be down in forty-five minutes or so, and then I'll go get her," he told his wife and handed her a plastic cup of red wine when she got back from putting Bobby down in the tent for the night.

The sky turned pale red and the shadows disappeared. Charlie looked down at his wine. Empty. "Well, looks like I'm out of reasons to delay it any longer," he said to himself as he got up and headed down to the boat. He heard Millie's singing coming from inside.

"Hey, little girl, time to call it a night," he said as he approached the StarCraft.

"OK, Daddy," Millie said, running to the bow and jumping into his arms.

As Charlie put Millie on the ground, something caught his eye. It was just above the water between him and Admiralty Island. He might not have noticed it, except the water was extremely smooth and quiet.

He gave Millie a kiss on the forehead and sent her off to her mother. He watched her run up the path, then turned back to try to make out the unidentified object.

It was getting dark now, but the objects—he could now see there were more than one—were getting closer. They were large, maybe three or four.

Charlie reached inside the boat and retrieves his Mossberg shotgun, checked to make sure a round was chambered, then looked back to see the slow flapping of four large birds heading his way. Charlie's gut told him that something was wrong.

Running back to camp, he told his wife to get Millie and herself in the tent and stay there.

Jean could tell something was wrong, and she hurried Millie to the tent and zipped the flap shut, but she did not go inside. She returned to her husband's side and followed his gaze to the flying visitors heading their way.

"What are they?" she asked not looking at him. They knew that whatever they were, they were not birds.

"I don't know, but I don't like the way they look." He wasn't surprised she hadn't listened to him.

They moved closer to the fire and Jean put on more wood, hoping it would keep them away.

Darkness was falling quickly now, but they could still see the creatures starting to split up, two headed straight at them while the other two started to circle, one on each side. They were about a hundred yards out.

"Find something to use as a club," he told his wife.

Jean looked at the hand axe, but then decided on the shovel. It was lighter and longer.

The two creatures that had flown straight in landed between the beach and camp. Their wings folded against their backs, like birds, but no, it was different, like they had arms that separated from the wings. Anyway, it was wrong. But when they folded in the wings they were almost invisible.

They just sat there. He could hear them making deep, short coughing sounds. Then they both started to change color, almost flashing as they went from a light gray to black; the one on the right had colors rippled like a large stripe running up and down its body.

Both Charlie and Jean didn't see the other two diving in from behind. Charlie was hit high on the right shoulder and neck. A talon ripped open his throat, severing his jugular vein. He was knocked facedown with the creature landing on his back, pinning him to the ground.

Jean's reflexes were quick; she had seen the movement of Charlie's attacker and dove to the left. The second creature hit her right arm, spinning her around, but did not drive her to the ground. Her attacker, having missed its mark, was off balance and hit the ground and rolled, knocking over the folding chairs and ice chest. Jean saw the beast perched on her husband, screamed, and swung her shovel as hard as she could.

Charlie heard the twang of the shovel hitting the creature's head, and that knocked the beast off him. He pushed himself to his knees, still holding the shotgun. He knew he was bleeding badly, but he brought the muzzle in line with his attacker and pulled the trigger.

Charlie's shot was slightly off target when he fired at the creature. The shot still blew a hole in a partially open leathery wing. Losing focus, Charlie tried to pump another round into the Mossberg but found it impossible to make this simple thing happen. He slipped to his right, looked up to see the second creature, the one he'd shot, had leaped on his wife, followed quickly by the other.

Charlie's vision narrowed, becoming unfocused, then went black. He saw nothing, he had no more feeling, and he heard nothing at all.

CHAPTER 11

BRAD HAD BEEN BACK in Juneau for a few days, continuing to go to the FAA office to check email and messages, receiving the standard bulk, general information crap, but nothing that really concerned him or his transfer. But dealing with emails, time sheets and travel vouchers still used up most of the day, so he decided on heading out for lunch a little later than normal, right before heading home, figuring to make it a short Friday.

Brad walked across the street to the local Mexican restaurant and saw Jim Straighter as soon as he entered. Jim was having a meal with a group of his co-workers. Brad had seated himself and ordered a beer before Jim looked up from his tacos, but as soon as he recognized Brad, he got up and came over to his table. Brad could see Jim's mood got worse with every step he took.

"Got a minute?" Jim said, obviously trying to control his temper.

"Want a beer?" Brad said, giving him a little time to cool off, and waved to the seat across the table.

"I'm still on duty," he said.

Brad was in a good mood, and his cool and confident demeanor calmed Jim down.

The waitress came up and asked if Jim wanted something to drink as she deposited chips and salsa between them and dropped off a beer for Brad. Jim ordered an iced tea.

When she left, Jim started. Still a little upset, but quite in control. "Bear, my ass!"

Brad knew the WCC had given him one of their canned statements concerning the four dead researchers.

Brad looked at Jim with an understanding nod and said, "First, I've been taken off the case. But even if I was still on it, I couldn't add to the official statement even if I wanted to."

This stopped Jim in his tracks. Now he was not sure how to continue, so he watched Brad eat a few chips with salsa. The waitress brought his drink and took Brad's food order and left. Jim continued, "Can you at least give me a name and a number of someone to talk to?"

"Yep, I can do that," Brad said between bites.

"But it won't do me any good, will it?"

Brad could see his shoulders drop and eyes shift. He'd given up.

"How'd the families handle the statement?" Brad asked, knowing Jim's frustration.

"They weren't surprised and even a little relieved, I guess," Jim said, pushing the lemon in his tea around with a straw.

"Right now that's what's important," Brad said, wanting to add more but kept quiet.

They sat in silence for a bit. Brad's food arrived and he started to eat, expecting Jim to excuse himself, but he sat there looking like he wanted to say something but didn't know how to start.

So without looking up from his chili relleno, Brad asked, "What's up?"

"We might have something else," Jim said.

This stopped Brad in mid-bite. He looked around to see if anyone was within earshot. "Have you called it in to my people yet?"

"No, they're still doing the investigation. But I can already see that things aren't going to add up on this one," Jim said, taking a drink. "It's really not like the other one, but I think they're related. I'm not sure why I think that they are, but I do."

Jim saw that he had Brad's interest and continued, "On one of the smaller satellite islands near Admiralty, they found a family of four. The bodies were not ground up like the others, but they were partially eaten. So far, they haven't been able to identify the number or type of animals involved. My first thought was black bears, but they located no clear tracks, the bite patterns are inconsistent, and the claw marks are wrong for bears. And, the two kids' remains were found in the nearby trees. It just doesn't figure."

Brad had put his fork down and was listening intently. "Did the bite patterns look strange and vary in width?" Brad saw the answer in Jim's eyes. Then before Jim could speak, asked a second question. "Only four claw marks?"

Jim's mouth just stayed open, but didn't say anything.

Brad held up his hand, stopping anything Jim might have said.

"Call the number you did before. Tell them what you told me about the new incident." Then Brad added, "Don't tell them you talked to me."

Jim got up without a word and let Brad finish his lunch. But Brad couldn't finish. He got up, paid his bill and went home, not sure what to do.

CHAPTER 12

SUNRISE SATURDAY FOUND BRAD drinking coffee from a stainless-steel mug at the helm of his C-Dory in route to Sweetheart Lake, hoping to gather information from the friendly Rhunken about the attacks on Admiralty Island. Scout was on the mainland and might not be aware of activity on the island, but he had to start somewhere.

Brad expected a quick trip, so he'd packed light, but this time a big stainless-steel Smith and Wesson .50 caliber was on his side and a .338 was in its waterproof case along the gunwale.

The trip through the light rain and two-foot chop was done on autopilot. Not electronic, but mental, and Brad's body took over automatically piloting the boat to the anchor point while his mind danced between the thoughts of the unusual aspects of the all but certain Rhunken attacks: the bodies in the trees, and the fact there were bodies and not just smears. Then his thoughts shifted to being fired, or the better-sounding term "reassigned," then to this trip to make contact against orders, and of course, when a redheaded, smart-ass lady kept intruding into his thoughts.

Once anchored, Brad decided to leave the rifle on the boat, but double-checked the 500 to make sure it was loaded with the 440 grain CorBons. This was the first time he'd felt anxious when heading into a contact. Brad knew the Rhunken would sense it, and he was a little worried about how Scout would react.

Sitting next to the fire, Brad's mind snapped to the realization that he had been so preoccupied with his rambling thoughts that he couldn't recall 90 percent of his trip. For all he knew, he could have run over a whale and not noticed it. While autopilot might be OK to use when commuting to work back in Juneau, it could be a sure way to get your ass in deep shit out here.

Brad had been unable to sleep; in fact, he really didn't even try. Something was really wrong, and with Bob gone, he knew he was the only one that could deal with it. The main office wasn't going to be much help.

It was 1:30 AM when he smelled bananas. Bananas? Brad looked up wind in the direction of the smell and spotted Scout's movement as it stepped into a small clearing a little farther away than the last time they'd met. It already knew he was upset.

Then he remembered he'd given the Rhunken bananas on his last visit. This was its way of letting him know it was there—to call him, in a sense. When he first started out, Bob told him he had commonly used a call scent to attract the Rhunken, but after a while he stopped, as he had found it unnecessary. But he also said that sometimes the Rhunken gave people a "call scent," and if that happened, it would be best to keep it secret. Brad smiled and said, "I'm glad Bob isn't here for this. I'd have a new nickname."

Scout stood in the open, watching Brad, hesitant. Brad forced himself into a more relaxed body position, seated with his legs extended, hands folded across his stomach and allowing his shoulders to relax. This posture worked instantly and the Rhunken came forward, but stayed just at the brush line, still tense then looked south toward the lake.

"People?" Brad asked. He had not seen them, but he really hadn't looked.

The relaxing facial muscles along with the eyes answered his question. "Yes. But at a safe distance." Once again, this told Brad how off his game he'd been.

As Scout squatted on its haunches, Brad saw its throat vibrate. He actually felt the sound more than he heard it. It was a low frequency thrumming. Brad knew instantly the large male was communicating with another Rhunken, so he looked around and saw a smaller male just behind and to his right.

Brad forced himself to remain calm, mentally going over the body language training he'd received from Bob. He was tense, therefore so were the Rhunken. After a minute, not knowing how to start, he asked outright.

"Do you know of any human killing by Rhunken?"

The Rhunken gave him a bored look, which indicated no.

The smaller Rhunken squatted and sat on its heels. Brad normally didn't give names to Rhunken, but "Junior" came to mind.

Brad was hoping they would have known something. Now he was at a loss.

The Rhunken waited patiently as Brad contemplated his next move.

Something caught his eye across the small clearing in the brush, not more than three feet wide and twenty-five feet long. At the end, Brad could just make out a set of eyes looking at him through a large huckleberry bush. It was a juvenile Rhunken, probably the same one he'd seen on the last visit, but he couldn't tell. It was trying to hide. Its color was perfect, but it was backlit, and too close to the front. As soon as Brad's eyes focused on the youngster, it knew it was busted and retreated farther into the brush—and in doing so moved the bush. Another mistake. Brad smiled, it was learning. He knew it wouldn't be long before it would be all but undetectable, at most just a silent shadow to most humans

Finally, Brad asked, "If the humans were killed by Rhunken, will you help me find them?" He raised his arm, pointing in the direction of Admiralty Island. The height of his arm indicated a long distance.

The eyes of the Rhunken became interested ,and both stood up and walked toward him.

"Well, I'd better break camp," Brad told himself.

CHAPTER 13

AFTER DROPPING OFF THE two Rhunken on Admiralty Island, Brad just wanted to get back home and crash. He was working on a thirty-six-hour day by now and was starting to feel it. So when he saw Jim Straighter waiting for him on the dock in the bright early morning sun, he cursed himself for stopping at Auke Bay harbor for fuel and breakfast instead of heading straight home.

"That's what you get for being the only one in Juneau to own a blue twenty-five-foot C-dory." But hell, it was still too small of a town to really hide anyway.

Jim helped Brad secure the boat to the dock and waited until Brad had finished refueling and headed up the path towards a local waffle company for a late breakfast before saying anything.

"They didn't know what I was talking about."

Brad wasn't sure if he was surprised or not, so he asked, "What'd you tell them?"

"Just what you told me to say: no identifiable tracks, variable bite patterns and the claw marks."

"Who'd you talk to?"

"Some receptionist, I guess. She took my information, said she had no idea what I was talking about but would forward it to her boss, and then if they could help, or had any questions, they'd call back. But I could tell she didn't give a shit. Well, I got pissed and demanded to talk to someone in charge and was finally forwarded to a man that didn't identify himself, but he gave me the same bear attack story. I told him I didn't believe his bullshit. I hung up after he started to threaten me."

Brad could tell Jim was completely frustrated and was looking for help, but Brad was tired, hungry, and the walk uphill had his leg muscles burning.

"I'm sorry, but I can't help," Brad said with a bite in his voice.

Jim stopped, and then said, "I knew those people, Brad. I went to church with them."

"Shit!" Brad said, stopping short. He took out a pen and wrote down the only other number he knew at the WCC, Bob's old office number. He also wrote a name.

"You'll have to wait until tomorrow and I don't know who'll answer this number anymore, but ask for Erica Hunt and tell her everything." Then Brad added, "If you do reach her, talk to her, and only her. Tell her I told you to call."

Something that Jim said finally registered in Brad's brain. "Did you say you were threatened?"

Jim had to stop and recall. "Yeah, when I refused to take the bullshit bear attack story from the rude guy, he actually said I could also disappear if I didn't leave it alone."

Brad wasn't sure what to do about this but finally said, "I'll try to talk to someone about the threat."

Before Jim could go on, Brad turned and headed for his truck. He changed his mind about breakfast at the waffle company and decided he needed his favorite fishing breakfast instead. He started up his Ford and headed to the supermarket, got a pound of bacon, spicy bloody Mary mix and cheap vodka and headed home.

By the time Brad got to his office on Monday, he was pissed off. He dug out his day planner and found the number that should be the direct line and dialed it. Brad decided to try to give Dr. Clark the benefit of the doubt. Clark answered on the third ring.

"Yes?" he said with a hint of surprise.

"Sir, this is Brad Michaels and I'd like to have a word if you've got a minute?"

The pause was long enough to be discomforting before the CEO replied, "What can I do for you?"

"I received a complaint from a Juneau–based Fish and Game official, that he was threatened by someone from our Seattle office."

"Is this about the Juneau incident?"

"Yes it is."

"Well, Mr. Michaels, I think you need to leave this to the professionals."

Brad paused so that his temper didn't build; it wasn't working.

"Dr. Clark, I guess I'm not sure what we're talking about here. Are you saying you knew of and condoned these threats?"

"Mr. Michaels, believe me, they are not threats. They're promises and they need to be heeded by all those who are not part of the solution to this problem. And to make it clear, you are not part of the solution."

Now Brad paused long enough to make his own point. "Dr. Clark, I know *you* would never try to enforce your 'promises' personally, so that means you'll have to send someone, someone you'll have to pay. So let me promise you something. If I have an encounter with your enforcer, you'll know it's been dealt with, because he'll never come asking for payment." He paused for a beat. "But you may rest assured that in my own sweet time I will personally come to you for payment."

Brad hung up the phone.

CHAPTER 14

A WEEK PASSED WITH no word about the Rhunken attacks. No news was good news, Brad thought. He figured the new administration would blow some smoke up the butts of enough Alaskan officials to get the troopers and the Fish and Game to back off, then send in a PCO or two to take care of the problem. He'd even seen Jim in passing and received a friendly wave.

Expecting his transfer back to the FAA, Brad started working his way into the maintenance and equipment troubleshooting being done by the local technicians. Monday morning, heading to the air traffic control tower to work on the air-to-ground transmitters with a communications technician named Mark, Brad spotted Erica and a group from WCC that had just arrived on the morning Alaska Airlines flight. Other than Erica, he recognized only two of the others. A short woman in a light blue jacket, the kind of person that looked a little overweight but in reality wasn't. Brad believed her first name was Sandy, but couldn't remember her last name. He was pretty sure she was a biologist that worked with Erica. The guy in the high-dollar safari outfit that looked completely out of place was the one he'd seen in the CEO's office the day he'd been fired. One of the other guys was younger and obviously a nerd, but the last four looked like capable outdoorsmen.

Brad excused himself, letting Mark head to the radio room alone while he stayed in the lobby of the airport and followed the WCC crew, staying out of sight. The surveillance only lasted about a minute as the crew of eight already had their bags and walked out the front door to a waiting van that would shuttle them to the heliport.

The sight of the four rifle cases made him worry. "That's all we need," he thought, "is a bunch of government idiots running around southeast Alaska with guns." Well, maybe that was normal, but those guys were not from Alaska.

Brad went to the payphone and called Erica's cell. She answered on the first ring.

"What's going on?" he asked.

"Wow! That didn't take you long," she said in a surprisingly pleasant voice.

"Small town," Brad said, then asked, "You in charge?"

"No, and I can't talk now. Can I call you back?" she said, obviously not wanting to be overheard.

"I'll head to my office. It'll take me about five minutes to get there."

"OK, bye," was all she said, and then hung up.

Brad remembered that he had ridden with Mark, who had the keys. But it wasn't far, so he took off at a trot and used the shortcut behind the Flight Service station.

The phone was ringing when he entered his office ten minutes later. Caller ID said it was Erica, so he started right in. "Can you tell me what's going on?"

"After I received Jim's call—oh yeah, and by the way, thank you very much for that," she added sarcastically before continuing. "Anyway, after the call, I did some research and found out what you already knew about Rhunken attacks. I put together a report, and then took it to the CEO. This generated quite a bit of excitement and a flurry of meetings, but in the end, it was decided that we did have to respond and it was a good opportunity to get a new group of people trained."

"Are there any PCO's with you?"

"Rick Chapmen and Peter Smith. They are from the southeast region, Mississippi or Louisiana, or someplace down there."

"Southeast? No one from up north?" Brad said. This was starting to sound bad.

"Everyone else was on the plane or not available. That's why we have Jack Spelling and Doug Wilder with us, they're professional hunters." Erica stated, trying to sound like this was a positive.

The silence on the phone made her worry. "They have hunted in Alaska before, and Africa too, and they both have experience working with research groups in capturing and releasing dangerous game," she said thinking it would help. It didn't.

"Do you and Sandy have to go with them?" Brad asked, but already knowing the answer.

"Yes, we do," she said with a little annoyance and then said more calmly, "Brad, we need to rebuild our expertise. We know we're behind the curve on this, but that's why we're taking eight people. We'll be fine."

Brad was wondering if he should tell her about the Rhunken he'd taken to the island, but he was pretty sure they'd have swum back to the mainland by now. So he decided not to mention it.

"Where are you setting up camp?"

"On Admiralty Island. Richard said they used the two attack locations and came up with a search area and base camp location."

Brad paused, and then said, "Admiralty's a big island. You'll need to be more specific than that."

"All I know is, Richard said they have a place to start. I guess if he's wrong we'll just be doing some camping."

Brad figured they were taking a wild guess and would most likely come up empty-handed. "I still don't like it," he said, and then added, "but I'm close, and your cell phones will work from the island's eastern ridges." After a break he said, "I'm going to go right now and buy a cell phone. I'll call you on it, so you'll have the number if you need it."

Now it was Erica's turn to be silent, but she finally took the humorous path and said, "Brad Michaels with a cell phone. What's the world coming to?"

Brad felt his face redden and was glad that she couldn't see it. "Don't tell anyone," he said and quickly adding, "And just so you know, I'm going to shoot it when this is over."

Erica laughed and said, "Thanks, Brad. Really, but we will be fine." Then she hung up.

Brad wasn't so sure. He had a bad feeling about this.

CHAPTER 15

ERICA WANTED TO RENT a boat for the team's transport to the island under the guise of saving money and having transportation on site, but her real reason was to explore some of Alaska. Unfortunately, she was overruled, so the team jumped into a couple of cabs and had lunch at a Chinese restaurant and stopped by Fred Meyers for last-minute provisions before heading to the heliport and loading their gear onto two chartered A-Stars.

The helicopter trip to Admiralty Island was a short twenty-six-mile flight. If they took Erica's boat, the trip to their rented cabin would have been much slower and a hundred miles around the Glass Peninsula and back up the Seymour Canal. The rented cabin was located on the northwest end of the inlet, relatively close to where the "Hasselborg Lake" and "family of four" events had taken place, about 15 miles northeast and just a couple miles northwest of the locations respectively.

Once airborne, Erica looked out the window through the light drizzle at the docked cruise ships, made larger by the close proximity of Juneau's small downtown. It amazed her that the Rhunken could live so close to all these people and still remain all but unknown. She was happy that the WCC's group of eight was sent for the primary purpose to investigate, monitor, and learn why these events took place. The CEO assured her that any culling would only happen if it was absolutely necessary. Erica hoped that they wouldn't bring

PCO's at all, or worse, the professional hunters. But it was made clear to her that was not an option.

The group was made up of two professional hunters or "PH's," three biologists, two PCO's and one supervisor. One of the new WCC management team members, Richard was the head of the team, and Jack and Doug were the PH's, Rick and Peter brought the PCO expertise, and Erica was one of the biologists assigned, along with Mike and Sandy.

It was close to ten at night when the two helicopters lifted off from the cabin, leaving the team alone at their temporary home. They spent the remaining hour of light moving in and exploring what the cabin had to offer. It was located in a large opening that had been mown recently, and as remote cabins go, it was big, with a tin roof and unpainted plywood siding that had grayed with time and weather. There was one main room and two bedrooms. The owner had made sure there was plenty of firewood for the woodstove, and the water came out of a pipe from an unseen uphill source that poured into an overflowing cistern that supplied a small inside sink. The water was clear and cold. A small oil-burning heater stood in the corner with a full tank and spare fuel cans outside. There were some candles, a Coleman lantern, some canned food, and even blue curtains on the windows. Erica smiled, she loved it. Well, except for maybe the outhouse.

Richard checked the reception on his cell and finding there was none, gave a small grunt, threw it in his suitcase next to his cot, and asked everyone to gather around.

"OK, we're here. . . it's worse than I thought, but we'll just have to make do. I guess that's all the more reason to finish up and get out ASAP." He looked around the cabin with disgust before he added, "Get some rest. We'll start setting up the sensors in the morning."

Erica and Sandy walked outside and down to the water. The rain was gone and the clouds had opened up to show the reddening of the evening sky. The cackling laugh of a bald eagle caught Erica's attention, and she watched it soar down the canal heading south. The waters of the bay were like glass with the surface only interrupted by the occasional jumping fish.

"Damn it!" Sandy said as she slapped a mosquito on her arm, leaving a blood smear.

Erica smiled and handed her some insect repellent. "Bug Dope?"

"Aren't you the Alaskan?" Sandy said jokingly as she applied the repellent.

"That, a small knife and some waterproof matches were in the pockets of this jacket when someone gave it to me," Erica said with a small smile, still watching the eagle, which was now just a speck. But her mind was elsewhere, thinking of another Alaskan creature, wondering what he was doing.

For the next couple of days the group kept busy setting up cameras along with motion and heat sensors on some of the trails in the area, as well as taking short scouting trips into the local wilderness. During the off-trail explorations, everyone was introduced to the thorns of an extremely nasty plant. Rick looked it up after his introduction and supplied the correct and very appropriate name of the devil's club. They worked in groups of three, but quickly found that only five of them were in any real shape to hike in the steep vegetation-covered mountains of the island. So it was left to the PH's, Jack and Doug, the PCO, Rick, and Peter and Erica to do the field work, while the rest stood day watches on the cameras and sensors and made shorter trips afield.

At night everyone took turns standing watch. While the heat and motion sensors would give an audible alarm, the video cameras won't. Also, the first night they found out that the large number of bears and deer on the island sent the equipment into alarm several times during the night, so the audible alarms were turned off, allowing people to sleep.

Erica had no trouble believing the estimated population of 1,600 bears on this island of 1,465 square miles.

On the fourth day, Richard pulled both the PCO's and Erica aside and asked why they hadn't made contact.

Rick, the younger of the PCO's, started. "It's different here. We don't know the established meeting points, if there are any. And there's so much bear sign it masks everything else." His voice gave away his frustration. Then he added, "I am going to say it, even though you don't want to hear it. You need to call Brad Michaels and get him out here."

"That won't happen," stated Richard flatly, and then looked at Erica. "So we need to try something else."

Erica, looking dumbfounded, said, "Why are you looking at me? I'm not a PCO."

"You're the leading biologist and our Alaskan expert," Richard stated.

Erica had to smile, then shaking her head said, "I've only been to Juneau once before, and I've never seen a Rhunken in real life. If this makes me the expert, we're in trouble."

Richard was getting upset with her. "Erica, you're becoming part of the problem. We need solutions."

Her Irish temper flared in her eyes. "What?"

Peter had been content to remain quietly in the background, but finally joined the conversation to head off a possible battle. "Back home we sometimes used a call scent. I'm not sure what would work, because the scents are developed locally between the PCO and Rhunken. It could be anything. Normally it's something common, but not usually used in the woods. We used Listerine mouthwash."

Erica almost laughed but caught herself, then said, "I brought an electronic copy of Bob Strom's and Brad Michael's files and reports. I can look to see if a call scent was developed."

Richard looked at Erica then turned back to Peter and said, "Good work, Peter. Look into it and get back to me." Then he walked away.

Erica walked down to the water to let her temper cool a little. Sandy was already there, looking through a set of binoculars at something, but she removed them from her eyes, let them hang from her neck and greeted Erica with a smile.

"So how was the meeting with CEO junior?"

"Who?" Erica asked.

"Richard, the boss's son," Sandy said, and then added after seeing the look on Erica's face, "You didn't know?"

"No, I didn't. Wow! I don't know why that surprises me, but it does." Then after thinking for a moment says, "Wait, they don't have the same last names."

Sandy nods in agreement. "That's what I said when Heather, the CEO's PA, told me. But I guess Richard uses his mother's maiden name."

Erica shook her head. "It's sure not the same WCC, is it?"

"No, it isn't." Sandy raised the binoculars and continued her surveillance of two black-tail deer across the bay.

Erica enjoyed the silence for a bit, cooling off her temper, before excusing herself. "I'll talk to you later. I've got to go dig up some files." Then she headed back to the cabin, looking for Peter and hoping to avoid Richard for a little longer.

Erica didn't find Peter at the cabin, and Richard wasn't there either, so she grabbed her laptop, closed the door to the ladies' bedroom and started going through Bob's and Brad's reports.

Finding the call scent was easier than she'd hoped. A word search on one of Bob's early reports brought it up. "Old Spice." Erica recalled what Peter had said, "Something common, but not usually used in the woods."

She said to herself, "No mouthwash or aftershave in the woods. Except for calling Rhunken." She had to smile to herself. "Heathens."

As she read about the scent, Bob had specified it was used on the mainland groups. This raised the question: would the same scent call Rhunken on this island?

It was close to midnight when Sandy came in to find Erica still reading reports on her computer.

"Still up, I see," breaking Erica's spell.

"Yeah, I'd better shut this down. Batteries are getting low," Erica said.

The camp was quiet; the small engine generator had been turned off at ten.

Sandy could see Erica was deep in thought as she prepared for bed, so she had to ask, "Find something in the files?"

Erica looked mystified. "There are no Rhunken on this island."

This stopped Sandy, but before she could respond, Erica continued. "Neither Bob's nor Brad's previous reports mention anything about Rhunken on this island. Either this is a completely new contact, or a group has moved. I hope it's the latter because the call scent might work."

Sandy asked, "What about Brad's report on the Hasselborg Lake event?"

Erica watched the computer shut down and then said, "His initial report gave locations of the smear and suggestions of a follow-up, but he was fired before he could complete it."

CHAPTER 16

ERICA WAS SURE RICHARD would be upset when he received the information she found about the lack of reported Rhunken on this island. But he took the data as proof that Bob and Brad had not done their job correctly, which lent further support to the decision to terminate Brad. Richard was sure that some of the mainland Rhunken had migrated and that the aftershave call would work. The two PCOs did not enter an opinion one way or the other.

No one was surprised that Mike had Old spice aftershave in his shaving kit. As a lab scientist there were few better, but the affable nerdy biologist was just about as far from an outdoorsman as possible. He was not having a good time on his first field trip. He seldom stepped out of his room, much less the cabin, and when he did it was usually to go to the outhouse, which anyone could tell was one of the worst experiences of his life.

They decided to use the aftershave call on the trail about two hundred yards from the cabin. If that didn't work, they'd start moving it farther into the interior of the island. The scent dispenser, a toilet paper roll stuffed with a washcloth with a tail of three inches left hanging out of the bottom, was then soaked with Old Spice. This was left hanging in a tree in view of a host of cameras and sensors, hoping to catch the Rhunken's approach.

Richard asked the PCO's how long it should take. Both shrugged and Rick finally said, "It depends on the wind, how far from the

Rhunken we are, and even then it could be all for naught if there are too many people in the area."

Richard didn't like that answer and turned to Erica. "Do you have anything to add?"

"They're the experts, but the weather should help. There will be a slight wind blowing inland and no heavy rain for the next few days," she said, and then added to answer the look she saw in his eyes, "Rain would limit the scent dispersal."

This seemed to satisfy Richard, who finally said, "OK. I guess there's nothing else we can do, except wait."

The next two days were some of the most beautiful days Erica had ever seen. The third morning after hanging the scent dispenser, she was up before anyone else. Even Paul had fallen asleep while on duty, and his chin rested on his chest in front of the monitors. She didn't wake him as she went outside to enjoy the clear morning sky. It was light enough to see, but the sun was still behind the mountains. No wind, not a wisp. The bay before her was perfectly still, and she could see the mountains in mirror image. Walking down to the water, Erica was still in her sweats and had tennis shoes pulled over her bare feet. She hadn't wanted to wake Sandy by getting dressed. She pulled her raincoat closed to keep the slight chill away.

A ripple in the water that caught her attention was close, but it made no sound. At first Erica didn't know what it was until it rose out of the water a little more. A seal, a harbor seal if she remembered her lessons in marine biology class correctly. The seal turned its head, looked off to its left, and exhaled, its breath a cloud of mist in the cool morning air, and then as quickly as it appeared it vanished. But she had a smile on her face. It changed to a frown when she realized she regretted not having a cup of coffee with her. Something, she decided, that she'd have to remedy quickly, then returned to continue her morning musing.

As she was heading back to the cabin, the sound of rocks clicking stopped her. It sounded like someone walking on the rocky shoreline.

Erica quietly made her way closer to the water, in order to enable her to see around a patch of alders and farther down the beach. Erica gasped as she saw the grizzly, a relatively young one, but it was still bigger and closer then she liked or ever expected to encounter, probably sixty yards away and coming in her direction. It hadn't seen her yet, at least she hoped so. It was slowly walking and sniffing the seaweed that had washed ashore.

Erica slowly started to back up, along the trail leading back to the cabin as quietly as she could. She was starting to feel better when she heard the huff. She froze, turning her head slowly she saw a second grizzly, a twin of the first, not more than twenty yards away, standing on its hind legs looking at her, Erica was petrified. She couldn't move.

After what seemed like forever, the bruin raised it head slightly, opening and closing its nostrils, sniffing, trying to catch her scent. Erica watched, unable to think or even breathe. Then the sound of the cabin door opening up made the bear's head jerk toward the sound. It dropped to all fours and took off like a shot back into the woods. After a few seconds Erica took a breath. She was relieved, but at the same time, after seeing it move, realized it was so fast, and that if it wanted to, it could have been on her before she could have screamed.

Sandy's voice snapped her back to reality. "Want some coffee?"

Erica looked at Sandy, then back to the bears. They were gone. Not a trace. She realized Sandy hadn't seen them.

Sandy handed her a cup and said, "It's a little strong. It should help wake you up."

Erica took the coffee, her hand shaking a little, and then said, "Thanks, Sandy, coffee sounds great, but as for being awake, that's taken care of."

Erica started to tell Sandy about the bears, but was interrupted by loud voices coming from the cabin.

Both of them slowly made their way back to the cabin and waited, just outside. Richard was reprimanding Paul for sleeping on the job and saying something about an inoperative video camera. Then they heard Richard say, "Where the hell are Erica and Sandy?"

They both took this cue to go inside. Erica was thinking to herself, "What a way to start the day."

"What the hell is going on in here?" Richard said, red-faced and barely in control. "We're not at summer camp, ladies and gentlemen."

Richard turned to the professional hunter that had fallen asleep on watch. He was about to jump down his throat when Peter, looking at the monitor showing a black screen with the words "no input signal detected" on the bottom of the screen, said quietly, "They're educated."

He might as well have yelled out the words, with the reaction it got. Everyone looked at him and froze.

Erica broke the spell and asked the question that they were all thinking. "What do you mean, educated?"

"In well-established colonies, one or two scout Rhunken are educated about commonly used sensors and cameras." Peter could see the disbelief in everyone's eyes, so he continued. "We started to do this after a group of Big Foot hunters tried using electronics in the Northwest."

"You mean, we taught these things how to disable our own equipment?" Richard said, as if he couldn't believe what he was hearing.

Peter shook his head. "Not necessarily to disable, but to avoid them." Then he added, "Although it wouldn't be much of a leap for them to figure out how to destroy them."

Jack broke in with a more sarcastic tone, "I'm not so sure about this bullshit. If they did do this, and are that smart, why didn't they take out the rest of the sensors?"

Peter took the question easily, ignoring the attitude. "You have to remember, while these are animals they are extremely intelligent, more so than dolphins. My guess, they took out the video because they considered it the most threatening, and by doing so, they will force us to do what they want."

Richard asked, "And what's that?"

Peter calmly said, "To draw a smaller number of us back out there."

Doug, one of the quietest of the group, walked to the rifle cases stacked next to the wall, and said to no one in particular, "'Bout time. Let's give 'em what they want."

Paul and the other two biologists looked like they were in shock. Erica couldn't believe it. "Wait a minute. Why the guns? We're not sure these are the Rhunken that were involved in the incidents."

Peter looked at her and said, "We're not sure they're not, either."

Erica began to worry when both the professional hunters and the PCOs started to ready the weapons. She turned to Richard, "I was told we were to investigate, monitor only. No killing!"

Richard's look told Erica one thing, but his lying mouth said another. "The weapons are just a precaution. We just need to make contact."

"Right. Now I feel so much better," she said sarcastically, and then added, "When do we leave?"

Richard started to gather his gear. "You won't be required on this outing. You can relax and continue to watch the remaining monitors."

Erica was so mad it was hard to breathe. She was trying to think of something to say when Mike came up to her and put a hand on her shoulder. "I really don't want you to be out there with them."

His concern caught her off guard, and when she looked over and saw the agreement in Sandy's eyes, her temper cooled instantly. "OK, I guess there's nothing I can do. And you're right. It's not a good idea to go out there with those idiots."

Richard over heard her comment but let it slide. They needed to get ready. He was smiling.

CHAPTER 17

THE GROUP OF FIVE headed out just before ten. The professional hunters, Jack and Doug, led the way, weapons at the ready. Both of the professional hunters had been contracted by the WCC at Richard's request. They had years of experience hunting and guiding in Africa, Russia and the northern U.S., including Alaska.

Jack held the dubious distinction of being one of the foremost experts in hunting primates. Erica had strongly opposed the use of these men but had been quickly overruled. Jack was glad she was left behind; he didn't like her and knew the feeling was mutual. While he had hunted with larger groups, he wished he could have been by himself; he was more successful when he hunted alone. The biggest reason was he didn't have to worry about which laws to follow.

Doug was the more likeable and ethical of the two PH's, but was also happy she wasn't along, but for a different reason. He believed the fewer people on any mission, the better. Rick followed the two hunters, then Richard, leaving Peter to bring up the rear.

The weather had been better the last few days, so the trail was a bit drier, but still damp, allowing the group heading up the lightly used trail to make little noise. The two hundred yards to the scent dispenser and camera site was covered quickly, and Jack held up his hand, stopping the group when he saw the dispenser still hanging in the tree where they'd left it. Slow scanning the surrounding forest gave no indication of any recent visitors.

Jack spread his fingers on his upheld hand, indicating that he wanted the group to spread out and check the area. Doug slowly made his way to the makeshift dispenser looking for any sign of visitors, but he found none. Both PCOs headed straight for the disabled camera. It had been placed fifteen yards off the right side of the trail, slightly uphill, about five feet off the ground and attached to a pine tree. It had been crushed. By the looks of it, the Rhunken had used a limb or thin tree trunk to destroy it.

Jack continued up the trail another twenty yards to a slight rise and surveyed the area. Due to the trees and thick underbrush, he was only able to see sixty to seventy yards, and the only sound he heard was coming from his companions. He looked back, seeing the PCOs checking the destroyed camera. The other PH was crouched down studying the ground next to the scent dispenser, and Richard was standing in the middle of the trail, holding his rifle. He looked more like a scared rabbit than their leader.

A scent caught Jack's attention: bananas? Then it was gone. He decided it was nothing, and he quickly dismissed it. He walked back to Richard and, using hand signals, called everyone together.

"Well," Jack said to the PCOs, "what now?"

Peter glanced at Rick. "I'm sure we're being watched. It, or they, are now studying us to see if we're friend or foe."

Rick added, "We need to relax and try to project an unthreatening appearance."

Annoyed, Jack looked around, slinging his rifle over his shoulder. "OK, now just how do we do that?"

Rick shrugged. "It knows who we are and it will follow us back to camp. So I suggest we just head back and have some lunch."

Richard looked dumbfounded. "Lunch? Back to camp? What, will this thing just come into camp and knock on our door?"

Peter smiled. "No. But this is a good sign. It will follow us, just as Rick said, and it will watch us for some time before it feels comfortable enough to show itself. Or it won't, and we'll never know."

Jack was not pleased. He didn't believe Rick and Peter, but he didn't have a better idea either. "All right, we'll try it your way. For now." Then added, "Let's go back."

The five headed back down the trail toward the cabin. The forest was dead quiet and every little sound they made seemed extremely loud. With each pop of a twig or kicked rock Jack was getting more upset.

The biologists were surprised that the party had returned so soon. Erica was also pleased that they had not encountered the Rhunken out on the trail and felt better when she learned that the encounter might happen here, where she had a better chance to affect the outcome. She hoped anyway.

Also, the boat delivering supplies had arrived and the extra hands moving them off the beach and into the cabin was appreciated.

At Peter's suggestion, they took turns sitting outside next to the fire ring, keeping a low-key watch. "Read, daydream, eat, whatever, just try to look non-aggressive, but keep your eyes open."

The rest of the day was a standard southeast day filled with light rain and overcast skies, but uneventful overall, other than Peter giving Sandy a lesson in firearms, showing her how to load and shoot a shotgun safely. As soon the sun started to drop toward the mountains, a front moved in and dropped the temperature.

Erica was inside the cabin preparing the evening meal of spaghetti with spicy reindeer sausage. It was a first for everyone and most of them would partake, all but Jack anyway. He almost always made his own meals and ate alone. This didn't hurt Erica's feelings at all.

During Mike's turn as outside watch he was sitting alone by the fire, trying to keep the chill away. He was thinking that if they wanted unthreatening, he was their man, but he didn't care. He just sat back and enjoyed the fire and some of the fresh fruit brought in by the supply boat this afternoon—a slightly overripe banana.

Mike stared at the fire, it was hypnotic. His thoughts roved among his companions, one by one. He generally liked them, but he really didn't like Jack; he was afraid of him. Mike knew that Jack despised him also, mostly for being a wimp. Jack occasionally made disparaging remark towards him, and would probably do more than just make remarks if given a chance. It had started on the first day, when Jack made a smartass comment about him having to make multiple trips to carry his luggage. Erica had shut him up by staring him down as only a redheaded Irish lass can. Mike knew he was a wimp, but he'd made peace with it a long time ago.

A movement caught Mike completely by surprise, and when he looked at the thing that caught his attention, he knew it was a Rhunken. He'd only seen photographs of them before, but it was unmistakable. Mike wasn't sure what to do. Amazingly, he wasn't frightened. He was actually worried he'd scare it away. Mike forced himself to sit back and relax, look at the Rhunken and greet it as he would a friend. "Hi there, it's good to see you."

Mike could see the Rhunken relax, its shoulders drop slightly and its head more erect. The reaction made Mike smile.

What Mike couldn't see was that Jack had been watching him. Jack had a feeling the Rhunken would show when Mike was on watch. It made sense. Mike was the least threatening of the bunch. Jack had set himself next to the window overlooking the fire ring and waited. When he saw Mike freeze, then start talking to something just out of sight, he knew what was going on.

Jack slowly got up, made his way to his rack, and retrieved his rifle. "Head call," he announced to the group. He'd made it a habit of always taking his weapon with him to the outhouse, so no one even gave him a second look as he headed out the door.

The cabin's arctic entryway gave Jack the opportunity to load the .375 H&H and remove the scope covers. Jack could hear Mike's voice, though he still couldn't quite make out what he was saying. But he really didn't care. The cabin door opened quietly and the door covered his movement as he raised the rifle to his shoulder. Jack's eyes skimmed over Mike, noting the direction of his focus. The cabin entrance was slightly behind and to Mike's right; the Rhunken would be over Mike's right shoulder.

Jack stepped to his left, just clearing the corner of the cabin, bringing the Rhunken into view. The adrenaline Jack felt running through his veins gave him the rush he was hoping for. He'd hunted for years and taken numerous dangerous game trophies, but over the years the thrill had lessened. But he felt it now. It burned in his blood.

Simultaneously, Mike turned to address the new movement he'd heard over his shoulder. Jack, sighted through the 1x4 Burris rifle scope, centering on the chest of the Rhunken. The creature shifted its focus from the man sitting at the fire to a man with a weapon pointed at it. The Rhunken's body tensed, bending at the knees as its leg muscles contracted, loading the power it needed to move it out of harm's way.

The roar of the .375 took everyone but Jack by surprise. The concussion felt was just as shocking as the sound, due to the closeness of the high-powered rifle shot. The world seemed to freeze as everyone's brain dealt with the sensory overload. Erica was the first to move; she knew instantly what had happened. She ran for the cabin door, throwing it open, screaming as she cleared the entryway. "No!"

The first thing Erica focused on was Mike getting off the ground. Apparently he had dived to the ground as the shot was fired, upending his chair. The sound of the bolt being worked on Jack's rifle gave a new direction for Erica's attention. Jack was walking away from her toward the tree line with his rifle at the ready.

"What the fuck are you doing?" Erica screamed at Jack, but his focus on the downed Rhunken stopped him from hearing anything she'd said.

The others were making their way out of the cabin, still in shock. Peter and Rick had rifles in their hands.

Then Erica saw it. The Rhunken lay in the weeds a few feet from

Jack. She was instantly sick to her stomach. "No," she said quietly, more to herself than to anyone else.

Doug, Rick, Peter and Richard came to where Jack and the downed creature were, as Sandy joined Erica still standing next to Mike.

As Jack approached the Rhunken, he knew it was dead. The shot had gone through its neck, killing it instantly. Jack was amazed at the wound. He'd aimed for the chest. He knew he must have jerked the trigger as the Rhunken moved to get out of the way. But today luck was on Jack's side. His bad shot had hit its mark only because the Rhunken had been much faster than Jack had expected, moving it into the path of the bullet. Of course, he would never tell anyone that. He would say the neck shot was planned to drop it instantly, if anyone asked.

Richard turned back to the biologists. "Sandy, Mike, let's get some samples as quickly as possible." Then as an attempt to get Erica away from the scene, he added, "Erica, make sure the stove in the cabin is off." Then he added, "On second thought, make us a fresh pot of coffee."

But Erica ignored Richard. Her temper had finally cleared the fog of shock and she picked up a piece of firewood and headed for Jack, hate in her eyes.

Peter had been half expecting this and was in position to stop her. But, then he thought, "What the hell," and he let her walk by and get in the swing. The blow wasn't as good as it could have been, but it was effective, catching Jack at the base of the neck, dropping him like a rock.

Peter and Doug grabbed Erica and hauled her away before she could get a second swing in. Richard started screaming at Erica as he rushed over to Jack, helping him up. Jack looked dazed but OK. Peter smiled as he led Erica away, noticing that Jack's rifle scope had smashed against a rock and shattered when he'd gone down. Peter knew Jack would recover quickly from the hit upside the head, but he'd never recover from the destroyed rifle scope. But Peter also knew Jack would never confront Erica about it.

Even though she felt better after she'd clobbered Jack, Erica was still pissed. No one questioned Jack as to why he shot the Rhunken, especially after they'd found a weathered ladies hiking boot in its hand. The consensus was that it must have belonged to one of the eco-tourists that had been killed in the spring. Erica was afraid they were right.

Even though they were completely disgusted with the killing, Erica, Mike and Sandy went to work taking samples and measurements of the dead Rhunken. Erica noticed Sandy was getting some assistance from Peter, and noticed a lot of eye contact. "Well, good for Sandy," she thought and got back to work.

The Rhunken was a young male, in good health and well nourished. If this was the Rhunken that was responsible for the killings, there was no obvious medical reason for it. A full necropsy would have to wait until they could get the body back to the lab. In the meantime, they wrapped the body in a blanket with what little ice they had. With the help of four men, they moved it into a small shed normally used to store ATVs.

After the biologists completed their tests and stored the samples, Richard called the group together. Looking at the two PCO's, Richard asked, "Is this the problem Rhunken?"

Rick said, "Could be, but we'll never know for sure."

Peter remarked, "It was in the area of the events, it was definitely capable, and it had an artifact in its possession." Then Peter shrugged and added, "But that is a problem in and of itself. I can't think of a reason for it to have the boot, unless someone asked it to find it."

Jack said, "It kept a trophy. I've seen chimps do the same thing in Africa."

Richard looked at Peter. "Could this be the case?"

Peter shrugged. "It's possible, I guess."

Erica wanted to say something but bit her tongue, knowing they were full of shit. But she also knew that if they believed this was the rogue Rhunken, their mission would be complete and they could leave and she could get out. She had to get away from these men.

Erica's silence made Richard's decision easier. "OK, I think we have our culprit. I'm going to call in the Coast Guard for extraction. It will take a little longer, but we can't risk any attention that using a public charter might bring when we transport the Rhunken out." Then he added, "Good work, everyone."

Looking at his watch, Richard could see it was after hours in Seattle. He'd make a bigger impact if he waited for morning to call the main office on the satellite phone to report his success. There would be more people present during working hours, and it would be easier to request their extraction. Besides, they needed a night to celebrate anyway.

CHAPTER 18

RICHARD WAS AMAZED AT the amount of alcohol that surfaced for the "celebration." Drinking had not been off limits during the trip, but no one had imbibed, at least not openly. Even Erica was drinking a summer ale. Her choice surprised him, since he had not figured her for a beer drinker. But it appeared she was not really celebrating as some were—more like she was drowning something. But right now Richard didn't care. His task was complete, earlier than expected and under budget. His father would be happy.

Erica, Mike and Sandy were by themselves in the kitchen area, drinking and eating mixed nuts, jerky and other miscellaneous snacks. Talk between them was light and directed away from work. Mike and Erica were amused at Sandy's split attention; she was constantly glancing at Peter across the room, while he talked guy stuff with the guys. The only way Erica kept her temper was to remain seated with her back to the rest of the cabin.

Richard was already starting to feel the alcohol. He felt great, in fact. He watched Sandy from the rear for a minute, but he really wasn't interested in her. But when he looked at Erica leaning on the counter, slightly bent over, he thought, "That's what I really want."

He had hoped she would have warmed to him by now, but she hadn't, and time was now running out. So when she got up and told the other biologists that she needed to get some fresh air, he watched her as she put on her raincoat and went outside. Richard gave her a couple minutes, then followed.

Erica heard the cabin door open. Even though she was out of sight, down the trail, near the water where she had had the encounter with the bears, she heard Richard call her name. Not feeling social, and certainly not wanting to deal with him, Erica stepped off the trail and stopped behind a large blueberry bush and under the boughs of a giant Sitka spruce, thinking she should be hidden from the trail. She knew Richard wouldn't stay outside long. It was late, the sun was down behind the mountains, but not yet completely dark. It was cool and a light mist was falling, and as he came into view she could see he was not dressed for it.

Erica's hiding spot wasn't good enough, though, and Richard saw her. He stopped and said, "Keeping out of the rain?"

"Not really," was all she said in response and started back to the cabin.

But Richard stepped in front of her, a little too close for comfort, and said, "When we get back to Seattle, I'd like to have dinner with you."

Erica was taken aback. "I don't think so."

Richard smiled, reaching for her arm, and asked, "I think it would be good for us to get to know each other better, don't you?"

Erica wrenched away from his hand. "No, I think I already know more about you than I care to."

Richard's smile changed slightly. "This is a very important decision you're making. I'm not saying it will make your career, but it could break it."

Now Erica was mad, probably the maddest she'd ever been at a man. She said, "Fuck you, Richard. If you ever approach me like this again, I will file charges against you." She turned her back on him and headed back to the cabin.

Richard watched her go, listening to the sound of her footsteps on the gravel path, wondering what he was going to do about this one. Finally, he shrugged and pulled out a miniature bottle of vodka from his pocket.

Erica looked back to make sure she wasn't being followed and saw that Richard was heading down onto the rocky beach. Then she saw that something must have caught Richard's eye, drawing his attention to the south. Whatever it was, it was out of her sightline. As Richard started walking down the shoreline trail, his focus fixed, she thought she'd better warn him about the bears she'd seen earlier, but decided to let him take his chances. Soon Richard was out of sight, and she made her way back to the cabin.

Erica was almost at the cabin when she stopped. She could hear the loud, happy conversations from within. She wasn't ready to rejoin the party. She shook her head, knowing the revelry was at the expense of an innocent creature. Without thinking about it, Erica glanced at the shed that held the body of the Rhunken.

The door was open. She stopped in her tracks. It was dark enough, so she couldn't make out the interior.

"Now what?" she asked herself as she walked over to the shed, almost afraid to look inside. It was empty. The dead Rhunken was gone!

Erica snapped her head around as if to catch whoever or whatever had taken the body, but she saw nothing. A chill ran up her spine. Richard was still out of sight, so she ran the short distance to the cabin, opened the door and rushed in.

The quickness of her entrance caused the door to slam against the wall, making a louder noise the she'd meant, catching everyone by surprise and silencing the room. Erica quickly did a visual muster. Everyone was here except Richard.

"What's wrong, Erica?" Peter asked.

"The Rhunken is gone," she replied.

"Gone? What do you mean, gone?" Jack snapped and started for the door.

He pushed past Erica and was followed by the others. As Rick passed he asked, "Where's Richard?"

"He was on the beach," Erica said as she followed the men outside.

The group quickly reached the shed and confirmed Erica's observation. Peter still had most of his wits about him and tried to stop the group from destroying what was left of any remaining sign indicating what happened to the Rhunken. "Look around for any evidence, tracks or drag marks," Peter stated.

The group fanned out and searched for sign, but found none. Some of the less experienced members actually destroyed what little there was. After fifteen minutes, Rick asked again, "Where's Richard?"

This time the question stopped everyone in their tracks. They knew something was wrong. Erica started for the rocky shore where she'd last seen him. A sick feeling in her gut told her that he was in trouble. No, she knew it was worse than just trouble.

Jack stopped the group before they got too far down the trail, telling them to wait while he headed back to the cabin to retrieve their weapons, quickly followed by Doug, Rick and Peter. This time no one complained.

The missing Rhunken vanished from everyone's thoughts as they reached the rocky shoreline. A light rain started to fall again. It was as dark as it was going to get this time of year, and the overcast sky made it even darker, but it was still light enough to see. The lack of contrast made the forest look dull, even ominous.

Jack took the lead, following Richard's tracks. They stood out on the well-worn but rained-out trail. Even Erica could have followed them as they headed south. She looked back to see Peter bringing up the rear. Erica could see the worry in his eyes. The same look was in everyone's eyes.

The tide was out, exposing more of the shore and with it batches of seaweed and mini geysers of water expelled by clams. The trail Richard had left ended on the rocky shore. Jack continued on without slowing, following sign Erica couldn't see. She shifted her focus from the ground to the terrain ahead hoping to see Richard now that more than a mile of shoreline came into view. Nothing.

The noise of a murder of crows momentarily caught her attention. One of the crows carried something into the air and dropped it from about thirty feet in the air. When the object struck the rocks and shattered, Erica identified it as a clam. The crow dove to dine on its meal, but was immediately joined by other crows, and a small fight was ensued for the meal.

"Here!" Jack said. Erica turned from the crows to see him pointing at something on the ground.

"Looks like he started to run," Jack said, and he started inland, heading for the tree line. The rest of the search party followed.

Erica could barely see the depressions of the footprints Jack was tracking in the rocky ground, wondering how he could derive anything from these, but she didn't doubt his skill.

Jack, Doug and Rick froze at the same time, bringing their weapons to low ready. The others followed their gaze to a black patch of liquid on the ground and flattened grass. Erica knew it was blood, but there was so much of it. It couldn't have come from a human. Could it?

Sandy must have figured it out also, because she threw up and this made Mike do the same. Peter walked past the biologists with a glance at Sandy and joined the forward group.

"Where is he?" Peter asked.

Doug raised his rifle and pointed at a stand of alders. "There," was all he said.

Erica pulled herself together and her eyes filled with resolve. "How do you know that?"

"See the droplets?" Jack said, pointing at the grass, then to a bush of some kind. Erica could then see the blood trail leading to the alders.

"Shouldn't there be drag marks or something?" But as soon as she'd asked, she realized that they were asking themselves the same question.

Doug finally said what the others didn't want to. "He was carried."

The PH's spread out and led the way, followed by the PCO's on their flanks, weapons at the ready.

Peter called over his shoulder without looking back, "You three head back to the cabin."

Mike and Sandy instantly obeyed the order, happy to get as far away as possible, as quickly as possible. No one was surprised when Erica ignored the order and continued to follow the search party to the stand of trees.

The PH's stepped over something as they moved forward, and when she arrived at the object she looked down at a large glob of coagulated blood. She knew it hadn't been there long. She still could not bring herself to believe this was from Richard.

The sharp movement of Jack raising his fist to halt the group did exactly that. Erica could see past him to the point of his focus, a matted area in the waist-high vegetation. The others silently spread out, checking the surrounding area with tense professionalism.

Erica stood still just out of sight of what lay in the center of the matted area, not sure if she wanted to look. The sudden realization of the fact that she was unarmed frightened her. She had never felt the need to arm herself before, but she knew she'd remedy that from now on.

Peter came in from the back after circling from the left and Rick from the right.

"Nothing?" Doug asked. The PCO's just shook their heads.

The men advanced into the matted area, Erica waited just out of view. The edge of the circle was stained with what she knew to be blood. Her hopes that the blood was from something other than Richard were dashed when Jack took his rifle barrel and picked up a shredded jacket. It was Richard's.

Erica turned around and sat on the ground with her back to the scene. She didn't want to be there, but she couldn't leave. She wasn't sure what she felt. She knew she was in shock, but she felt in control. She could not lose control, especially now.

She took a deep breath, stood up and called out while turning to the men, "What happened?"

The question caught the men off guard because no one answered. Erica took a step toward the group. "Well?"

Peter started to speak, but Jack cut him off. "He was eaten."

Jack's attempt to shock her went unrealized as Erica kept her poise and said, "That's it? That's all you can tell me? Was it a bear?"

Doug stepped between them and began, "Whatever they were, they attacked Richard back there." He pointed back at the first area.

Erica interrupted, "They? There was more than one?"

Jack came forward but was stopped by Peter, who said, "Yes, looks to me like at least three, maybe—."

Peter interrupted, "Four. You can see where they knelt as they fed. It looks like Rhunken did this, young ones."

Peter squatted over an area of matted grass. "They're not very big. It's odd that an adult is not with them."

Erica stayed just out of sight of what remained of her late boss. "So, you're saying we have an unsupervised group of juvenile Rhunken running around killing people?"

Peter stood up. "Yes, that's exactly what it looks like. And we probably made it worst by killing an adult, if not the only adult in the area."

The wind shifted and brought a scent along with the realization that she had reached her limit. But she still refused to show it. "I need to call in and report what's happened. Is there anything else you can surmise about his death?"

No one answered for a minute, and then Jack looked at her. "He didn't die well."

"Get him ready to go home," was all she said as she headed back to the cabin.

CHAPTER 19

THE RINGING OF THE phone came as an annoyance not because of the hour, but because Scott Clark had to put down his glass of brandy to answer it.

Looking at the caller ID, he recognized the generic display of a satellite phone. Probably Richard, but maybe not.

"Yes," his standard greeting.

"Dr. Clark?" came a women's voice.

Scott knew instantly who it was, but as a rule he never let anyone feel they were important enough for him to know them by their voice. "May I ask whose calling?"

The question surprised Erica. "Oh, I'm sorry. This is Erica Hunt, and I was calling for Scott Clark."

"Erica, this is Dr. Clark."

Erica took a deep breath. "Sir, I'm sorry I have to be the one to inform you, but there's been a problem up here."

With an annoyed voice, "Yes, yes, and why are you the one to inform me? Where's Richard?"

Erica's pause actually told the story. "I'm sorry to inform you that he was killed."

His thought shifted back to Russia and that PCO that died there. He couldn't remember his name. He wondered if Richard had died that way. He was surprised that he didn't feel any remorse. "Any details to report?" he said with a cold edge.

Erica said shakily, "A full report will follow when all the facts are gathered. But, as of now, we are all but certain Richard was killed by a group of four Rhunken. He appears to have been partially eaten."

Erica continued reporting the ongoing recovery arrangements, pending autopsy schedule and the standard cover story that would be released to the press upon his approval, but Scott wasn't listening. He was picturing Richard's body torn apart.

"Was he alone when he was attacked?" Scott said, cutting off Erica's report.

"Yes, yes, he was, sir."

"Why?"

"We're not sure. The group was occupied with the discovery that our Rhunken specimen had gone missing. We calculate he was alone for about fifteen to twenty minutes when we noticed he was gone. We're not sure what made him walk down the beach and out of sight."

"Miss Hunt, did Richard appoint you as second in command, or were you elected after the fact?" he said, anger building in his voice.

"Neither, sir. I just kept things going. I didn't mean to take command."

"But you did. And it's apparent you're doing a good job. So I'm going to keep you there and task you with the completion of the assignment. And your first obligation is to tell me why Richard was alone."

Erica sounded stunned by the request. "Richard made some unwanted advances toward me. I'm afraid we had some words, and I assume he went for a walk to cool off."

Dr. Scott paused. He knew Richard had issues with women in the past, most had proved to be gold diggers and were easily scared off. Others had cost money to avoid legal trouble. Erica was one of the original employees he respected. But, she was a strong woman and he was worried how she would respond to being treated disrespectfully. "Do what it takes, get the people you need."

She said, "I'm going to bring Brad Michaels in to assist."

There was a long pause this time as he recalled Mr. Michaels' file. He knew Brad had the propensity to be trouble. His military background along with being a fucking boy scout, always following the rules—he'd never even gotten a speeding ticket. He knew he could never control him. And teamed with Erica. It could be a big problem. The CEO finally asked, "Is Jack Spellings around? I'd like to speak with him."

Erica looked toward the beach and the group bringing Richard's body, wrapped in a blue tarp, up the trail. "Yes sir, I'll hand him the phone."

She walked down the trail and met the group. The men carrying the body continued to the shed as she held out the sat-phone to Jack. "Dr. Clark would like a word."

Jack took the phone and walked back down the trail. When he saw that Erica was leaving, he brought the phone to his ear. "This is Jack."

"Mr. Spellings, are you alone?"

"Yes sir."

"Ms. Hunt said Richard made some unwanted advancements toward her. Did you witness this?"

A small smile came across Jack's face. "No. Every interaction I saw between Richard and Erica was done strictly professional. I have no idea why she would say something like that."

After a few seconds' delay Dr. Clark inquired, "She said a group of Rhunken attacked Richard. Is it possible that she had anything to do with this?"

Jack's smile didn't fade. "I'm not sure. I don't think she has the ability to call Rhunken, but she could have easily left him in a situation that would have put him in harm's way, especially if she didn't raise an alarm when she should have. But why would she do that?"

"I don't think Ms. Hunt liked Richard, and now that he's gone, she wants to bring in Brad Michaels to assist."

Jack's smile went away. "I don't think that's a good idea," he said with a little acid in his voice.

"I agree, but I've decided that a few adjustments need to be made, and having Mr. Michaels and Ms. Hunt in the same location may help, especially in an area with such a high probability of hunting accidents."

Jack's smile returned. "I might be able to help a little in that regard."

Dr. Clark said, "No, just do your job. I'll bring in some specialists."

The line went dead in Jack's ear. He turned off the phone, looked around at the sky, noticing it was starting to lighten, even with the morning sun still hidden behind the low-hanging clouds, and said to himself, "Looks to be a nice day."

Back at HQ, the CEO picked up the phone and dialed a number from memory even though he hadn't used it for a very long time. After all, it wasn't a number he would want found in his possession if things didn't go as planned.

It was answered on the first ring. "Yes."

Dr. Clark paused, then said, "I need two items handled quickly."

There was no reply, just silence.

Then the CEO said, "I'll leave a package for you at the Alexis front desk in Seattle on your way to Juneau."

The line went dead and the CEO closed his phone and smiled.

CHAPTER 20

THE COAST GUARD PILOT that had responded to Erica's call was overseeing the crew lifting the body and securing it in the chopper when he overheard Sandy ask Erica, "After what they did to him, do you think Brad gives a shit, and even if he does, do you know where he is? And after what you've told me about him, I'm sure he'd rather be back at his house, drinking beer."

Before Erica could answer, the helicopter pilot responded, "Would you be referring to Brad Michaels?"

Both ladies looked at the pilot with a shocked look that told him that was precisely who they were talking about.

The pilot finished securing Richard's body and then turned to Erica. "Hi, I'm Skip Nelson, and I'd bet my boat I know where he is—if he's not at home drinking beer, that is."

"Can you take me back with you to Juneau?" Erica asked

"No problem. We'll be lifting off in about ten."

Erica ran back to the cabin to grab a few things.

Just after lift-off, Skip asked Erica, "What happened to your co-worker, if you don't mind me asking?"

Without looking in his direction, she murmured, "Bear attack."

Erica knew he didn't believe her, but she also knew he wouldn't push the issue. Sometimes you have to love the military, she thought.

After a few minutes of just the sound of the helicopter rotors muffled by the headset, Erica asked, "Skip, how do you know Brad?"

"I've been picking him up or dropping him off in various remote locations for a few years now. Brad used to tell me he's working for the FAA, doing site surveys for new equipment. But he doesn't even try to explain anymore. And I know it's better not to ask too many questions. Questions like, what would Brad or the FAA have to do with this here bear attack?"

Skip couldn't see her looking because she was seated behind him, but he could feel her eyes on him. "Skip, I'm glad you know better than to ask questions."

Skip and his copilot just smiled, and the rest of the flight was made in silence.

Brad gazed out the window that overlooked Auke Bay as an eagle soared by effortlessly. He never got tired of seeing them. The sun was still shining even though it was near ten o'clock in the evening.

The numbness in his cheeks told him he needed to stop drinking or resign himself to a cab ride home. But the jalapeno ale he was enjoying was a seasonal draft that was only available every few years and it had higher alcohol content, so Brad ordered another one.

The bar was busy for a Wednesday night. Locals were talking about local stuff, stuff he could ignore if he liked or join in if he chose. This evening he was happy to just sit and look out the window. The tour buses had finished taking the last run of whale watchers back to their cruise ships, and a few sport fishing boats were slowly making their way back into the harbor, cutting V's through the calm waters.

Brad's musing was interrupted by an odd sound. The sound was coming from him, a foreign sound, catching him completely off guard.

Terri, the bartender, could see the confusion on his face. She smiled knowingly and shook her head. "It's yours, honey. Hell, I didn't know you had one."

Brad's cell phone was ringing.

Holy shit!

Brad dug it out of his pocket and opened it. It displayed a number he didn't recognize. How do I answer it? he thought.

A distant "Hello" came from the device. "Oh!"

Moving it to his ear, Brad asked, "Hello?"

"Brad?" Erica asked. Just her voice allowed a release of tension that was surprising. Shit, he had no idea he was even worrying about her.

"May I ask who is calling?" Brad asked, smiling, gathering himself.

"Eat shit and die!" was her response.

"Hi, Erica," Brad said, smiling even more.

"Look, we need to talk." Her voice told him something was wrong.

"Are you back in town?"

"Yes, just got off Coast Guard copter, but I've got to get back soon."

"I'm at a bar in Auke Bay, called Squirez with a z. You can come here if you'd like, or if this place won't do for conversation, well, you'll need to come get me anyway. I've had a couple and I really don't want to drive if I don't have to."

The phone went dead. Brad looked at it inquisitively.

"I figured that," came a voice from behind him.

Turning around, Brad smiled at the sight of her. But his expression quickly changed to a perplexed look. He was about to ask her how she knew where to find him, but then the truth dawned on him. "Skip's an asshole."

The bartender came up to Brad and, looking at Erica with a smile, "What can I get for you?"

Before she could order, Brad said, "Erica, this is Terri, with two r's and one i. Terri, this is Erica, with one pain in my ass."

Erica said, "It's nice to meet you, Terri, I'll have a margarita, rocks, salt, not sweet, please."

Terri nodded and went off without a word.

One of the locals asked, "Brad, who's the lady?"

Brad just flipped him off, and then the two moved to a table at the far end of the room, where their conversation would remain theirs.

Brad could see she'd been outside by her color. She wasn't wearing any makeup, and she looked great. He also could see the stress in her eyes, though.

"Run into some shit?"

Erica frowned. "I'd say that's an understatement. But for some reason, I don't think you're surprised."

Brad took a long pull of his beer and waited for her to continue.

"Richard was killed." Erica looked up and he wasn't even the least bit shocked.

"Richard? Your new boss, right?"

"Yeah. He was a real jerk. But he didn't deserve to die like that."

Brad didn't respond to the statement. "Any other casualties?"

"Just a rogue Rhunken."

That got a response. Brad went from happy to pissed off in a blink of an eye. "What do you mean, rogue?"

"Well, that's what the PCO's and the PH's said it was. But now I'm not so sure."

"Did it attack anyone?" Brad was trying to control himself. He knew it wasn't Erica's fault, but it didn't help to lessen his anger.

"No. Mike said it was just standing there looking at him when one of the PH's shot it."

Brad's blood pressure was rising fast. He took another pull of the beer and calmed himself down, and as he gained control, something else crossed his mind.

"Was it a young one, or was it a large adult?"

"The PCO said it was young. Why?"

"I took two Rhunken over to the island to do some scouting for me some time ago. I thought they'd be gone by now. But now I'm not so sure."

"I'm sorry," Erica said honestly.

Brad wasn't sure if he wanted to get too far into the details right now. He needed to cool off first.

Erica broke into his thoughts. "I really need your help. Can you go back with me?"

Brad thought this might happen, but didn't actually believe that it would. So it surprised him a bit. "I thought I was fired."

"Well, the transfer hasn't happened yet, and the CEO put me in charge after Richard's death, telling me to do whatever I need to do to complete the mission. Well, I need you."

The challenge was more than Brad could pass up. Still, he wasn't sure he wanted to walk into somebody else's fight. So she made up his mind for him.

"Let's go get your stuff together. I'll call and set up the helicopter for the morning."

Brad nodded. He did care about the Rhunken, and he wanted to talk to the idiot that shot one. He finished his beer and paid the tab, then asked her to wait while he hit the head.

Erica stood at the U-shaped end of the bar, waiting, when Terri came up and asked, "Are you here to help Brad?"

Erica looked puzzled and replied, "No, I'm here to ask for his help."

Terri smiled. "Good, I think that might be what he needs." And she went back to work, leaving Erica a little perplexed.

Brad soon walked by and tossed his car keys to Terri without a look. He followed Erica to her rental car and climbed into the passenger seat.

While she followed his directions to his house, she finished briefing Brad on what happened in the last few days. As she rounded the bend on the dirt road, she stopped in mid-sentence, stunned by the view. Brad's house was right on the water of Beardsley Bay.

Brad was used to the reaction. "Yeah, it's tough to take," was all he said.

Erica was even more shocked to find the house unlocked. Following him inside, they shed their coats and shoes in a small room. Taking off her shoes made her a little uneasy, but she followed Brad's lead. He passed through the mudroom door and into the kitchen. He started to set up the coffeemaker to automatically brew a full pot. "6:00 AM OK?" he asked

Erica nodded. "That's fine. I have a helo scheduled for eight."

The kitchen was large and open with plenty of cabinets. But her attention quickly shifted to the large windows of the dining and living rooms, or more correctly the view beyond. She walked past him into the living room, stopping in front of the fifteen-foot windows, looking out at the bay, bathed in the evening light. "Beautiful," she said.

With the coffee set, Brad followed her in and found Erica looking out on Beardsley Bay. Her body was back lit with the incoming light, allowing him to see her silhouette through her white blouse. She turned and caught him looking, and smiled. Embarrassed, he quickly shifted his gaze. She wasn't the first woman he'd brought back to his house after Kate had passed. But there was something different about this one. He knew he felt something, but he really didn't want to deal with it right now. But he didn't want to ask her to leave either.

Feeling awkward, he continued past her, pointing to the spare room. In a voice he managed to keep steady, he announced, "That's your room. Towels lower right. If you want something to eat, go for it. See you in the morning."

Hiding his embarrassment, he headed for the master bedroom. She looked perplexed. "You're leaving me? Just like that?"

Without turning around, "You'll be fine, sleep tight."

That was real smooth, Brad, he told himself as he closed the door behind him.

Erica looked out the massive windows overlooking the bay. She noticed a spotting scope and went over to watch a pair of seals floating lazily just offshore before they disappeared in the water. Backing away from the scope, she looked around the house. Lots of wood, tongue-and-groove knotty pine paneling, oak hardwood floors and pine furnishings gave the living room a warm cabin feel. A large mule deer and moose mounts looked over the room and to the bay outside. She walked over to the shelves and checked out the pictures, knickknacks and other mementos, telling her a lot of Brad's past. There were pictures of a younger Brad in a Navy uniform, his daughter at various ages, and his late wife, all with happy faces. A shadow box held some military shooting medals, some dating back more than twenty years, and eight fancy championship belt buckles with recent dates from state, territorial and national cowboy shooting events. A current photo of Brad in a cowboy outfit at a shooting competition made her smile. "Boys will be boys," she said quietly.

Erica looked out once more at the view, grabbed her bag and headed toward the guest room. As she spied the closed door to Brad's room, she paused. A smile grew on her face, and then she went into her room.

A loud noise startled Brad out of his sleep. He automatically grabbed the .45 on the nightstand. Looking at the clock, he figured he'd been asleep for about an hour. The noise sounded like something had fallen in the guest bathroom or maybe the kitchen. Keeping the 1911 pointed down, thumb on the safety, he opened his door.

As on cue, the guest bathroom door opened and Erica stepped out. Her hair was wet and she was wearing only a baby blue tee shirt. She grabbed the bottom and pulled it down to just cover her lower front, pulling hard enough for the neckline to almost bare her breasts.

She smiled coyly. "Sorry, didn't mean to wake you."

Turning, she said, "Sleep tight," giving him a little wave as she retreated with bare feet and bare ass back into the bedroom, closing the door.

Brad stood stunned for a moment, then grumbled, "Jesus Christ."

Brad looked at the door for a few seconds, shaking his head, trying to clear the image that had just burned itself into his corneas.

CHAPTER 21

ERICA WAS JUST AMAZED at how quickly Brad packed. Most of his weapons and field gear were already in heavy-duty travel cases. Erica wanted to see what he was bringing, hoping to learn what an experienced outdoorsman would carry. She did see him pack the biggest revolver she'd ever seen, along with a couple of boxes of ammo in his waterproof day pack. His clothing took all of five minutes to throw together. The item that perplexed her was a plastic container with four bananas in it. Erica didn't ask, and Brad didn't explain.

For breakfast Brad set out a bag of bagels, cream cheese and a jar of smoked salmon. She wasn't sure of the salmon until the aroma hit her and started her mouth watering. She looked up between bites. "How'd you sleep?" she said with a smile.

He finished chewing, then said, "Funny you should ask. I didn't sleep as well as I normally do. Too much beer, I guess, because a nightmare woke me up." He was unable to hold back a smile.

"Oh, is that so? I'll remember that," she said with a big smile of her own.

The thirty-minute drive to the Coast Guard base gave Erica time to fill in as many of the blanks as she could about the recent events. Brad's expression was blank. Erica wasn't sure if he was mad, worried or the least bit excited about the assignment.

"You're awful quiet, what's on your mind?" she asked.

"A lot. I know you didn't start this thing, but I feel like I'm walking into a disaster that could have been avoided if I'd been included from the start."

Erica nodded, "That's exactly what it is. I hated to ask, but you were my only option if we are going to salvage the mission. You know we have to do something. People are dying."

"Is there any way we can send those professional hunters home?"

"I don't think so. Dr. Clark was adamant about having them on board. He took some convincing to include PCOs."

"That older one is going to be trouble," he said.

"That's Jack, and I think you're right," she agreed.

Brad used his FAA badge to open the airport gate, and then drove to the waiting Coast Guard copter. Skip waved them over with a smile, and he broke out laughing when Brad flipped him off. As Brad approached a still smiling Skip, they shook hands and he said, "Hope I didn't do you wrong by telling her where to find you."

"No, I'm glad you did. I just hate being that predictable is all."

Skip laughed again. "Squirez is about the only thing that is predictable about you."

Together they loaded Brad's gun case and waterproof bag into the bird, strapped in, and were airborne in a matter of minutes. Brad and the pilots chatted as the orange and white helicopter cut around the north end of Douglas Island, then angled south.

The trip was fast and smooth, and soon they were landing in the clearing next to the cabin. They were met by the whole group, but it was actually three small sub-groups. The two PCO's came up quickly to greet Brad, to introduce themselves and welcome Erica back. Sandy was all smiles when greeting Brad, then hugging Erica while whispering something in her ear that caused Erica to blush. She introduced the other biologist on the team, a small, nervous man that purposely kept away from the last two in the group. The two professional hunters had hung back, sizing him up. Brad knew who Jack was and he could see his obvious dislike for Erica. He could also see it had been automatically transferred to him. He also knew his presence was challenging Jack's self-proclaimed "alpha male" standing in the group and that it would cause strife. The other PH introduced himself as Doug, shook his hand and seemed quite affable at the start, but quickly backed off to stand by Jack. Brad understood that he was just showing his support for his partner.

Brad's gear was stored and sleeping arrangements were made, all of which took about ten minutes. Then Erica called a group meeting as the Coast Guard copter lifted off.

Erica requested that Brad tell everyone about his experience in the area and share his knowledge of the local Rhunken population. But he didn't know anything about the local colony, or even if there was one. He didn't want to tell them about Scout right now, nor did he want to let them know about the colony just across the channel. So he talked about his experience, and kept it to the minimum. He was done in less than a minute. He could tell by Erica's expression that she had expected more. But Mike came to the rescue and started asking questions. Brad was obliging and answered not only his questions, but questions by the others as well. Everyone but Jack asked questions. Even so, he stayed around and listened.

Mike finally asked a question directed at no one in particular. "OK, what's the plan now?" But everyone looked at Brad.

Brad responded quickly, "I need to contact the Rhunken scout, if he's still around."

For the first time Jack spoke, his resentment thick. "What makes you think you can do that?"

Brad didn't answer him but looked at Erica. "I'm going out alone tonight to see if I can find him."

"I don't think going out alone is wise. It's extremely dangerous out there right now," Erica said with little conviction in her voice. They both knew it was necessary.

Brad couldn't have asked for a better segue. "That's why I'm requesting everyone to stay here. I'm likely to shoot first and identify the noise later."

Mike looked worried. "Won't you shoot the scout?"

"The scout won't make noise," was Brad's reply as he got up, ending the meeting.

Brad spied the slightly over ripe bananas on the counter. He now knew why the Rhunken came into camp. Brad reached over and took the remaining four bananas and stuffed them in his day pack without an explanation to the small group watching him pack. No one asked any questions.

Just before sunset, Brad grabbed his stainless steel mariner shotgun, checked to make sure it was loaded and slung his backpack over his shoulder.

Erica stood by the end of his cot, looking concerned, but said nothing. Brad walked behind her and lightly touched the small of her back as he made his way out the door. He was sure no one else would notice.

He was wrong. Sandy made a low "ah ha" sound but said nothing more and turned to go about her business.

Erica made no response, but her face turned red as she watched Brad leave the cabin and head west and disappear into the wet undergrowth.

Brad headed off until, just above the camp where the trail had one of its rare clearings overlooking the bay, he stopped and gazed back. The light was softer as evening closed in. The smoke from the cooking fire rose only slightly higher than the cabin roof, and then slowly drifted horizontally southward, carried by an unfelt breeze.

The bay was busy. From his vantage point, Brad could see six boats plus light coming from some of the established camps. This part of southeast Alaska was well used by locals as well as a few tourists, so a Rhunken colony should have been discouraged from being established. He feared that just the opposite had happened for some reason.

Brad heard someone coming. It was human by the sound; nothing that belonged out here would make that much noise. Brad eased off the trail and sat in the shadows at the base of an ancient Sitka spruce, waiting for the unwanted guest.

Brad was in plain sight of the trail. He wasn't trying to hide, as he wanted to confront the person following. Brad was pretty sure it was Jack Spelling. The mariner 12 gauge lay across his lap. His wait wasn't long. Movement and the sound of small branches raking across synthetic clothing came from just down the trail. Brad's hands automatically moved to their place on the shotgun.

Mike stepped into the opening. He was trying to keep quiet, watching where he put his feet. He would have walked right by if Brad didn't stop him.

"What the fuck are you doin'?"

Mike just about jumped out of his skin. "Jesus Christ, you scared the shit out of me."

Brad didn't respond. He wasn't sure if he should be mad yet.

"I'm sorry I followed you. I just didn't want to be at camp with Jack so pissed off."

"Why is he pissed?" Brad asked, though he knew the reason.

"You're here, and he's no longer the top dog, and that makes him mad. And I know he'd take it out on me."

"Guys like that can be assholes. But I need to be alone for this, you know?"

"Well, I think I can help. The first one came out when I was alone, so I thought the others might as well."

"It was the bananas."

Mike looked completely lost.

"Was someone eating a banana shortly before the Rhunken showed up?"

"I was."

"That became my call a while back. The Rhunken thought I was there."

Mike was silent, thinking.

"I'm not sure how Scout will react to the scent now, and they don't like crowds anyway. So I need you to head back to camp."

Mike looked like a whipped puppy. Brad reached into his vest pocket and withdrew a derringer, one that filled his entire hand, and handed it to Mike.

"It's a .45 long Colt loaded with .410 shells. If he screws with you, shoot him in the guts."

Mike looked like he was holding a rattlesnake, and he quickly gave it back. "I'll be OK," he said as he turned to leave, physically shaken.

Brad took the belly gun and tucked it away. "The day you can actually shoot him in the guts is the day he'll leave you alone." Then he added, "You won't have to actually do it. He'll know that you would, and that'll be enough."

Brad stood up and started up the trail. He didn't hear another noise from Mike.

Brad knew Scout would be close—he hoped so anyway. So after another mile up the trail, he came to a slight clearing near the top of a ridge. He thought about starting a fire but decided against it. He broke out the bananas, split open most of them and tossed them around to increase the scent pattern. Taking off his pack, Brad removed his canteen, found a bag of smoked almonds and made himself comfortable, figuring it would be a long night.

The two black eyes peering out of an almost black hole in the underbrush was what caught Brad's attention. It startled him a bit, for he'd only just got settled. It must have followed him. As soon as Brad's eyes focused on the Rhunken, it disappeared into the underbrush. Brad knew this was a signal to follow it to a more remote location to converse. Well, he hoped it was to converse.

The thicket was dark, too dark to walk quietly, so Brad removed a small flashlight with a red lens. The red light could not be seen as long as he kept it pointed downward. Brad continued to follow his guide, only catching a glimpse of him from time to time. Its path took a seemingly random course, but Brad knew better. He was suddenly brought to a halt when he stood up after coming out a heavily overgrown section of trail, a tunnel through the patch of salmonberry bushes. Bears had cut the well-worn trail over many years.

Scout appeared just inches from him. Brad looked up into its eyes. He could see the conflict. So he walked over to a downed log and sat down. He surveyed the spot where the Rhunken had brought him. It was an overgrown notch in the side of the hill. A creek ran through it, and a waterfall just upstream and another just downstream would mask any sound they made.

The darkness made it hard to read the expressions, but Brad knew what it wanted to know. "I'm sorry," Brad said more for himself than for Scout. Rhunken didn't really understand "sorry."

Scout's shoulders relaxed a little. Maybe Rhunken didn't understand the words, but they were better at reading our body language, Brad judged, than we could ever imagine.

Scout moved closer and squatted down, sitting on its heels. Brad followed suit, moving closer and joined him in what might be a Rhunken pow-wow.

Brad could now see the sorrowful questioning in Scout's eyes. Brad knew it wanted to know why the junior Rhunken was killed.

Brad really didn't know what to say. After all, he wasn't there. So he shrugged his shoulders and said, "It was a mistake."

Surprisingly, this seemed to work. Scout held up his hands in a small cupping gesture, as if holding something small. Brad's blood went cold. This was the sign for Tacks.

"A Tack is here?"

The Scout held up five fingers. Brad knew this didn't mean there were five, but many, more than one. The possibility was almost unthinkable. How could this be?

"Are these Tacks responsible for the killings?" Brad asked, but he already knew the answer and Scout's eyes confirmed it.

"Shit, I've got to get back to the others." Brad rose, and then looked back at Scout. "Do you know where they live?"

The large Rhunken stood, towering over Brad and looked north by northwest into the darkness.

Brad waited until he had left Scout behind before turning on his red flashlight. Then he started back toward the trail as quickly as he could, not too worried about stealth. Brad's mind started to work, recalling what little he knew about Tacks. The only person he'd known to have ever dealt with a grown Tack was Bob, his mentor. Bob had talked about them in some detail, so he wasn't completely ignorant. But multiple Tacks?

Brad reached the trail and was just about to double-time it when he almost ran into the back of Scout standing in the trail.

Brad quickly switched off his light and came around to the side of the Rhunken. Was there anything down the trail? Not sensing anything, he looked at Scout. Its eyes were focused and alert, and Brad knew it had seen, heard or smelled something that was dangerous. And dangerous to a Rhunken was something to worry about.

Brad started down the trail but was quickly overtaken by the Rhunken and he had to almost run to keep up. This part of the forest was more open, allowing filtered light from the half-moon. Soon Scout came to a halt, slipped off the trail and disappeared into the brush.

Brad stopped and waited, bringing up the twelve-gauge with his thumb on the safety. Nothing, not a sound. Shit, he hated this. Brad retrieved his light and turned it on. The red light seemed extremely bright because his eyes were adjusted to the darkness of the night. Starting slowly down the trail, he shifted the red light left to right, always pointing downward, not wanting to give away his position or highlight Scout in case others were around.

An object came into view, sitting in the middle of the trail. Brad knew this hadn't been here when he came through earlier. As he got closer, he could start to make out the details of clothing, shiny black. Brad knew what it was but unscrewed the red filter from the lens of the flashlight. The almost blinding white light showed the blood-soaked coat, ripped and completely missing one sleeve. A quick sweep of the light showed upturned soil, pine needles and twigs mostly covered in blood. Bringing the light back to the coat, Brad realized he'd seen it before. It was Mike's.

CHAPTER 22

ERICA SNAPPED AWAKE. WIDE-awake. She sat up and listened, but heard nothing except Sandy's rhythmic breathing. She pushed the button on her watch and saw that it was just after three. The sun was just lighting the sky, and in the distance, the crows were making their annoying cawing noises.

Erica's thoughts shifted to Brad, and she slid out of bed. She made her way to the main room to see if he was back. She doubted it; she would have heard that—if not Brad, she'd have heard Mike for sure.

The room was lightly lit from the glow of the surveillance monitors and power indicators of the electronics equipment. Rick was sitting in the "watch chair," but by the position of his head she knew he was asleep. All was normal in the world; she thought and turned to the kitchen area to get a drink of water before heading back to the warmth of her bed. The sight of a silver shotgun lying across the dimly lit dining table stopped Erica. Her eyes shift to the right, and she jumped when she spotted Brad sitting in the dark watching her.

"Jesus Christ, you scared me," Erica said with an edge in her voice.

Brad just nodded, saying nothing. Erica's anger vanished when she saw the look on his face and realized something was wrong. Remembering Mike had gone after Brad, she quickly checked Mike's cot in the corner. It was empty. Erica knew instantly he was dead.

"Was it a Rhunken?" she asked as she joined Brad at the table.

"Tacks," he said, and gulped down the last of the wine he had in his hand. Erica's still waking mind was questioning if it was too early or too late to be drinking wine, so she really didn't listen to what he'd said.

After a few seconds, when the words sank in, she said, "Tack! As in a little flying Rhunken?

"Yes, Tacks," this time emphasizing the plural.

Erica's mind was still trying to get wrapped around the possibility of a Tack causing this, so she still missed the emphasis.

Brad understood the disbelief, so he let her have some time to digest the information. Hell, he still didn't have a complete grasp of the situation. So he got up and filled his mason jar with merlot from the box. While common for him, drinking wine from a box was camping for most folks, he thought.

With Erica up, Brad started a pot of coffee brewing. He knew that would wake everyone, but that was the idea—get everyone up and briefed on the situation.

"Did you say Tacks with an *s*?" Erica said after a few minutes.

Brad smiled. "Yes, as in multiple Tacks."

"But that isn't possible. There isn't a single report of multiple Tacks that I know of."

Brad went back to his bunk, opened his gun case and removed a revolver, holster and a box of ammo. He walked over and handed it to Erica.

"Here, you may need this, but I hope not."

Erica took the small .357 magnum; it was just like the one she trained with in Seattle. Somehow, she knew this wasn't a coincidence.

By the time Brad had downed his wine and Erica finished her first cup of his overly strong camp coffee, he'd filled her in on the events of the night. The others were starting to stir. Sandy was the first to join them at the table, and she grimaced when she tasted the coffee. Seeing Sandy's reaction, Erica volunteered to make a second, more civilized pot. It would help get her mind off the thought that Mike was dead.

Brad, not wanting to waste the last of the pot, had Erica pour him a cup, switching from the merlot. Hell, he needed to switch, he was getting a little buzzed.

After everyone had breakfast, Brad got the crew caught up with the latest events. Quietly, Jack and Peter volunteered to go up the trail and retrieve Mike's remains, wrap them up and put them in the shed.

Jack slipped inside, grabbed the sat phone, and took it down to the beach. He found the WCC number he wanted stored in the directory and hit send.

"Doctor Clark's office," said a woman's voice on the other end.

"Is Dr. Clark in?"

She must have seen the number and recognized his voice. "I'll connect you right away, sir."

"Yes?" came Dr. Clarks voice after a short pause.

"Sir, it's Jack, I have just received some information you will want to hear."

Jack waited for a response but didn't receive one, so he continued. "Brad Michaels came in yesterday and last night made contact with a Rhunken. He reports the deaths, including your son's, were caused by Tacks, multiple Tacks. This report explains some of the evidence I saw at Richard's attack site. I also know you were involved in a Tack training program at one time and thought you might be interested in a lair that held multiple Tacks."

"Yes, this does interest me. It does change the situation slightly. For now, gather as much data as possible and . . . I know it's a long shot, but if some of the Tacks can be captured, do so."

Jack responded, "I don't think that will go over well with Erica, and I'm damn sure Brad Michaels will be dead set against it."

After a long pause Dr. Clark said, "Things are being done in that regard. Just continue on as planned," hanging up the phone.

Jack got the phone back just before Erica came in, looking for it.

Erica called for a helicopter and the body was gone before noon.

Over a late lunch a plan of action was made, mostly by Erica,

Jack and Peter. Brad already had his own plan, and as it turned out, the group's plan was similar enough to his that he agreed to all of it but the start time. They wanted to depart as soon as possible, but Brad needed rest, so he "suggested" the group prepare for an early morning departure, and then he went off to bed.

CHAPTER 23

TWO MEN GOT OFF the Alaska Airlines morning flight and waited for their luggage. The small duffel bags came around the carousel quickly enough, but the gun cases took a little longer. They were delivered through a small side door, where they had to show the claim ticket to the attendant to take them. Still, the process took less than twenty minutes, a lot faster than expected.

The walk over to Coastal Helicopters was not even far enough to stretch the legs, but it was long enough to make both men wish they had dug out their raincoats before they left the main terminal. Being located in a rain forest and with a light but steady rain coming down, Juneau weather was holding true to form.

An attendant whose badge read Barbara greeted the two men with a smile. "I'm guessing you're the John Smiths we're going to fly out to Admiralty this morning. We've never had two John Smiths fly with us at the same time."

One of them nodded without any emotion, handed Barbara six hundred-dollar bills and walked away without the change, which made a very nice tip. "Thanks. Your pilot today will be Doug, and he'll be right with you," she said.

Black was the in color these days, but these two were taking it to the extreme. The pilot escorted the two of them out onto the ramp and loaded them and their gear on the Ranger. Everything they were wearing, and all their gear, was black and tactical. No exceptions.

After a quick safety briefing, and a quiet twenty-minute flight, Doug landed on the beach of a finger of land on the north end of Seymour Canal. The landing was easy due to the fact that it was precisely at extreme low tide.

The two men were off-loaded and Doug asked, "I understand you'll call when you need a ride out?"

The two men nodded and moved their gear slightly away from the chopper to allow it to take off.

Doug was in the air before he realized the two men had not spoken a single word.

Of course their names weren't John, but Tony and Frank knew no one would question them. This was not their first time to Alaska. They had done a job in a small town called Talkeetna the year before. It wasn't this remote, and the little town was a lot busier with tourists than they had expected, but they were still successful.

When the helicopter was out of sight, they dug out their black raingear and put it on. The constant drizzle was starting to make them shiver. Opening the gun cases and getting the two Colt M4's and Glock 9 mms loaded and ready took less than three minutes. They left the rest of the gear where it lay. Tony turned on his GPS, allowing it to acquire satellites, and noticed that it was 0935.

They were dropped off three miles from the targets and in the next valley over. The plan was to get to the site in three hours, do the hit, get back, and call for a return pick up the same day.

Tony retrieved a satellite phone from a side pocket on his day pack and dialed a long number from memory.

After a long pause, the call was answered, "Yes."

"We're here. The issues will be resolved shortly."

Without an answer, the line went dead, and Tony put the phone back in the side pocket and slung the pack on his back. Frank was already twenty yards ahead.

Now that they started to hike across the flat toward the ridge, it looked a lot more like a mountain. But they were in great shape.

It might take a little longer to get there than originally planned, but with the long daylight hours up here this time of year, no problem.

At the low point in the flat, a small stream crossed their path. The crossing wasn't as easy as it looked. The flat was mud, and the mud was getting deeper. Still, the creek was shallower than feared and the streambed was firm gravel, so the crossing barely got their boots clean of the mud.

Frank pointed to a smooth area of the mud flats that looked easier to cross and led the way. Tony was heavier than Frank by forty pounds and sank deeper in the mire. Then he made the mistake of stopping to catch his breath. He looked around at the creek they had just crossed and noticed it looked wider. Not just a little, but a lot wider. He started to bring it to Frank's attention, but he was already far enough away that Tony didn't want to yell, so he tried to take a step. Tony's feet were stuck.

Frank's feet were getting stuck also, and he was focused on getting the hell off this mud flat. He looked at the rocky shore ahead and figured it was still two hundred yards off. He was breathing hard. "I hate this shit. Fuck Alaska," he said.

Tony could see Frank was now more than halfway to the rocks. Tony yelled, trying to get Frank's attention. But Frank must not have heard him because he didn't turn. "Shit," Tony cursed as he tried to dig his right foot out. Then he noticed the water—it was somehow all around him. He looked back at what had been a large mud flat and a small creek, and now more than half the inlet was full of water. Tony started to panic, he yelled, and then whistled loudly for Frank.

Frank stopped when he heard Tony's whistle, turned around, and was instantly terrified. Tony was in the middle of a huge body of water. He knew what was happening, but could not believe a tide could come in that fast. By stopping, the mud started to grab his feet also, and Frank knew what was going to happen.

Struggling, Frank got his feet free and broke for the shore. He didn't know when he lost his rifle, but Frank thought of it only for a split second, then focused on getting away from the water that was about to reach him. A quick glance showed Tony splashing about in water up to his waist. Frank didn't care, he had to get out.

Tony could see Frank scrambling through the mud, but he was going the wrong way. His M4 was gone, lost under the water. He probably would have shot at Frank if he had it. Tony tried to dig at the mud that was now up to his crotch, but he couldn't get free. He ripped off the pack, hoping that less weight would help, but it didn't. Now Tony had to hold his breath and bend over in the water to try to dig himself free, but he couldn't, and he started to panic. The ice-cold water was reaching for his armpits. Terror finally gripped Tony and he started to splash wildly, grabbing for anything he could, but there was nothing but water. As the frigid water reached his chin, he stretched his neck to keep his mouth above it. All he could do was scream.

Frank finally made hard ground. The water lapped at his feet, but he could move. He ran to the first bunch of large rocks and driftwood logs that had washed up to the high tide line before he turned around and looked for Tony. It took a few seconds before he found him. Frank couldn't believe how far out he was. All Frank could see was Tony's head and flailing arms. Frank watched helplessly for the next five minutes until Tony's arms stopped moving and his head was no longer in sight.

In shock, Frank sat on a rock for an unknown amount of time. At last, he mentally reset and broke loose of what just happened. He knew the plan, pulled out his GPS, and turned it on. He watched the display light up and go through its self-test before acquiring satellites.

Frank was covered in mud and shivering, more from exertion than the cold, but he knew he had to get moving. He decided right then that he was going to demand both his and Tony's pay when he completed this. The job was going to be harder now that he only had a pistol, but that shouldn't be a problem. He stood up and began heading south, hiking up the hill, to the ridge, following the route the GPS provided.

Frank's shivering stopped quickly once the climb began. The

ridge was much steeper then it appeared. The ground was slick with loose rocks, wet, moss-covered trees and dense vegetation, some bearing large thorns, making every step forward a painful task. By now his clothes were completely soaked, and his high-dollar black calfskin gloves had holes in them.

After what seemed like hours, the incline became more gradual and the vegetation opened up a bit, allowing the gray filtered light to reach the forest floor. Frank headed toward the south side of the ridge and found himself on the top of a sheer rock cliff that disappeared into the treetops below. Frank checked the GPS in his hand; it had him going straight off the cliff and heading south for another two miles.

He looked down and cursed, "Fuck, I hate Alaska."

His best guess was to head west and follow the cliff edge up the valley, mostly because of a game trail that skirted the rim, making it easier to walk that way.

He made better progress on the ridge trail, and as Frank caught his breath, his confidence came back. As he walked, his leg brushed up against a large-leafed plant and it felt like he was bitten. Frank stopped and looked at the plant more closely. The stems and underside of the large leaves were covered in large, sharp thorns. Frank recalled from his research that these plants were called devil's club. At the time he thought it was a cool name for a plant.

After traveling less than a hundred yards, the game trail vanished and Frank found himself bushwhacking along the cliff edge. He didn't want to stray from the open sky and possibly miss a way down. The rain didn't let up, and the way was slick.

A black-tailed deer jumped up from its bed not more than ten feet away. The sudden movement caused Frank to jump to one side. Frank stopped his sideways movement and kept his balance, digging in his heels. The deer was long gone when he looked at where he was. He realized he had jumped farther than he thought, almost over the side of the cliff.

Frank shifted his weight to the downhill foot, but as he started to move away from the edge, his foot slipped a bit. Frank instinctively grabbed for a branch to keep himself from sliding. His hand felt like it caught fire and he let go of the devil's club and pulled back from it. But his back foot slipped again and Frank found himself flying in space. He grabbed for anything he could, but he could grab nothing but sky.

Frank never hit the ground. Last winter's snow load had been too much for the young Sitka spruce, and the top one-third of the tree had snapped off. It was waiting to impale him. The jagged six-inch trunk pierced Frank's skin, broke his back, lacerated multiple organs and protruded from his abdomen. Frank was still awake and looking at the world upside down, twenty feet off the ground and bent in half.

It was impossible to get enough air in his lungs to yell, and he fought for a few minutes to free himself, but he knew he was finished. So he pulled his Glock from his shoulder holster, put the muzzle in his mouth and pulled the trigger.

Brad woke up when he heard the muted shot in the distance, well north of camp. He looked at his watch to keep the time as a mental note, just in case. It was 2:02 PM.

CHAPTER 24

AT 3:30 AM THERE was enough light to start up the trail. The group had been awake most of the night. They all knew something was going to happen, and that it was not going to be pleasant. Brad had long ago acquired the ability to sleep when and where he could. So he had slept most of the day and catnapped in the evening. He was fresh and ready to go.

Sandy stood in the cabin door and watched them leave, relieved she didn't have to go, but also a little scared that she'd be there alone. Brad wanted two of them to stay behind with her, but most of the group, Sandy included, voted against him. Erica was the only one to vote with Brad and almost used her authority to overrule, but Sandy assured her she'd be fine, so she let the group consensus stand. Sandy glanced at the shotgun leaning next to the door. Funny, she'd always hated guns, but now, after some basic firearms training and the realization that sometimes a gun is the only thing that is going to give you a chance, she was happy to have it. It reassured her.

The morning weather was starting out to be nice for southeast Alaska as they made their way up the trail. The forecast was for a small front to move in later in the day, but for now they were making good time over the soft, wet trail. Jack seemed pleased by how quietly they were traveling, Brad noticed. He was probably thinking they would be able to make it to their destination unnoticed. Brad, on the other hand, knew they were making enough racket to alert Scout that they were on their way. The Rhunken would have no problem following their sounds, allowing it to stay out of sight.

Brad smiled to himself; this was better than he had anticipated. His plan was to draw the Tacks out of the forest and hit them near the cabin. He had presented the idea to the rest of the group when they were planning this outing, but to no avail. Jack wanted to hit their lair, and he was sure they could find it and destroy it in complete surprise. He was also sure that the cabin's location out in the open would deter the Tacks from attacking it. The others went along with Jack's assessment after the PCO's agreed with him.

After thinking it through, Brad agreed to go along with Jack's plan. He actually thought it might work out OK, but not quite as Jack had planned. No way would the group ever manage to sneak up on the lair, but the Tacks might show themselves. Brad's experience showed that Rhunken were curious and they would follow the group, especially if it was "sneaking" toward their lair. He hoped, for Sandy's sake, that the Tacks focused on the group.

An electronic crack followed by Sandy's voice came over the headsets that Erica, Peter and Jack wore. "I see you at trail cam one."

Erica gave a double key of the hand-held radio's PTT button to silently acknowledge the report.

"Roger, trail cam one," Jack repeated in a whisper, ignoring Brad's request for total silence.

The team only had three working headsets and one spare hand-held radio that was in Erica's pack. This limitation had originally pleased Brad, not wanting to deal with the distraction of communications and the inherent possibility of becoming perturbed. But Jack still found a way to piss him off. And he wasn't the only one that got mad. Erica gave Jack a look that shut him down quickly.

At noon Erica stopped in a clearing on the saddle and raised her binoculars, focusing them on the compound where their cabin was located. The view was obscured by the trees, but a wisp of smoke rising from the cabin was visible, as well as one of the sheds and the outhouse. Erica took in the view; their campsite was peaceful, set in a picturesque postcard setting of southeast Alaska, belying the danger at hand.

Erica gave the handheld radio's PTT button two presses. She saw Jack and Peter's attention shift to her, thus confirming her transmission.

A moment later, "I see you at trail cam five. Nothing to report on the other cameras or sensors, other than a doe and a fawn," came Sandy's voice. Then she added, "Will wait until next check point," acknowledging that the party would be behind a ridge for some time and most likely out of range of communications.

Brad watched as she secured the radio and adjusted her pack, getting set for the next section of the trail. He noticed she was not breathing hard and hadn't broken a sweat like some of the others. He was impressed with her confidence, and for now there was no doubt that she was in charge. But so far this has just been a hike. Things could change quickly when the shit started to fly. He reassured himself. "She'll do well. I'll make sure of it."

This break could not have come at a better time for Sandy: she had to pee! And she didn't even stop to change to her outside shoes before she dashed outside.

Sandy grunted in disgust when she noticed it had begun to rain, a light rain but enough to get her inside shoes wet. But as she raced to the outhouse, she thought of Erica having to deal with peeing in the woods with all those guys hanging around. She felt grateful for this facility; it had a light bulb that was always left on to keep the chill out, well, at least a little. The slight breeze that came out of the hole was refreshing at times, but she knew the ventilation was necessary and it did keep the odor down.

Sandy stopped. Something was squatting next to the wood pile, near the outhouse. She felt it before she saw it, she didn't know how, but she had, just like she knew she'd find more if she looked around. But she couldn't, she just started to cry. Sandy turned around and slowly started back to the cabin, no longer having to use the outhouse. Fear had erased that concern for her. Sandy wanted to run, but she merely looked at the slightly ajar cabin door. "I guess I didn't close it," she thought. The sight of the open door gave her some hope, but the sound of moving gravel to her right quickly removed it.

The blow came from the left, she never heard it coming. The wind was knocked from her lungs, Sandy's face hit the gravel walk hard, and she saw stars. She tried to push her hands beneath her so that she could raise herself up to run. "This time I'm going to do it," she told herself. But she couldn't get her arms to move.

Sandy started to sob. She could feel the gravel on her face; she was being dragged. She heard clothes being ripped, but she couldn't feel anything other than the pebbles against her cheek. Then Sandy realized she was holding her breath and she tried to inhale. Nothing. Again she tried, but she couldn't get her diaphragm to work.

Sandy forgot about the beasts sitting and feeding on her body below her broken neck. She was alone with the fading heartbeat in her ears and the narrowing of light in her vision. "Breathe, I just need to breathe," was her last thought.

CHAPTER 25

THE TRAIL HAD DWINDLED to a small deer path, so Brad didn't mind when it turned south and he took the group north, higher up the ravine and deeper into the woods. Erica caught Brad's eye and held up the radio with an inquiring look on her face. Brad nodded his head and pointed to a rock outcrop just ahead.

As they reached the rocks, Brad left the group so that they could rest and make contact with Sandy, while he scouted ahead. But his true intention was to make contact with Scout. And like he figured, the Rhunken was waiting for Brad just out of sight of the others. Sitting on its haunches, it did not shift its gaze when Brad approached. The Rhunken was a light gray and green color that blended into the background perfectly in this light. Brad followed its gaze up and slightly across the top of the valley to a dark and extremely thick stand of spruce. Even from this distance, Brad could make out the large leaves of the devil's club that enveloped the base of the trees.

Without a word being said, Brad knew where they needed to go. Brad nodded and turned to head back to the group. Yet when he looked back, Scout was gone—no trace, no sound. Brad smiled; the stealth still amazed him every time. They were close to the lair and he hoped the Tacks were still unaware of their presence. But he knew better, subconsciously readjusting the shotgun positioned on his back.

Brad could hear their voices before he could even see them. Everyone was talking, and at first Brad was upset, but the tension in the voices told him something was wrong.

Erica was on the radio. "Sandy, come in! If you can hear me, we can't hear you. Go stand by the woodpile and wave."

With the end of the transmission, everyone looked through their binoculars, pointing down the valley toward the cabin, where the smoke from the chimney had stopped.

No movement at the cabin site. With every passing second, the group became more concerned. Peter finally broke the tense silence. "I'm going back." He headed back down the way they came.

Erica spoke up before Brad did, but just barely. "Wait. You can't go alone."

"If one goes back, we all go back," Brad said.

He was missing something; a thought had been stirring in the back of his mind since Mike had been killed. He was still unsure what was bothering him, but he knew splitting up was a bad idea.

Jack interrupted Brad's thoughts. "No, I think we need to hit the colony while we're up here. It might even be easier if some of the Tacks are down at the camp."

Peter became livid. "What the fuck are you talking about? Sandy could be in trouble! We need to get our asses down there, now!"

Erica held up her hand. "OK, I really don't think there's a large number of these things, so I think we can afford to split up. Peter, you, Jack and Rick head back to the cabin to check on Sandy. Brad, Doug and I will go look for the colony."

Brad looked at Erica in disbelief that she would even think about contradicting his suggestion not to split the group up. They made eye contact and he could see the conflict in her eyes. Bad call or not— and he was sure it was a bad one—at least she made the call. And he knew that the only way to get true field experience is to screw up sometimes. He also knew she needed his support, so he let it drop. But every second that passed allowed the group's uneasiness to grow.

"I don't give a shit, I'm staying," Jack announced.

Doug must have seen the anger rise in both Brad's and Erica's eyes because he quickly said, "I'll go with Rick and Peter."

Everyone was onboard with the split except Brad, but he didn't really have a good reason other than his gut instinct, so he decided not to press the issue. Brad looked up towards the location of the Tack colony; it was out of sight. At least that was something positive.

Brad grabbed Erica by the shoulders and turned her around. Before she had the chance to protest the manhandling, he unzipped the side pouch and dug the backup radio out of her pack. Handing it to Doug, he said to the rescuers, "Don't worry about making noise, just focus on speed."

Rick nodded and turned to see that he had to move fast. The others were already headed down the hill at almost a run.

When the others left, Brad told Erica and Jack to stay put. If they had been discovered, which he was sure they had, the Tacks might think the entire group had headed back, hopefully allowing their little attack force to regain the surprise factor, if they actually ever had it, a notion Brad was starting to doubt. Going back to Erica, he zipped up her pack, "Sorry, I spun you around."

"It's OK," she said over her shoulder.

Brad saw the smirk on Jack's face. At first, he thought it was in reaction to his apology to Erica, but it wasn't. For some reason he seemed most pleased with the split. Then it dawned on him. The fewer the people, the better the chance for Jack to get kills. The only thing that would have been better for the asshole was if he and Erica had left too. If he had his way, he'd let the son-of-a-bitch try it alone. Because right now the chances were good, that Jack would need Brad to save his miserable life.

Brad watched the other group until they were out of sight. In this terrain that took about thirty seconds. Then he said to Erica, "OK," and started up the ridge.

"You think it's a bad idea, splitting up, don't you?" she said to Brad.

"It was a tough call. I would have done it differently. But who's to say I'd be right. They'll probably be fine as long as they don't split up."

The second part of his statement was more for his own benefit then hers, but the uneasiness in his gut had not subsided. In fact, it was worse.

CHAPTER 26

BRAD WAS EXTREMELY HAPPY with their "off trail" conditions. The path they chose was not too rocky or overgrown, and the change in elevation was gradual. Normally he would speed up the pace until people started to lag behind, but he was going as fast as he dared and these two hung in right behind him, so they were making remarkable time.

The weather helped with the stealth part of the plan, as it had taken a turn for the worse. The wind and moderate rain would help cover their approach, but the loud chatter of one of the resident squirrels didn't help them. Brad knew any Rhunken would be alerted by the noise, not frightened, and they would already be more focused in this direction anyway, because it was the obvious approach. They were also close to the lair and, with time, he knew they could find it, but having Scout with them he felt good about their chances of locating it quickly.

As they made their way higher up the mountain, the rain turned to snow and it started to stick to the ground and vegetation. Brad looked at this as a good thing, as even Rhunken would have to leave tracks in the snow. Of course, there were ways to hide what sign was left, but the act of covering up sign left even more information for those who knew how to read it. The snow wouldn't last long this time of year, even at this altitude, maybe just minutes, but Brad had learned to take advantage of opportunity when available.

In the end, the tracks didn't give Scout away. The old log was just wrong. It was partially hidden in a small stand of Sitka spruce saplings. Snow was sticking lightly to the young needles and had settled on the bark of the old fallen tree, but a small section of the tree, about five feet, had no snow. While this might not normally catch his eye, the new snow under the log where it shouldn't be did. Brad calmly stopped and turned to the others. Erica and Jack stopped and looked at him blankly, not surprisingly; they had no idea of what was just a couple of feet away. Brad took a deep breath; it was time to introduce them to Scout.

Brad edged back toward the other two, not only moving closer so he could quietly speak to them, but also wedging himself between them and the Rhunken. "I didn't tell you this, but we've had help while we've been out here."

The blank look on their faces almost made him smile, but looking at Jack quickly replaced that feeling with one of disgust. "The Rhunken you killed at camp was only one of the two I brought over here to help us."

Jack's eyes quickly darted away from Brad's and scanned the brush around them. His hands tightened their grip on his rifle but he saw nothing. Jack looked back at Brad with a glimmer of fear in his eyes. That made Brad smile.

Erica looked even more lost than before. "What? Is it here? Where is it?" she said a little too loudly for Brad's liking.

Before Brad could point out the Rhunken, Scout stood up. Jack jumped in surprise, bringing up his gun. This is exactly what Brad had expected. He probably would have reacted the same way himself. So he reached out and grabbed the barrel, pushing it aside so that it would miss Scout if it went off. Brad figured it would take a few seconds before Jack regained his composure.

But Jack didn't stop. He jerked his rifle out of Brad's hand, stepped to his right and began to raise his rifle again. Scout let out a low rumble, a sound that was felt more than heard. Brad didn't see fear in Jack's eyes, but hate, murderous hate. Brad was about to jump on Jack when Erica's shotgun butt caught Jack behind the ear, toppling him to his knees, and his rifle fell harmlessly to the ground.

"Asshole," Erica said, stepping around Jack and retrieving his rifle.

This happened all within a couple of seconds, and Brad wasn't sure whether he should kick Jack in the head or hug Erica. So he just smiled in amazement at how well she handled the situation. Brad looked over at Scout. The Rhunken was looking up the hill as if nothing had happened.

Jack recovered quickly, physically anyway, but he was quiet and it was easy to see he wasn't happy. Brad couldn't blame him for that; his ego was damaged more than his head.

"You stupid bastard. You try that again, I'll let him shoot you. If I don't do it myself." Erica removed the round from the chamber of his rifle and handed it back to him. "Keep it together. If you can't do that you need to leave right now."

Jack knew it would take a couple of seconds to re-chamber a round, and that would be more than enough time for all three to react, so he just slung it over his shoulder and rejoined the march without saying a word.

Scout led the way, followed by Brad, Erica, and then Jack. The weather wasn't getting better as they climbed. Visibility was down to one quarter of a mile or so, but the snow had turned back to rain, melting the snow that had stuck and soaking everything.

Scout led the way, and soon the route they were traveling angled up a steep slope covered in large fiddlehead ferns and devil's club growing up between fallen and rotting old growth trees. The trees towered overhead, blocking out most of the infrequent sunlight. The rain had stopped, or at the very least wasn't penetrating the thick canopy above them, but an occasional water drop would remind them this was a rain forest.

They'd traveled about twenty minutes when Scout stopped next to a sheer rock wall covered in mosses, lichens and small spruce trees trying to grow in seemingly impossible cracks.

Scout was gazing at the wall and his shoulders became tense. Brad's rifle came to the ready, his finger on the safety. Both Erica and Jack saw this and readied their weapons.

Scout grabbed a handhold and easily climbed the wall to an almost invisible crack about fifteen feet up, then disappeared. The three looked at each other in amazement. Erica and Jack had never seen a Rhunken lair. Brad had to admit this one was the best concealed of any he'd ever seen.

Scout reappeared after a long minute and jumped to the ground. He sank to his haunches, waiting. Brad's heart raced even more, because he knew what the Rhunken's body language meant. Something was home.

Brad leaned his shotgun against the rock, then pulled out the Smith & Wesson .50 caliber handgun, checked and reholstered it. He dug through his pack to find his tactical flashlight. Meanwhile, Jack set aside his rifle, and pulled out and checked his two modified 1911's and attached a rail-mounted light to one.

Brad shifted his attention to Erica. "Stay here with that scatter gun, but don't shoot us when we come out. Well, me anyway," he said with a smile.

Erica swallowed and looked out of sorts, but her hands tightened on her shotgun. "Well, you may want to announce yourselves then," was all she said. Brad and Jack both nodded.

The Rhunken led the way, and what Scout did easily in a matter of seconds took Brad and Jack a great deal longer and required much more effort. Neither one was a practiced rock climber, nor did they have the proper gear. With Brad in the lead they finally made it to the ledge that led to the entrance. Jack put a hand on Brad's shoulder, and with his eyes asked to go in first. Brad nodded in agreement, actually feeling better with Jack in front.

The entrance was bigger than Brad expected, not large by any means, but a good-sized slit in the rock wall. Most Rhunken lair entrances were difficult for a man to enter. A Rhunken's pliable skeletal structure allowed them to ooze through small and irregular openings.

Both men, with lights ready but off, pulled out their handguns and quietly slid through the crack in the rock wall.

It wasn't as dark as Brad had expected: they could see thirty feet in from the lair entrance. Probably a combination of the larger opening and their eyes being better adjusted because of the day's overcast skies. But just the same, Jack and Brad stepped toward opposite sides of the entrance and kneeled with weapons ready, allowing their eyes to completely adjust to the darkness while they listened to the sounds of the cave.

As their eyes adjusted, they could see that the entrance was more of an elongated room with a relatively flat rock floor and three passages leading deeper into the mountain. The first one was level with the floor, but the other two were higher; the second one to the left about ten feet up, and the third one, to the right, was all but invisible about fifteen feet above the floor with no obvious means of access. Scout was nowhere in sight.

There was no sign of Rhunken, but there was almost never any sign. The only indication that this cave was used was the lack of dust or debris in the middle of the floor.

Brad nodded to Jack, giving him the okay. Jack clicked on his light and proceeded down the floor-level tunnel. With a deep breath, Brad turned on his tactical flashlight and followed, trying to keep an eye on Jack while watching their six at the same time. Brad was pleased to see Jack had training in room clearance, and they moved efficiently through the maze of rocks, holes and offshoots until they came to a larger cavern. The ceiling must have been fifty feet high and was covered with stalactites, the floor was covered in broken and well-worn stalagmites, some so worn they were small humps in the floor. Another sign the cave had been used for many years.

The only sound was their footsteps grinding gravel against the cave floor. The flashlight beams darted from side to side and up and down. Brad's light crossed something that caused him to pause. He was not sure why at first, just something odd. The frozen beam of light got Jack's attention, and he moved his light to the spot that Brad's was fixed on. With both lights, Brad could see that the something had straight edges. It was man-made. Something was concealed with an old tarp that was covered with dust so it blended in with the surrounding rocks.

A small stream of dirt fell on the tarp, and both lights darted up the cavern wall, searching for the cause. Both lights illuminated the Tack staring down at them. Brad had his .50 caliber handgun pointed squarely at its chest with the hammer pulled back and his finger on the hair trigger, but he didn't fire. No threat, not yet.

The deafening reports of both of Jack's .45s surprised Brad, causing him to flinch, and the big revolver thundered. He instantly knew his shot went a little high. The concussion of the .45s and the 500 caused dust from the cave walls and ceiling to fill the room, obscuring everything from view. Both men froze, hoping they'd hit the Tack, but more importantly, they hoped that the mountain wouldn't fall on them.

After what seemed like hours, the room cleared enough to see the shelf where the Tack had been. They spotted nothing other than a handful of tiny brown bats still trying to settle down after what must have seemed like a major explosion. Brad's ears were ringing; he couldn't imagine the shock to their sensitive ears. Jack seemed not to notice Alaska's rare little cave dwellers.

"Shit," Jack said as he started to scan the cave with his light, pistols ready.

Brad's light went to the ground under the ledge and spotted the Tack wing sticking up slightly behind the canvas-covered object. "Here it is."

As they approached the Tack, the exit hole from one of the .45s in its back gave them good reason to believe it was dead, but the .50 caliber wound that took off most of its head guaranteed it.

Jack smiled. "My shots were faster."

Brad put away his Smith & Wesson. "Yeah, but mine was final."

Leaving the Tack where it lay, the two men completed the search of the cavern and didn't find anything else, not even Scout. Brad knew there must be other hidden passages, but they really didn't have the time to look for them. They needed Scout to show them.

"Must have been the only one," Jack stated, more to himself than to Brad.

"Let's see if Scout is outside and get Erica. She'll want to look at the Tack, and I think we should look at what's under that tarp," Brad said.

"Coming out," Brad yelled as they neared the entrance.

Squinting as they exited the cave, they found Erica looking up at them with the shotgun in a relaxed position. She knew they were okay.

"You don't seem too worried about us," Brad stated.

"I must be getting better at understanding Rhunken," Erica replied.

Erica shifted her gaze to her right and the two men followed it to see Scout sitting on its haunches, casually looking back at them like there was nothing wrong in the world.

Jack said, "I don't see how that Rhunken got past us to leave the cave before we did."

Brad said, "He must have been in one of the other chambers. It appears the Tack was the only thing at home."

Erica looked at him. "He did it three times. It came out twice and just looked at me, as if to check on me. Then it came out just seconds before you did."

Brad smiled, "I think he just likes you better than us. But seriously, this tells me Scout was more worried about a threat outside the lair than the inside."

Gathering up their equipment, they hurried back into the cavern, Brad could see that Erica had shifted gears; she was in biologist mode now. She was excited in a new way, and happier. He offered a hand to her when she started to climb to the entrance, expecting to help with her load, but she must have thought he wanted a drink because she just handed him a water bottle from a pocket and scaled the rock face with ease. Brad smiled, thinking to himself. "Hell. She's in better shape than I am."

Watching her from behind, Brad smiled, lost in a thought.

Erica looked down at him. "What are you thinking about?"

"A recent nightmare." He said as he climbed to the ledge.

"Oh" she said blushing.

Jack looked puzzled, but didn't ask.

Brad followed her back into the cave with Jack right behind him. All three wanted to explore what was under the tarp and Erica couldn't wait to examine the dead Tack.

CHAPTER 27

PETER WASN'T SLOWING DOWN even though he knew he should. He was very worried. Both Rick and Doug had fallen behind. He heard one of them slip and the other stop to help. Peter hadn't even turned around to see if anyone was hurt.

Peter pushed past the camp overlook without stopping. The on-again, off-again weather was on again, and the rain had increased to a steady drizzle; everything was wet. He figured it must be raining harder higher up in the mountains because little rivulets were making mini-waterfalls all along the trail, causing enough noise along with the sounds he made splashing through the water as he ran down the trail to drown out any sounds coming from the camp. Peter mumbled, "I hate this shit! Why would anyone live in this crap?" He knew he was close to the cabin when he could smell the smoke from the cabin's woodstove, so he picked up his pace even more. All he could think about was getting to Sandy.

Peter broke into the clearing surrounding the camp compound, and headed straight for the cabin, focusing on the open door. At first nothing seemed out of place. He was about to call out when movement off to the right caught his attention. He stopped in his tracks and froze.

Peter knew instantly that it was a Tack, even though he'd never seen one. It was only ten yards away on the path heading to the outhouse, but he didn't recognize what it was sitting on at first, and he probably wouldn't have even cared if he hadn't seen the hair. It was Sandy's, but what the hair was attached to wasn't Sandy. It didn't have any skin. Peter looked up to see the Tack's flat face, its eyes focused on him, its mouth in what looked like a bloody, toothy grin. The Tack changed color from a light gray to almost black almost instantly.

"What the fuck?" Peter didn't see or hear the other Tack that hit him.

The blow knocked Peter to the ground, and his rifle slid away. He turned and saw what hit him, a second Tack. His breath had been knocked out of him, but he rolled to get clear. He began to scramble toward his weapon, which lay just out of reach, but as he got to his knees a second blow came, rolling him onto his back and allowing him to see both of the Tacks that had attacked him. Quickly, he rolled back over and lunged for his gun, but a large, hooked, thumb-claw sank into his right shoulder. The first Tack jumped on his back, immediately followed by the second.

The world went silent for Peter as shock and fright overtook him. He couldn't hear his own screams as the Tacks ripped off his jacket and shirt and started to lick his skin with their rasp-like tongues.

CHAPTER 28

THE TACK WAS JUST as they'd left it, wedged behind the tarp. Brad wouldn't have been surprised if it was gone, with the way the Rhunken cleaned up after themselves.

Brad and Jack pulled the dead Tack into the center of the cavern, giving Erica room to work. It was a lot lighter than Brad expected. He could have easily lifted it by himself. They laid it out on its back, folding and positioning its wings close to its body. Erica excitedly pulled a LED headlamp from her pack and turned it on. The sight of the head caused her to grimace slightly, but she quickly recovered.

"Did you have to make such a mess?" she asked.

Brad and Jack looked at each other. Brad said, "It's not like we planned it, you know."

Jack added, "He's the one with the cannon."

She shrugged and, without another word, opened a small surgical kit and went to work. Brad could see she was in her element.

Brad returned to the tarp and grabbed one end, throwing it back to reveal an old Army footlocker. The faded name stenciled on the lid stopped him in his tracks. "What the fuck?" was all Brad could say.

The tone in Brad's voice made Erica stop and look up. "What is it?"

Jack came over and looked over Brad's shoulder and read the name. "Robert Strom. Who the hell is Robert Strom?"

Erica looked at the box. "Holy shit. Is that Bob's?"

Brad ignored both questions and knelt in the dust. The footlocker wasn't locked, so he opened the latches and lifted the lid to discover an oil lamp, spare oil, matches and some bottled water along with a stack of notebooks. The water bottles and matches looked new. Brad took out the lamp and lit it with the matches, bathing the cavern in light.

Erica and Jack came over to the trunk and peered inside. Brad picked up one of the books and read from the handwritten document dated less than a year before.

"'Number two is more aggressive each time I visit—for that matter, I think they all are. The lack of an adult Rhunken seems to allow this tendency. The tests came back to confirm what I thought; the reason the Tacks lick or eat the skin of their pray is to enjoy what I believe to be the taste of fear, i.e., the chemicals released through the skin when an animal is frightened. This appears to be a delicacy. They will lick the skin completely off a highly terrified victim even if they've already fed.'"

Jack broke in. "Jesus Christ, and what's this number two? How many are there? What the fuck is going on?"

Brad looked at Erica. "Looks like Bob had his own little experiment going on."

Who's Bob?" Jack almost shouted. They could hear the fear in his voice.

Erica answered, "Bob was one of the best PCOs we ever had, if not the best." She grabbed one of the other books and started to page through it.

Erica came across an entry in the book that referred to one of the Tacks as a number five, as well as an extremely large newborn. All three looked at each other, then at the all but forgotten dead Tack behind them.

"Looks like we may have four more of these to deal with—no, make that five more adults, if this is the newborn Bob referred to," Brad said in an extremely calm voice as he put the books back and shut the footlocker. He started to quickly gather his equipment.

"Fucking great," was the only thing Jack could say, but he was also repacking.

Erica was confused. "What's the rush?"

Brad looked at her. "Where do you think the other Tacks are?" Seeing the blank look on her face, he explained, "They're the reason Sandy didn't answer the radio."

The light came on in Erica's eyes. "Oh, shit, we've got to get down there and help!"

Brad pulled out a large hunting knife. He cut off one of the Tack's hands at the wrist and roughly stuffed it in one of Erica's specimen bags. She nodded, acknowledging that the odds were slim that the body would still be there when they returned. She placed a set of forceps on the Tack's chest for scale and took several pictures before she started to repack her gear. They knew the footlocker would be fine.

In a matter of minutes the trio exited the cave and raced down the hill.

Scout was nowhere in sight.

When they weren't far from the last communications check point, Erica stopped and keyed her radio. "Rick. Doug. Rick. Do you copy?"

No response. Erica looked at Jack, who instantly understood. Jack tried his. "Doug, Rick, anyone, do you copy? Say again, do you copy?"

No response. Without a word the group continued on as fast as they dared, unaware that their broadcast had been received.

Peter's earpiece had been knocked free and lay next to him. The call startled the Tacks, causing them to retreat a short distance from the unconscious Peter. Their faces flattened as they focused on the small device, not sure what to make of it. Both Tacks' colors changed from dark brown to brindled gray and they sniffed the air.

Whoever was making those noises would be the next to die.

CHAPTER 29

RICK'S ANKLE HURT LIKE a son-of-a-bitch, and he couldn't put any real weight on it. Doug had cut him a walking stick, allowing them to start down the trail again. Doug carried both rifles and daypacks. It was slow going. After a while, the ankle warmed up and the pain subsided to a dull ache, but Rick knew when it got cold again, the agony would be a lot worse, so they needed to keep moving.

Not long after, Rick slipped on the wet spruce needles and slid off the trail and down a rock face, ending up in a stand of devil's club, so he not only had a sprained ankle but his left hand and arm was burning from the hundreds of embedded thorns from the nasty plant. No wonder it was called the hiker's bane.

Peter had gone ahead a good twenty minutes ago. They had thought about trying to stop him, but it was probably a good idea for someone to reach camp as soon as possible. Neither of them thought Peter would have stayed behind even if they'd insisted.

The scream stopped them in their tracks. Neither of them had ever heard such a sound, but they knew it had to be Peter.

Doug told Rick, "I'm going to run ahead and check on Peter." Then Doug started to set down Rick's rifle and pack.

Rick stopped him. "I don't think that's a good idea. We should stay together."

Fear more than logic made Doug agree.

Leaving their packs behind, they started toward the cabin. Doug held his weapon in both hands. Rick carried his with one hand and used the walking stick, forcing more weight on his injured foot. He hobbled as fast as he could. He figured it would take close to a half hour to get to the cabin at this speed. He knew they would be too late. The screaming had already stopped.

They made their way through the wet forest as quickly as possible. The rain had picked up again, and the pattering it made got louder. Rick hoped this would cover the sounds of their approach. The trail had flattened a little and they picked up some speed— not as fast as a Doug could manage by himself, but not bad considering. He was still torn between the feelings of getting to the cabin as fast as possible and staying with Rick, but he kept his concerns to himself.

From behind Rick managed to ask between pain-gritted teeth, "Should we wait for Brad and Jack?

The question snapped Doug out of his reactionary thinking mode and into proactive mindset.

He stopped and turned toward Rick, his mind running through the possibilities. "Yes, I think that's a damn good idea." But his mind was also focused on fixing this problem.

Rick took a break and sat on a wet, moss-covered fallen tree. Rick could see Doug's mind working, but his own mind was too focused on his foot and the burning from the devil's club.

"We're only a few minutes from the camp," Doug said, then continued, "I think I should sneak forward to see what I can."

Doug indicated Rick's ankle, acknowledging his pain. "You stay here. I'll do a quick recon and get back as soon as possible."

Rick nodded in agreement. He watched Doug leave, quickly disappearing into the forest.

The pain in his ankle subsided to a throb, and Rick knew once it cooled down, he wouldn't be able to stand on it at all. So he got back up and, as quietly as he could, started to follow Doug toward the cabin.

Doug felt better about himself as he made his way down the path. It felt good to be doing something he considered positive and not a reaction to his fear. After a few minutes of walking, he looked around. The trail was still unfamiliar, so he figured he must be farther from the camp than he'd anticipated. He sped up a little.

The sight of the roof stopped Doug. He could see the cabin roof through the trees off to the left. He could only see a small part of the compound, but what he could see looked quiet. No movement or sound. He knew the trail from here. It would go down the slope for a quarter of a mile, and then hook to the left, coming in on the south side of the campsite. In his mind, he planned his approach, using the cover of the last bend in the trail.

Feeling confident, he slid back the bolt of his AR-10, spied the brass of the 7.62 NATO round, and then let it slide back into the receiver. He gave the bolt handle a hit with the heel of this hand, making sure it was loaded and the bolt was home. Then he started down the hill with a stone-cold look on his face.

CHAPTER 30

THE RAINDROP THAT STRUCK his right eyelid woke him, but Peter still felt as if he was in a dream. Slowly his vision started to clear. He was lying on the ground, on his stomach, the left side of his face on wet gravel.

He tried to sit up, but he felt heavy and tired. His hand came to his face and rubbed the rain out of his eye. When it refocused, he could see blood on his hand. At first it didn't make sense, but as if a switch was thrown, everything rushed back. With a jerk Peter rolled to his left side and got up on his left elbow and looked around.

The Tack was not six feet away, sitting on its haunches. It quickly shifted its flattened face toward the radio headset. The headset moved with Rick because the cable was still attached to the transmitter on his belt.

As the Tack looked back at Peter, its face seemed to stretch. Its teeth, for lack of a better word began to show. It leaned forward and started to come at him. The Tack changed from a mixed gray to solid gray, then almost black in color.

Peter was frozen, still in shock. Nothing seemed real.

The gravel between him and the Tack exploded, and almost instantly Peter heard the report of the rifle. Both the Tack and Peter jumped, but neither was hit. The shot snapped Peter back on line. He knew he was in trouble. Peter sat up and looked to his left, where the shot had come from. Doug was standing at the trailhead about fifty yards away with his rifle at the ready. A great feeling of relief came to Peter until he saw movement to his right. Another Tack flew from the roof of the cabin just to Doug's left, aiming straight at him.

Peter started to yell a warning, but the Tack near him started to race toward Doug as well.

Peter rolled slightly on his hip and pulled his Sig P229 from its holster. He pulled the trigger as the Tack was passing him. The Tack was focused on Doug, and Peter's reaction was lost in the Tack's narrowed peripheral vision. The .40 caliber hollow point caught the Tack under its left jaw, angled up and took off the right side of its head. The Tack slid to a stop without another twitch.

Adrenaline had set in. He snapped his head to see the Tack attack Doug. He had been defending Peter and never saw it coming. Peter tried to jump to his feet, but his right leg collapsed, sending him back to the gravel, and the pain seared though him, causing him to see stars. Peter could see an unnatural bend in the thigh, confirming it was broken.

Peter rolled to his stomach and started to take aim at the Tack now standing over Doug as he lay unmoving on the ground. It was a long shot with a pistol, so he focused on the front sight, aiming slightly high on the blurred Tack and started to squeeze the trigger.

The blow from a third Tack hit Peter in the back of the head, knocking his face into the gravel, breaking his nose and overloading his nervous system, causing a sudden white-hot flash, then nothing but black.

CHAPTER 31

RICK'S STOMACH REMINDED HIM he'd not eaten since breakfast. His thoughts shifted to the snacks in the packs they'd left up the trail. He mumbled, "The water's there too. Hell, and the radio."

Rick looked back the way they'd come, shrugged and made his way back to their packs.

He heard Doug's shot just before he reached them. The single shot was reassuring. Doug must have killed it. When the pistol shot rang out, Rick assumed Doug had just finished off the Tack.

Rick now recognized this place: it was the location of their first trail camera. Funny how places look different when looking at them from a different angle, he thought. Retrieving the pack, he calmly sat down on the edge of the trail and dug out the radio, water bottle and a protein bar.

Rick took a big bite of the protein bar and eyed the radio. He glanced down the trail, half expecting Doug to come back for him. But it didn't surprise him that Doug didn't appear. Rick held the green button down until it beeped three times, turning on the radio, and took another bite of the bar. He didn't even wait to finish chewing when making his first transmission. "Erica, Brad. Are you guys out there?"

Erica, Brad and Jack all came to a halt when Rick's call came over both Jack's and Erica's radio headsets.

Erica grabbed her radio off her belt and keyed the PTT. "Rick, is that you? You guys OK?"

Rick swallowed his bite. "Yeah, other than twisting my ankle and having sex with some devil's club, I'm fine. Not sure about Peter. He went ahead and we haven't heard a word. Doug went to check on him and I heard a couple of shots, so I'm pretty sure he got the Tack. So I think we have it under control."

Erica, Brad and Jack looked at each other. Then Brad summarized their mutual feeling: "Oh shit."

He grabbed Jack's radio. "Rick, are you in contact with Doug?"

Rick heard the tenseness in Brad's voice. "No, he doesn't have a radio. But I'm sure he'll be back shortly."

Brad shook his head. They had also heard the shots, but it hadn't given them the same reassuring feeling it'd given Rick. "Where are you?"

"I'm at the first trail cam site."

Brad surveyed the surrounding terrain and mentally calculated their position in relationship to Rick. "There's more than one Tack, so stay put. We're not far from you. We should be there in about fifteen minutes."

Brad could see the worry on Erica's face. He was sure his look had changed also. No one questioned or tried to second-guess him. There was no doubt that he was now in charge. He tossed Jack the radio and said, "Let's go." Then started down the trail at a jog. He didn't look back, but he heard the other two keeping pace behind him.

CHAPTER 32

IT WAS FIFTEEN MINUTES, almost to the second, when Rick heard the group coming down the trail. He got to his feet with a groan, his foot protesting as he applied some weight to it.

"Why did you split up?" Jack snapped as they approached.

Rick gave Jack a "fuck you" look, and then directed his attention to Brad. "What do mean, there's more than one?"

Brad could see Rick was in great pain, so he picked up the packs. Giving one to Jack, he grabbed Rick by the arm and started the group down the trail. "We found evidence in the cave of multiple Tacks. Not sure how many, but we are guessing five."

Brad could see Rick was upset, but he'd just have to suck it up. "We're not far from camp. There's a place we can see it, about a quarter mile away. We'll see what the situation is, then make a plan."

The four made their way to the bend in the trail that overlooked the camp through the tops of some small new growth spruce and alder trees. It limited their view, but it also gave them cover.

Brad unzipped his polar fleece jacket, pulling out a small set of binoculars. Bringing the optics to his eyes, he almost instantly saw a Tack sitting like a stone gargoyle on the roof of the main cabin. A second Tack half flew, half hopped across the center of the clearing, disappearing behind the north end of the cabin and out of sight.

"Well, I see at least two Tacks." Brad continued to glass the area. "No sign of Doug or the others."

Brad scanned his "brothers in battle," so to speak, and saw a mixed group. Jack appeared overly excited—if he wasn't pointed in the right direction, he'd be dangerous. Rick was hurting; he'd be slow in his actions for sure and possibly in his mental acuity as was well. Erica looked scared, but no more than most would and a lot less than she might have been, but she stood steady with focus. She was the obvious choice for his back-up, even with her limited training. And if the situation gets hot, he'd feel better if she was close.

Brad thought through a possible plan, and then knelt. Picking up a stick, he drew a sketch of the campground in the dirt. "There's one on the roof here, and I saw another one go behind the cabin here, to the north. I hope Doug took down one or two, but let's not count on it. So that leaves a possible three unknowns."

Brad drew a hooked line leading into the south end of the camp, representing the trail they were on. "Jack, I'd like you to make your way through the trees to the beach and come in from the east. Try not to show yourself. You're our cover. Once you're in position, key your radio. Erica and I will walk straight into the south end of camp. The Tack on the roof should be in view and the second will have to come from behind the cabin."

Brad looked at Rick. "I'd like you to trail behind us by about ten yards and watch our backs."

"And Erica, I want you on my ass, covering my right." He looked at her, and got a nod in response.

Everyone studied the makeshift map, visualizing the depicted plan. "Remember where everyone is and watch for the others. Any questions?" Brad concluded.

"Jack, we'll give you fifteen minutes to get to your position. That should be plenty of time. If we don't get your radio key, we'll assume something went wrong and we'll back out and reassess our options." Both he and Jack looked at their watches and noted the time. Brad's watch read 4:50. Still lots of daylight left this time of year.

Jack slipped off his pack and checked his weapons. Slipping away silently down the trail, he disappeared into the wet forest.

Brad watched Jack leave, checked his watch once more and took a deep breath. "OK, one last weapons check and let's get in position."

CHAPTER 33

THE WEATHER HAD CLEARED slightly, and patches of blue sky showed through the breaks in the high cloud layer. Lower heavy gray clouds still hung on the windward tops of the surrounding mountains. Most of the Seymour Canal was now in the spotted sunlight. In some areas it was still raining, though. This was one of them.

At five o'clock Erica's radio squelched twice, and she keyed hers once in acknowledgment. She looked at Brad and nodded.

Brad unhooked the holster's hammer strap on the .50 caliber handgun. He slid the bolt of the twelve-gauge back a half inch until he could see the brass of the 00 Buck shell, then sent it back into the receiver, thumb on the safety. Without a word Brad started toward camp. Erica was just to his right and half a step back, her breathing steady but a little faster than normal. And the sound of Rick's boots on the gravel put him well to the rear.

The trail's slight downhill slope ended just as it turned left to a small footbridge that crossed an unnamed creek. Only about sixty feet of wooded trail was left before the open grounds of the camp.

From the footbridge, part of the clearing was visible, and Brad could see Doug, Peter, and what must be Sandy. All appeared to be dead. Brad could also see a dead Tack fallen near Peter. Erica inhaled sharply and started toward Doug. Brad put out his arm and stopped her with a firm grasp. Erica snapped her head around, ready to protest his thwarting of her attempt to help their teammates, but the look in his eyes stopped her without saying a word. Yet Brad wasn't looking at her, or at their downed friends. Erica followed his gaze and saw a Tack sitting on its haunches just inside the tree line on the opposite side of the clearing, looking right at them.

Brad had realized the trap that had obviously worked on both Peter and Doug.

Brad knew the Tack was out of range of the shotgun, but that Tack wasn't the one that worried him. Brad started forward again, and Erica stayed next to him. He knew she must be scared shitless, but she stayed by his side just the same. At times like this, Brad's blood turned to ice. He became calm, almost cold. His hands remained steady and all his senses became heightened. Brad scanned left and right, scoping at ground level as well as in the trees. "Take your time," Brad said in a low voice, mostly to himself.

As Brad and Erica reached the clearing, he stopped. Erica had to force herself to look away from the Tack on the opposite side and scan to her right, her shotgun at port arms; Brad had the left side. She saw the dead Tack lying near Peter, its head partially gone. She forced herself to look away and continue scanning.

Slight movement on the roof of the cabin gave away another Tack's location. Brad could just see its left arm and folded wing before it disappeared again. A noise came from between the cabin and the shed. The Tack on the far side shifted its gaze toward it, and then quickly looked back at them. Brad told himself, "Number three. And the dead one makes four."

Brad was feeling a little more confident now that he knew the location of four of the Tacks. That left only one Tack's location unknown. Brad edged his way out into the clearing and angled toward the cabin. He was confident the attack would come from the roof.

The Tack across the clearing rose slightly and shifted to its right, bringing it more into the open. It started to flash; ribbons of white, gray and brown ran up its body, slowly, then rapidly. Its whole body turned white, then almost black. Brad and Erica couldn't help but watch.

Brad heard the slightest rapid flapping sound, not from the roof but from behind and over his left shoulder. Brad dropped to his knee and twisted to his left, bringing his shotgun to his shoulder. Before he even turned completely around, he could see the large Tack diving at him from the trees behind them. It had covered most of the distance and was only fifteen feet away when Brad's gun went off. Brad was off balance, but the shot was true, hitting the fourth Tack squarely in the chest, killing it instantly. But the dead Tack continued on its course and slammed into Brad, knocking him to the ground with the Tack on top of him, but unmoving. Brad's large revolver was thrown clear of its holster and was lost from his view, but he still had the shotgun and he jacked in a fresh round. Mentally counting, "Seven shells left."

Erica had been caught off guard when Brad spun around. As she watched what Brad was doing, movement on the roof of the cabin captured her attention. A Tack was spreading its wings and launching off the roof, coming at them. Erica swung her Mossberg around to engage it, but another Tack came from behind the cabin, running on the ground like a dog. Erica's shotgun came to bear on the running Tack first. She fired the shot at the same time as Brad, and the Tack he'd shot slammed into her, sending her to the ground. Her gun flew from her hands and slid across the gravel to settle ten feet away.

The loud report of Jack's .375 H&H sounded off to the right. His shot found the midsection of the flashing Tack. The large-caliber weapon all but cut the Tack in half.

Erica's shot hit the running Tack in the left side, knocking it down. The Tack coming from the roof flared and rolled in midair at Erica's shot, and by doing so Rick's shotgun blast went under it, missing cleanly. The airborne Tack shifted its focus on the biggest threat: the only one left standing, Rick.

Rick had been watching the Tack near the shed, and when it started to flash he knew something was going to happen. Ignoring the pain in his ankle, he ran up to Brad and Erica's position. When

Brad killed the Tack diving from the left, it knocked over both Brad and Erica just feet in front of him.

Rick couldn't believe he missed, but the real problem now was that the Tack was coming at him. He aimed at the Tack and pulled the trigger. Nothing happened. A sick feeling hit him. He hadn't pumped a new round into his gun.

Brad pushed the Tack off and got to his knees in time to see the Tack attack Rick. The blow knocked Rick onto his back as the Tack stuck to him as he went down. Its teeth sank into Rick's throat, causing an instant spray of blood as Rick was trying to push it away. Brad's shotgun fired. He pumped in a second shell without thinking about it and fired again in less than a second. Both shots, nine pellets from each of the 00-buck hit the Tack in the back, the tight patterns just inches apart. They knocked the Tack completely off Rick, and Brad automatically jacked in a fresh round. "Five shells left." Brad could see Rick gasping for air, but the gaping hole where his throat had been told him that Rick would be dead by the time he got there.

Brad got to his feet and started for Rick when Erica yelled, "Brad!"

Erica was getting to her feet when the Tack she'd shot got up and lunged at Brad. She picked up Brad's big revolver from the ground at her feet, aimed it and pulled the trigger. The sound and recoil was tremendous, and she barely held on to the cannon. But the hollow point hit the Tack just below the eye, removing most of its face, but amazingly not killing it. But before the sound of her shot died away, a second shot from Peter's Sig hit the Tack in the left side and through the heart and lungs. In what seemed like in slow motion the Tack went facedown in the dirt for good.

Both Brad and Erica looked to see Peter lower his pistol to the gravel and roll onto his back.

Erica eyed the dead Tack next to them. "They can fly."

"No shit," was his reply.

Erica ran to Peter's side, checking him over, and started caring for his injuries the best she could.

Brad gathered himself and cleared the gravel from his shotgun, then reloaded it with the last two rounds that he had stashed in his jacket pocket. "Back to seven." Scanning the tree line and buildings, he went to confirm that there was nothing that could be done for Doug. His eyes were open and glazed over, and blood had stopped flowing from the gaping hole in his throat. Then he checked on Sandy as well, then covered her remains with the blue tarp from the nearby wood pile. Brad started to relax. He guessed they got them all.

Brad saw Jack coming from the body of the Tack he'd killed. He was wiping his knife off and putting it away. The Tack had been scalped.

Even though he was disgusted, Brad wasn't at all surprised. Brad shook his head and said, "You're a sick son of a bitch."

Jack smiled, taking it as a compliment, but didn't reply.

Jack's eyes snapped to his right and narrowed to a focus and raised his rifle all within a split second. Without thinking Brad started to turn towards the new threat while swinging the shotgun off his shoulder and ducking to a kneeling position. But all Brad saw was Scout coming out from behind the cabin.

Brad exhaled the breath he was holding, and a feeling of relief came over him, Scout was letting Brad know for sure all the Tacks were gone. Then he saw Scout tense and start to twist. The concussion from the muzzle blast and report from Jack's rifle made Brad jump in surprise. He saw Scout flinch from the hit and complete the turn. Still kneeling, he brought his gun around and pointed it at Jack's face. "What the fuck are you doing?" Brad snapped, but Jack didn't even look at him. He just started off at a run towards Scout.

The look of disbelief in Jack's eyes made Brad look back at Scout. The Rhunken was nowhere in sight. Brad slipped while trying to rise, and cursed under his breath as he started after Jack, who already had a big head start.

Jack couldn't believe it when the Rhunken had taken the hit, then turned and ran into the woods behind the cabin. He knew the hit was not placed exactly where he wanted it, but he knew he hit it. Wanting to finish what he had started, he ran after the Scout as he worked the bolt of his .375, sending home a fresh round.

"Shit, that thing is fast." he told himself as he ran past the fuel tank next to the cabin, heading toward the overgrown brush that choked the entrance to the old growth forest.

Jack stopped. He couldn't see the Rhunken or even where it had entered the woods. The movement to his left came so fast, Jack didn't even have time to turn his head. The rifle was jerked from his hands before he had time to react. Looking down, all he could see was empty hands. As if time had a mind of its own, it slowed down, thus allowing Jack the opportunity to see what was happening. In slow motion Jack turned his head to his left to see Scout. Its right hand was gripping the stock of the rifle, poised to swing. Jack knew it meant to hit him and he tried to duck. But his body would not move. Jack could see the muscles of the Scout's shoulder tighten, and then the barrel of the rifle sped toward him.

Trying to catch up to Jack, Brad continued to curse under his breath as he sprinted toward the side of the cabin where Jack had disappeared. He continued around the building, his weapon at low ready. He found Scout was standing next to Jack. It held Jack's rifle in its hand, with blood covering the barrel. Scout dropped the gun and shifted his gaze to Brad. Scout could see the question in Brad's eyes, and Scout answered it by shrugging his shoulders. Brad recalled how he had answered Scout's confusion over the killing of the other Rhunken. An accident.

Scout's look changed to one of content, and Brad knew the job was done. Brad could see the wound caused by Jack's rifle shot. It had hit Scout on the left side. The bullet hole looked puckered and much whiter than the rest of skin, and Brad surmised Rhunken must have the ability to restrict skin and surrounding blood vessels to control bleeding. "Learn something new every day," he said to himself. Scout didn't seem fazed by the wound. It turned and walked into the brush, completely disappearing within a few steps.

Jack was alive, but just barely. Scout had hit him on the right side of his face, smashing his jaw and ripping a gash from his right ear down and across to his left collarbone. If Jack had been six inches closer, he would have been decapitated. Teeth were missing from his lower jaw. It didn't look as if the jugular vein was severed, but the wound was bleeding profusely, causing Jack to choke and gurgle.

Erica came around the corner of the building and rushed past him to help Jack. Brad realized he hadn't moved, but he quickly followed Erica to help. They rolled Jack on his back and Erica applied pressure on his wound. He was conscious, his eyes darting from Erica to Brad and back, pleading for help. She told Brad, "Go get something I can use as a bandage."

Brad went into the cabin and found the large first aid kit. Grabbing one of Jack's tee-shirts, he went back out and handed Erica the shirt. They made quick work of Jack's injury, using superglue and sutures supplied in the kit, before bandaging the wound. Erica seemed pleased with the work. "If you can get him inside without causing too much damage, go ahead. If not, I'll be back to help."

Then she got up and said, "I'll go see to the others."

Brad went into the cabin and grabbed a blanket. Using it as a drag tarp, he brought Jack inside the cabin, leaving him on the floor but covering him up with the blanket.

Jack looked better than he deserved to, and Brad told him, "You're a lucky bastard. If she wasn't here, I would have let you die." Then he turned and went outside.

Erica was still working on Peter. She had dressed his wounds as best as she could and was making him as comfortable as possible. So he headed over to the first Tack he'd killed with the shotgun to have a look at it. It had made a flapping or fluttering noise that the others hadn't, and he wondered why. The Tack was by far the largest in the group, almost as big as the one in the lair, but this one looked much older. As he rolled it over he could see a hole in its wing. Brad spread out the wing and could tell it was an old wound, made by a shotgun. This must be what disrupted the normal airflow and made the flapping noise. Brad shook his head and thought, "Whoever did this long ago saved our lives."

Brad made his way back to Peter. Erica was getting to her feet, and she looked relieved to see him. "Everything OK?" she asked.

Brad looked around at the carnage, then back to Peter. "Let's get him inside and I'll radio for a ride."

Erica helped Brad make a stretcher from two limbs and a blanket and carried Peter into the cabin and onto a bunk. Brad reached the Coast Guard station and reported a "bear attack." After giving the radio operator their location and what information Brad figured was "need to know" for the rescue, he learned that the helicopter would be coming from Sitka, with an ETA of two hours.

Brad caught Erica looking at her hands; they were covered in blood and shaking. She went to the sink and washed them. He knew it was the adrenaline and absolutely normal. After she dried her hands and they still hadn't settled down, she looked at Brad and asked, "Does this happen to you?"

"Used to, but not anymore."

He knew he didn't need to explain. She knew more about the adrenal system than he ever would. But he watched her process the new experience. She had impressed him. She'd kept her head in the game, moved well and improvised when needed. That was more than he could have hoped from anyone.

Erica asked Brad, "Can you get some blood and tissue samples from the Tacks?"

"I can do that. How do you want them marked?"

"Just one through five. And if you would, take a picture of each one, and we'll mark them the same. I should be able to keep them straight."

He watched as she went over to Jack, and looked at his wounds. Her hands were already calming down. "She's a lot better person than I am." He thought.

Brad grabbed five Ziploc bags labeled them one through five. Found the digital camera and went out and collected the samples.

It took about fifteen minutes to collect the samples, and Brad made his way to the ice chest in the cabin and put the plastic bags in for cold storage. While he was there, he grabbed two beers and walked over to where Erica was working on Peter. He handed one of the beers to her. He could see Peter was out again and asked, "How's he doing?"

"He needs a doctor, but I think he'll be fine." She took a long pull of the cool amber, followed by another. "That's maybe the best thing I've ever tasted."

Brad nodded with a smile. They hadn't had anything to drink in hours and he figured that's what they needed.

Brad downed half his beer in one swig, then looked at Erica. "You did great out there today."

She blushed and said, "Thanks, that means a lot to me."

After seeing that Peter and Jack were comfortable, Erica got up and followed Brad outside. Erica could see the sky had cleared a bit more and the wind had all but stopped. It was going to be a beautiful evening.

"They never cease to amaze me," Brad said, snapping Erica out of her musing.

Erica followed Brad's gaze. All the dead Tacks were gone.

CHAPTER 34

THE LADIES' PERFUME WAS overpowering, or was it a man's cologne next to her? Four people were talking on cell phones, six had some kind of fancy coffee, and everyone but Erica had a laptop. And this was just in the elevator. Even after being back in Seattle for three weeks, Erica still felt out of place. She knew she'd get back in the groove, but now she wasn't sure if she even wanted to.

She had finally finished the "after action report." The CEO had sent it back three times, wanting more detail, mostly about the final attack sequence. What Erica really wanted to do was to study Bob's journal. She had been given the option of taking a few weeks off, but she knew if she did, someone else would be given the task, so she reported to the office the next morning and immediately dove into Bob's documents, just as she knew Brad would do with his secretly copied duplicate back in Juneau.

Erica was excited to be at work today. She'd finished her analysis of Robert Strom's notes, typed her preliminary brief and was on her way to present it to the board. But that really wasn't why she was excited.

He was supposed to be here. Erica had requested the board to ask Brad to come in to help clarify and answer questions. He had responded to the invitation by saying he would attend. Erica also knew he'd been offered his job back, but she hadn't heard if he'd accepted it. Maybe she'd find out today. No, she would find out. She'd make him tell her, even if he didn't want anyone else to know.

As usual, Brad had arrived early. He was already in the large conference room and contemplating a refill of the coffee he just finished. His decision was made for him when a heavyset woman, wearing a light blue pantsuit, pushed in a cart. Brad walked over to the cart and waited until the coffee and assorted pastries were placed on the table in the back of the room. Ignoring the china, with its small fancy cups, he refilled his sixteen-ounce paper cup, grabbed a maple bar and went back to his seat in the back row. The only other person in the room was a technician checking the audiovisual equipment.

Erica walked in carrying an arm full of papers and made her way down the aisle to the front, focused on the technician. Brad just watched and kept silent. She stopped about halfway down and turned slightly, looking directly at him. She'd felt his gaze. Erica had a Mona Lisa smile and she might have said something if Peter hadn't walked into the room and caught their attention with his boisterous greeting: "Brad!"

Brad walked over to the man, still on crutches, his haircut close, keeping his scalp wounds clear and easy to clean. Overall, he looked like he was healing well. Brad was pleasantly surprised to see him. He glanced back toward Erica, but she was already heading to the podium. "It's good to see you up and about," Brad said, shaking his hand.

The room started to fill quickly, and Peter forced Brad to move to a set of saved seats in the front row.

Brad watched her relaxed, methodical preparation and noticed that she was much more confident than the first time he'd attended one of her presentations. Erica made a voice test of the audio system. Then looking satisfied with her prep work, she looked over to Brad and met his eyes with a smile. Brad rose and started over to the front of the stage to greet her, but was beaten to it by the CEO. Erica's attention shifted to Dr. Clark and almost covered up her disappointment of the interruption. But she smiled, shook his hand and joined the conversation. Brad took a right and headed back up the aisle to retrieve another cup of coffee, this time in the little fancy cup. But Brad did notice the CEO had a new attachment. It was about six-foot-five, two hundred and fifty pounds and wrapped in a cheap suit. A bodyguard. While this didn't surprise him, it still made him wonder, especially with the way the guy was tracking Brad's movements with intense interest.

After people watching at the back of the room, Brad put down his empty cup and headed for his seat, but along the way was forced into exchanging pleasantries with a few people he recognized but didn't remember their names. Once seated, Peter asked Brad, "You haven't talked to her since we've been back? Why haven't you?"

Brad didn't answer. Hell, he didn't have one.

"You're an idiot," Peter said with a smile.

Brad nodded, but still didn't reply.

Precisely at nine o'clock, the lights dimmed slightly and the large screen behind the podium came alive, displaying a map of northern southeast Alaska. Erica excused herself from the CEO, made her way to the podium and clipped a wireless mike to her lapel.

"Thanks for coming," she started. "Just so everyone knows, this presentation is not covering the successful, yet costly expedition to eradicate a colony of Tacks on Admiralty Island, Alaska. It is to present the findings of the review of the documentation found during the expedition."

The screen behind Erica changed to show Bob's footlocker with multiple notebooks arranged on top.

"When I started to put this together, I wanted to present just the facts, not conjecture. But I found this to be impossible. A lot of the information in the notes is captured as random thoughts and observations. So my plan is to present Robert Strom's information and share my understanding of what he wrote, but I will try to differentiate between the two." She checked her notes before going on.

"Anthropomorphic: Ascribing human characteristics to non-human things.

"This is how Robert Strom started his notes. Knowing Bob, this was one of his pet peeves, and I think this is a good thing to remind ourselves to remain objective. The first entry was dated. . . "

Brad watched Erica more than he listened. He didn't need to, because he'd read and studied Bob's notes. He was the one who went back, retrieved the books, and took photos of the lair after everyone had been evacuated. And once back in Juneau, he had stopped by the FAA office and made copies of everything before turning them over to Erica. He told her he'd made duplicates, but she just shrugged, telling him she really didn't want to know.

The briefing turned out to be anything but brief. A great many questions and comments were raised when Bob's notes on how the Tacks fly were presented. How they locked their arms with their wings, using the never understood bend in the ulnas, and used both sets of pectoral muscles for powered flight, and how they could only glide or dive in an attack, without their arms and associated muscles locked to the wings.

Well into the second hour, Erica finally reached the part Brad was waiting to hear about.

"We were able to take two sets of samples from dispatched Tacks. The first came from the tests of the five culled Tacks and didn't yield anything we didn't already know. All we learned was that it was part of the greater Alaska colony. This was no surprise. But the second. . . "

The screen behind Erica changed to the severed hand of the Tack killed in the cave. A slight gasp came from some in the audience.

She paused slightly before continuing. "I'm sorry for the graphic photo, but this particular specimen, along with Bob's notes on this individual, will write a complete new chapter in the Rhunken book."

Erica came out from behind the podium and walked to the front of the stage to stress the importance of what she was going to talk about.

"While it was the largest specimen we encountered, this Tack did not look, or act, like the rest. It didn't try to run or attack us, and it was by far the easiest to dispatch. While we didn't give the matter much thought at the time, tests now explain the aberration. It was a juvenile. Less than two years old, and its DNA was not completely consistent with the others. It looks as if it's a mix with a subspecies."

The conference room noise level rose considerably. Erica had expected it would and let the crowd settle down, ignoring the questions and walking back to the podium. Before long people figured out that she wasn't going to try to compete with the noise and it quieted down.

The screen changed to a graph with multiple lines depicting growth vs. age. A blue line was marked "Human," a green line marked "Rhunken" and then a brown line that was the last full line, was marked "Tack." Erica pointed out a short, incomplete red line with no identifier.

"This graph comes from some of the last entries Bob made. Until this time, we didn't have any growth information on Tacks. He was obviously aware of, and studying, the growth rate of this young oversized Tack until the tragic accident that took many of our top people."

The screen changed to a list of numbers. "Using the information from Bob's notes and measurements taken by us at the time it was killed, we have calculated two different scales that could apply to this special Tack. The first is based on what I believe is the more accurate, the Rhunken growth rate. The second, and what I think is least likely, the Tack growth rate. Now, the actual rate of growth is not really what's in question. Computer modeling for this is believed to be quite accurate. It's the lifespan that's the question. Both Rhunken and Tacks grow continuously throughout their lives. And thanks to Bob's data, we see that Tacks appear to live much shorter natural lives."

The CEO stood up and stopped Erica. "Are you saying that this new Tack would have grown at the faster rate and would have lived the longer lifespan?"

"Yes, I'm almost positive." Erica pushed the button on the remote and a new graph was displayed.

"The blue line represents what I believe is the least likely. It shows a projected size at maturity of five feet tall with a wingspan of eighteen feet. And—"

Erica pushed the button once more, adding a red line to the graph along with the blue.

The audience gasped.

Erica smiled. She'd hoped for this reaction. "If the computer and I are correct, the new Tack would have stood closer to ten feet and had a wingspan of thirty feet."

This time the crowd would not calm down without help. Erica thumped the mike and the sound got everyone's attention refocused on the stage.

Erica pushed the remote again and forwarded to the next slide, showing the data of the comparison of two different DNA sequences. "This shows the differences between the smaller and the larger specimens quite clearly. Bob wrote in his papers that he hypothesized this unknown subspecies is from an undocumented colony located near Yakutat, Alaska." She paused, took a drink of water, and then continued. "The Yakutat area was a glacial refugium during the last ice age, and allowed this allopatric speciation. But without further study this is just a hypothesis."

Erica could see more than a few expressions of bewilderment, so she restated her last statement in layperson terms. "Basically, the area around Yakutat was not covered by glaciers during the last ice age, and this allowed the local populations to develop separately from the rest of the world." Then she added, "We know this happened to a subspecies of pike in this area, so it would not be without precedence."

"That's all I have to present on the actual documentation we recovered from the Tack lair. Now, I know this brief raises more questions than it answers, but I think that it should. This briefing has taken a lot longer then we planned, but I think we can still take a few questions."

Dr. Clark took the privilege of rank and asked the first question.

"What is the likelihood of us seeing another one of these Super Tacks?"

Erica nodded; this was one of the anticipated questions. "I'm sure many of you are wondering the same thing. I know I did, so I calculated the answer as best I could. If you recall, the occurrence of a Tack birth is about one in 17,000, and while we don't know the exact combination of conditions required to produce this so-called 'Super Tack,' we calculate the chances to be around one in 150,000,000, given the culling practices. Without culling, the chance is about one in 150,000. Now, given the estimated number of Rhunken on earth, I figure we will be hit by a meteor long before we see any super Tack flying overhead, or as I've come to call them 'Dhraken.'"

Erica patiently answered questions for another half-hour, in which time her name for the new Rhunken firmly took hold. When the CEO got up to leave, he was followed by his bodyguard and what seemed to be a new assistant. No more questions were asked, effectively calling an end to the meeting.

Brad waited just outside the door to the conference room for another half-hour before he gave up and decided to leave. Looking at his watch, he figured he had just enough time to get a bite to eat before catching the last flight home.

Erica had been trying to work her way through the one-on-one questions as pleasantly as she could and get out of the auditorium. She could see Brad waiting just outside. When she saw Brad look at his watch, his expression changed and he disappeared down the hall. She knew he was leaving. So she excused herself and pushed her way out and into the hall.

"Brad!" Erica said a little more loudly than she wanted. Brad stopped and turned. They locked eyes, making Erica slightly embarrassed and unsure what she should do next.

Brad just gave her a little smile, nodded, then walked away. Erica smiled, but couldn't just leave it at that. She knew only one term of endearment that he would understand. She raised her voice loud enough so he would hear her, "Eat shit and die, Brad Michaels!"

Brad didn't turn around or even pause, but Erica knew he was smiling.

Just before Brad left the building, the CEO's private secretary, the one he remembered from the last visit, ran up to him, "Mr. Michaels, I have something for you."

Brad took the standard-sized envelope and turned it over. It was marked "Brad Michaels, Private." Brad stopped in his tracks. It was from Bob, dated the day before he died, and it had been opened.

CHAPTER 35

"IT DOESN'T MAKE SENSE." Brad had read the information multiple times and it was still kicking his ass.

The computer on his desk was off, and he sat looking out the office window across the Glacier Highway at a strip mall and motel, but not really seeing anything. He'd been back in Juneau for a couple of weeks, going to work at the FAA office without knowing if he was still affiliated with the WCC, so he decided to keep on operating as if he was.

The information in Bob's envelope would have been great to have before the last adventure; it might have saved lives. But it ended up in the wrong hands, and it took lives. The Admiralty crew used it to come up with its search area and base camp, putting them right in the middle of the Tacks' range. Brad also knew he still didn't have the whole story, as pages were missing from the envelope. Probably a third of the original data was gone by the look of the creases in the envelope, and this was confirmed by using the FAA's postal scale and comparing shipping charges with its weight.

The one piece that didn't fit and was giving him the most trouble was a handwritten note with azimuth and distance from a point called "First contact." According to Brad's WCC reports, his first official contact with a Rhunken was with Bob at the Sweetheart Lake, but using that point as the start, the direction and range put the far end in the center of the Juneau ice field, nothing close. Bob's first recorded contact starting point led to open water in the Gulf of Alaska. So he tossed the envelope in his backpack, hoping his subconscious would work it out. Brad reached over and turned on his computer, watching it go through its startup, and logging in when it requested it.

Alice walked into his office, put a yellow padded envelope on his desk with a smile, and walked out without a word, going through the rest of the mail in her hands.

"Thanks," Brad said to her back.

Mail? That's something he didn't get too often anymore. No return address, then he noticed the postage was cancelled in Seattle, but he couldn't make out the date. Using his hands, he ripped it open to find a key and a copy of the directions that were in Bob's package. Just the note and a key, nothing else. "Now what?" he thought.

Only one person to call. He picked up his phone and dialed the number from memory.

"Hi, Brad's office," Erica said with a cheery voice.

"You sound good. Everything OK?"

"Yep. It's slowed down around here for most folks, but I've still got tons of data to go through, so I'm keeping busy. Oh, and while I'm thinking about it, there's another issue that may concern you. Your local Fish and Game guy, Jim Straighter, has called multiple times, complaining and asking a lot of questions. I guess he wasn't happy with the answers he's received, so lately he's been throwing around a U.S. senator's name. It sounds like she's a friend of his, and he's threatening to get her involved if he doesn't get the answers he wants. The CEO has gotten really pissed off at him and at you for giving out the WCC's number."

Brad said, "Is Jim calling your number or the Public Affairs Office number?"

"He's using the PAO's number like he's supposed to, but the CEO is still mad at you," she replied.

Brad wasn't surprised and actually didn't care, so he changed the subject. "The reason I called was to ask if you sent me a package."

"No. Why?"

"I received a padded envelope today from Seattle with no return address on it."

"What was in it?"

"Just a key and the same note that was in Bob's package, nothing else."

"Nope, wasn't me. Looks like you've got a bigger mystery on your hands. Speaking of mysteries, did you figure out that point-to-point thing?"

"No. Going through the after-action reports, I found some first-contact points, but they don't lead me to anything."

The phone was silent for a bit, then Erica said, "If that note was for you and you alone, Bob would have used a point only you and him would have known."

"Of course," Brad thought. "I've got to go. Thanks," he said and hung up.

Brad looked out his window. It was still there. A blue compact rental car was parked in the take-out pizza place parking lot across the street for the second day in a row. It was actually parked at the side of the building, toward the back. No one ever parked there, so it stood out like a sore thumb. And there was somebody sitting in it.

CHAPTER 36

THE WHALE SPOUTED OFF the port side about four hundred yards away. Brad heard it first and turned his head in time to see the humpback's fluke as it dove deep in slow motion. The waters of Icy Straight lay smooth as glass, and the C-Dory sat still, just off of Sisters Island with its anchor rode relaxed with the slack tide. He got to the waypoint that marked the hump and set the hook. In less than ten minutes he dropped the herring baited, circle hooks over the side, let it settle to the bottom, put the pole in the rod holder, and headed into the cabin to get his breakfast. Before he could pour the first bloody Mary, the rod tip started dancing.

"One of those days," he said with a smile and started the three-hundred-foot battle. While not big, the forty-pounder was within tolerance for keeping, so he cut the gills and put it in the cooler. This time he got the drink and a piece of bacon before sending the baited rig back to the bottom. Taking a drink of his breakfast was delayed yet again, as a bookend to the first fish didn't even let the herring hit the mud floor. With the limit of two halibut taken, Brad finally sat down in the morning sun and enjoyed his morning meal.

Halfway through the glass, Brad fished one of the olives out of the Mason jar and put it in his mouth, then picked up the binoculars and scanned northeast as he chewed. There it was, as he predicted, one of John Tidman's rental boats. It was just on the other side of one of the smaller islands off Point Couverden, almost hidden, but the man standing in the small boat watching him through his own optics helped with finding it.

Brad continued to sweep the entire area, so that it would appear that he was just scanning the area, hoping not to tip his hand that he knew he was being watched. This same boat and operator had followed him yesterday when he wanted to explore the anchorage at William Henry Bay. Not sure at the time, Brad had altered his plan and went fishing off Vanderbilt Reef. When Brad shifted course, so had the rental boat.

Gut feeling told Brad that the abandoned William Henry Bay mine was the answer to the handwritten note. The "first contact" starting point was his and Bob's first meeting location, something only they knew. While not sure what he would find there, Brad suspected another Tack lair. What it actually was, and if the key had anything to do with it, there was only one way to find out. Get there and look, preferably without being followed.

Stuffing another strip of bacon in his mouth, Brad pulled anchor and headed back toward Juneau, which would take him right by his watcher. But the small boat kept far enough ahead that he couldn't get a good look at the operator.

Brad knew it was still forty-five minutes into the trip back to the dock. Watching the rental boat, still well ahead, making its way around Point Retreat and out of sight, the C-Dory was just passing the entrance to Funter Bay; Brad backed off the throttle and turned right into the bay. For good measure, Brad dropped a crab pot before making his way to the small public floating dock to tie up.

Brad figured the man following in the small boat was not prepared for overnight surveillance. The C-Dory, on the other hand, was supplied comfortably for a few nights. Plus, he had fresh halibut and, with any luck, a Dungeness crab or two for dinner. The only problem was, he hadn't stocked enough beer, but he could rough it if he had to.

Fortunately, John and Gail Haven saved the day when they pulled up and moored their sailboat to the other side of the dock with a healthy store of beer and wine. They were longtime friends and fellow members of the Juneau Gun Club, but Brad couldn't remember the last time they actually visited. It was still early when they saw his boat, but decided to spend the rest of the day and night here instead of their planned layover at Swanson Harbor.

John and Gail had just pulled their shrimp pots before pulling in and tying up. While not a large haul, the thirty spotted prawns, along with the three Dungeness crab Brad pulled from his pot, were cleaned and added to the halibut to make an afternoon meal about as good as it could get.

Just before four o'clock, a thirty-six-foot Tug pulled up to the dock and after introductions, Chuck and Joni from Ketchikan suggested dinner, so the lunch leftovers and more of the halibut were given to Joni and she added some hot sausage and whipped up a great gumbo.

More beer and wine was sacrificed and fishing tales were told. Brad and the others sat on the dock between the boats and watched the sun set. Brad thought, "Could be worse ways to spend a day."

The small surveillance boat never made an appearance.

CHAPTER 37

WHEN THE C-DORY DIDN'T come around the point, Dave figured it must have turned into Funter Bay. He checked his phone and was surprised to find he had cell service, so he selected a number in his contacts list and hit send. Spike answered on the first ring: "You back yet?"

Dave replied, "No. I'm at the south end of North Pass. It looks like he pulled into Funter. I'm pretty sure he'll be there for the night."

"OK, come on in. We'll check on him in the morning. Besides, we've picked up another job to do this afternoon, if you can get back."

Dave said, "No problem. I can be back in about an hour." Then he hung up his cellphone, stored it in a waterproof case and brought the ninety-horsepower outboard to life as he pushed the throttle all the way forward and headed back to Auke Bay as fast as he could.

Spike waited forty minutes before he dialed the Douglas Fish and Game office. Jim Straighter's direct line was listed on the ADGF website. When Spike called the number, it went to a recording stating he wasn't in the office, and gave another number to call for issues that couldn't wait. So Spike called the new number.

Jim answered on the third ring. "Fish and Game, this is Jim."

Spike said, "Hi, Jim. I'm John Gillespie and I found a deer tangled in some wire and it's thrashing around. Would you be the one I talk to?"

Jim wrote down the name and the time, and then said, "Yes, I can take your information. Can you tell me where it is?"

"There's a turnout a few miles north of Yankee Cove. It's near there."

Jim paused and then said, "Would you be able to meet me and show me exactly where it is?"

Spike smiled. "No problem, I'd be glad to help. I can be out there in about forty-five minutes. I'm driving a red Ford sedan."

Jim wrote the information down. "Well, it'll talk me about an hour and a half to get there. But I'll hurry," Jim said, then hung up.

Spike's phone buzzed, telling him he had a message. Dave was back, waiting to be picked up. Spike called Dave back.

Dave answered the call. "I'm at the hamburger joint in the parking lot."

Spike said, "We'll be there in ten. We'll all head out from there to take care of the job. Do you need anything from the hotel?"

"No, I've got everything I need with me."

Spike hung up his cell and called Tom's room with the room phone.

Tom answered after one ring, "Yes."

"Let's roll," Spike said and hung up.

Spike looked at the rifle case, but decided against it and opened the small hard plastic waterproof case and took out his Beretta M-9. He checked to make sure it was loaded, de-cocked the hammer and left the safety in the off position. He slipped the pistol in the breast concealment pocket on his jacket and closed the Velcro flap.

Tom was waiting in the hallway. "Which car?"

"Mine. I told him to look for a red Ford," Spike answered.

The drive to Auke Bay took eleven minutes, and was done in silence and they saw Dave standing outside the hamburger shop with a black backpack slung over his shoulder, sucking on a straw protruding from a white Styrofoam cup.

Spike drove around the circular parking lot, full of pickup trucks with empty boat trailers attached, and stopped in front of the shake shop. Dave climbed into the back seat. Spike drove out of the parking lot and headed north on the Glacier Highway, out the road.

Dave said, "The burgers looked good in there. Maybe we can stop by on the way back and have dinner."

Tom asked, "What's the job?"

Spike said, "One man, a Jim Straighter, no special requirements."

"Will he be alone?" Dave asked.

"Don't know. If he's isn't, we'll deal with that too," Spike said.

The thirty-five-minute drive went smoothly. Spike stayed just under the speed limit and none of the other cars heading in the same direction pushed him. Everyone else had turned off the highway by the time they passed the Eagle Beach campground. The only noise in the car was Dave slurping the last of the chocolate malt through the straw.

Spike pulled off the road at the turnout and parked the car closer to the road so the target would have no problem seeing it. It would also force him to park near the edge, away from the road.

All three got out of the car. Tom leaned casually against the trunk, Spike walked to the edge of the road and looked back the way they came, and without a word, Dave pulled his 1911 out from inside the waistband holster, checked and replaced it, then walked over to the safety rail, stepping over it and climbing down the rocks to the water line. Satisfied, he turned south and walked the thirty feet to an alder and stepped out of sight.

Thirty-eight minutes later, the green Fish and Game truck came into view, Spike saw Jim was alone. When the truck was a quarter of a mile away, Spike waved and walked back to the Ford and stood next to Tom.

Jim pulled past the red car and parked next to the guard rail and got out. Spike and Tom walked over, and Spike stuck out his hand. "You must be Jim. I'm John and this here is Bob," he said with a smile.

Jim smiled back and shook their hands. "Good to meet you. So there's a deer in a bad way around here?"

Spike nodded and said, "Yep, it's down by the water over here."

He stepped over the rail and made his way down the rocks, Jim keeping up with him. Tom stayed up on the road, watching as they climbed down the rocks. The way was rough and the men needed to keep their eyes on what they were doing, so Jim didn't start looking for the deer until they stopped at the water's edge. He looked right, then left.

Not seeing the deer, he turned and said, "Where is. . . ?" Jim stopped when he saw the pistol pointed at his head.

Spike pulled the trigger; the bullet hit Jim in the left eye and came out the back of his head, killing him instantly.

Careful not to step in any blood, Spike and Dave pulled Jim's body to the water and put rocks in his pockets and zipped them closed, then pushed him into the water. Tom looked up and down the road and gave them an all-clear. Dave pulled out his .45 and shot Jim twice in the chest, once in each lung, then once in the stomach. He sank slowly into the cold water as the current took his body south down the channel.

Spike and Dave collected their brass and climbed back up the rocks to join Tom. Still not seeing any traffic on the highway, they got in the car and started back to town.

At the halfway point Spike said, "Pizza sounds better to me. That OK?"

Both Tom and Dave replied at the same time, "Sure."

CHAPTER 38

AT THREE-THIRTY HE had enough light to get under way, so Brad started the main motor and untied the moorings, leaving the dark sailboat and tug with their occupants still asleep, slowly cutting through the still waters of the bay. The boat's windows were fogging on the inside because of the coffee percolating on the stove, prompting him to open the windows and turn on the fans in front. The fog outside limited his visibility to half a mile, so he turned on the radar to help with navigation and avoiding other vessels. It wouldn't slow him down, for he was used to the fog. Plus, it limited the capability of others to follow him.

Clearing the mouth of Funter Bay, he turned north up the Lynn Canal and brought the C-dory on step while adjusting the trim tabs to improve the ride and efficiency. Brad looked at the radar display and didn't see another boat, so he left the helm, poured a cup of coffee, grabbed a granola bar, then settled back in the captain's chair for the trip to William Henry Bay.

A little over an hour into the uneventful trek, he had just passed the north end of Lincoln Island when the fog lifted. The sun had not cleared the Coast Mountains, but the light overcast sky promised a beautiful day. Scanning the water with his binoculars, Brad identified three commercial fishing boats and one sport boat heading south, but no sign of the rental boat, so he continued on with his plan.

Just less than three hours from the start, Brad backed the C-Dory down, picked up his binoculars and glassed the canal one more time before he slowly entered the bay he'd traveled past many times before but never taken the time to explore. Watching the depth reading on the sonar, he eased to the back of the bay. A pair of otters watched curiously from still water as he located a depth he liked, with plenty of arc. No wind and a low, slack tide helped make the anchoring easy. With the hook set, Brad untied the raft from the top of the boat and set it in the water, securing it to the starboard side. The William Henry Bay mine was reportedly on an unnamed tributary of the Beardsley River that flowed into the bay, not quite a mile from the mouth of the river.

Brad put on the bandoleer holster with the .50 caliber revolver, grabbed his daypack and shotgun, and put the mystery key in his pocket. He climbed in the raft, untied it and pushed off, paddling to the shore on the north side of the mouth of the small clear river.

Stepping out of the raft into the shallow water, Brad let out an almost silent growl when he felt the wetness seep into his boot, but he put it out of his mind and carried the raft above the high tide line and secured it to a tree.

Checking the big revolver and shotgun again to make sure they were loaded and ready, he looked at his watch checking the time and started up the valley. The noise of a small plane flying up the Lynn Canal just outside the bay made him stop and turn around. The Cessna 207 was owned by one of the local operators that provided service between Juneau, Haines and Skagway, and one he'd used many times himself. It seemed early for a scheduled flight, but Brad didn't have the schedules memorized, so he let it go and continued his trek to the mine. The trail at one time was a full-fledged road, but now it was overgrown and washed out in areas, but still made for easy walking, except for the elevation change.

He took less than an hour to reach the old mine. The main shaft appeared to be sealed, and the worn, rusted milling equipment spent its time watching the weathered gray, moss-covered buildings rot away. To most the site would look completely unused, but Brad could see signs of activity—stunted and flat ground cover, moss and small twigs cleared on almost invisible trails and spider webs across these trails clear below six feet told him something tall had used them recently. With few exceptions, man wasn't this good at hiding his trail, so that meant Rhunken.

An old sign near the mine's sealed entrance looked wrong; it wasn't as old as everything else. Making his way around an old rusted vertical boiler tank, he saw a "Danger" sign hanging on a newer metal door built into the side of the cliff face. The door was painted to make it look old, and it had a flap of rubber protecting the bolt latch. Brad lifted the rubber flap and with no surprise at all he saw a shiny new lock.

Pulling the key from his pocket, he knew that it would work even before he tried, but when it turned and the lock jumped open, he still flinched in surprise. He took a deep breath and removed the lock, then slid back the bolt. The door swung silently open on well-oiled hinges, allowing the mid-morning sun to fill the chamber behind it. The fifteen-by-twenty-five-foot room was carved out of the hill, and Brad could see the mine tunnel at the back. A cot, folding chair and small camp table furnished the room. Ignoring the plastic tote that held food and water next to the table, Brad spied an unopened package of tree shaped car air-fresheners and a well-used logbook with the initials A. J. M. on its cover set on a twelve-pack of Summer Ale. No dust on anything.

Brad set the logbook aside, opened the twelve-pack, pulled out one of the cool beers, picked up the air fresheners and the chair, and went outside. He placed the chair in a sunny opening in front of the rusted boiler, opened the air-freshener package and hung one from the arm of the chair. He dug out the Swiss-army knife from his pocket, opened the ale, and took a long hit then settled in the chair and waited.

The slight breeze hit him on his left cheek and carried the fake pine scent smell of the air-freshener away from him, down the valley toward the bay, so Brad couldn't smell it. He knew it was a waiting game with no time schedule, so he opened the logbook and started to read. But with the final pull on the first ale, the light air current that hit the back of his neck carried a strong pine scent that ended his wait.

Brad calmly got up, put the chair and air-freshener back in the cave and locked the door, taking the logbook and remaining beers with him.

"OK, who's the new player?" he asked himself as he made his way back to the bay.

CHAPTER 39

A.J.M. WAS ANTHONY J. Morris. Brad knew of him and may have even met him once. He was a senior PCO, not up to Bob's level, but pretty high up. He was also one of the passengers on the plane that crashed.

To Brad's knowledge, Anthony had never worked in Alaska, but his logbook clearly said otherwise. While the format was different, the basic premise was the same as Bob's logs that they retrieved from the other Tack lair. Anthony's data wasn't as complete, but it did report on what he called a terminal colony. The log stated the three remaining Rhunken, one male and two females, were old and unable to reproduce, so once they died, so would the colony. But it also reported that three Tacks lived in the colony, all males, and just like Bob's colony, the Tacks were allowed to live and be studied. But unlike Bob, Anthony went one step further and started to train the Tacks with basic working dog commands—hunting dogs, to be more precise. He had even given the Tacks names and had listed physical characteristics of each to be able to identify them. As Brad read the narrative on the training the writing changed, it became forced, more mechanical, no commentary toward the end. For some reason Anthony wasn't happy in the end.

Not having a scanner at home, Brad went to the FAA office to scan and email the log to Erica's personal email without any questions asked, not that anyone would, since it was a Sunday. At the last minute, he removed the first page that identified the lair's name and location. Just in case. He'd call her with that information tomorrow, if she didn't call him first.

At 10:30 AM Monday Brad called Erica's cell, but only got her recording to leave a message, so he called her office phone and got the same thing. Not a big deal, it was just about lunchtime in Seattle, but it didn't feel right, so he called Peter's cell.

"This is Peter." answering the phone, not recognizing the number.

"Hey Peter, it's Brad."

"Hey, Brad. How are you doing?"

"I'm good. You back to normal?"

"More or less. You in town?"

"No. Still in Juneau. Actually, I was trying to get hold of Erica. Have you seen her?"

Peter said, "Yep, saw her this morning. She was called in to the CEO;s office; she was on her way in when I ran into her. Then I saw her again later, leaving the building with another guy. A big guy, really good-looking and loaded with money." Then he added, "Why, you checking up on her?"

"Kind of. Can you have her call me if you see her?"

"No problem, I can do that." Peter paused. "Hey, I was kidding. I'm sure the guy was just walking her to her car."

"Don't worry about it, I'm sure it's fine. I'll talk to you later," Brad said, and hung up.

Brad went into the FAA facility manager's office and informed him that he'd be taking the rest of the day off. Then he headed to the store to get ammo, batteries, food and pine scented car air-fresheners.

The short drive to the store didn't take five minutes and collecting the items on his list only took ten. While standing in the checkout line at the sporting goods counter, Jeff Turner, an acquaintance from the gun club, got in line behind him carrying a new fishing pole, and Brad nodded his head in a silent hello.

"Hey, Brad, how are you doing?"

"Good, Jeff. And you?" Brad replied.

Jeff said, "I'm doing OK, but did you hear about Jim Straighter?"

Brad could hear the excitement in his voice so he turned and faced Jeff. "No. What's going on?"

"They found his body washed up on Eagle Beach. Looks like he was murdered."

Brad's first thought, had Dr. Clark responsible, but he told himself not to jump to conclusions. "No shit. What makes them think it was murder?"

"Well, JPD hasn't actually called it a murder yet, but my daughter was one of the EMTs that retrieved the body, and the four bullet holes are going to be too hard to explain in any other way."

"That's interesting" was all Brad could think of to say. Now he was sure the bastard Clark had it done.

Brad was quiet while he paid the cashier for his selected items. Then he turned back and said, "It's good to see you again, Jeff, and I'm sure I'll see you at the range sometime."

Brad headed out to his truck, only to find it was raining again. So he got in and pulled out his cell phone and dialed Erica's cell. It went straight to voicemail. He hung-up without leaving a message. He was starting to worry.

Tuesday morning had Brad back at the office at his normal 6 AM; he read the history about William Henry Mine and studied the topo for the area. He mapped an alternate route to the mine if he decided to anchor the C-Dory in Boat Harbor and hike in. Even with this he still only made it to 9 before calling Peter.

He answered his desk phone on the second ring, "This is Peter."

"Hey, Peter. It's Brad."

"Wow, twice in one week. I guess you still haven't been able to get hold of Erica."

"No," Brad said, "I haven't. And there's some weird shit going on around here and I'm starting to get a bad feeling."

"Well, buddy, I don't think there's anything to worry about. I had dinner with a gal that works in Erica's section, and she told me Erica is on some kind of detail. She didn't seem concerned at all."

Brad felt himself relax. "OK, thanks. But I'd still feel better if I knew more. Can you ask around?"

"No problem, I can do that. What's this 'weird shit' you're talking about?"

Brad thought about it for a few seconds before replying. "I'll tell you about it some other time. And just to let you know, I plan on taking a trip this weekend, so you won't be able to get hold of me." And he hung up.

Brad looked out the window and noticed that the car that had been watching him wasn't there today.

Wednesday crawled by—nothing happened in the FAA to give him something else to focus on. The town was buzzing about the death of Jim Straighter. Still no official word yet, but everyone pretty much knew what happened. Of course, no suspects in custody, and Brad knew there never would be. This was a professional hit and Brad was sure he knew who ordered it, but he also knew he'd never be able to prove it. So he added it to the bill.

Brad watched for, and didn't see, his tail again today. He thought about driving by the hotels to check for the rental car that had been watching him, but was sure the driver was long gone by now.

Brad left the office at the regular time and stopped at the bar for an early dinner and a beer or three. Terri was as nice as always when she brought his beer, but she didn't stay around to talk. His burger and fries came and he ate in silence. The locals continued their bantering, but steered clear of him. Brad knew he'd grown his bark again. His late wife called it his fight face, and she helped to keep it to a minimum, but with her passing it completely redeveloped. His "bark" was something he'd subconsciously developed in the military, a shift in mindset, both protective and aggressive. Other than not smiling much, Brad didn't think he'd changed, but the reaction of the people around him was undeniable. Everyone stood clear.

So after his second beer, he paid his tab and headed home, having decided to begin preparations for the weekend trip.

CHAPTER 40

BRAD WOKE UP EARLY, called the office and left a message that he'd be taking off the next two days. Looking out the window at the water, he could see waves breaking on the rocks opposite the entrance of the bay. While the wind was calm here, the winds in the channel must be up.

The C-Dory was ready, but he went through the complete list again, one last time. Brad decided he'd head to the mine tomorrow after checking the marine weather. It reported winds today of twenty to twenty-five miles per hour and seas to five feet, and the forecast for Friday was better with lighter winds and seas down to two feet or less, which was better than the forecast for the weekend. A weekday trip would also avoid the chance of a weekend boater anchored in William Henry Bay.

Brad wasn't sure how long he'd be out, but he figured at least three days. So he packed for a week.

To get a head start he launched the boat and moored it at a neighbor's dock two houses down, then walked the two miles back to the launch to retrieve his truck and trailer and park his rig back in his yard.

"Time for something to eat," he told himself.

The phone was ringing when he walked in the house. Caller ID showed a Seattle area code.

"Hello."

"Hey, old man," came Peter's voice.

"Hey, Peter. What's going on?"

"I did some asking around and found out that Erica is on a field assignment."

"Oh, where?"

"That's the funny part. It's in your neck of the woods."

"In Juneau?"

"I can't find out the exact location, but from what I hear, they had to go through Juneau."

"When did they leave Seattle?" Brad asked after a pause.

"Tuesday morning, if my information is correct."

"Any details about the assignment?"

"No, but that's not unusual. Would you like me to go ask the CEO?"

"No. If she came through here, I can find her. Thanks," he said and hung up.

Brad dialed the phone and it rang once before a woman answered, "Alaska Cargo, may I help you?"

"Hi, Marlene."

"Hi, Brad. Wow, it's been a while. How are you?"

"I'm great. Hey, Marlene, I need a favor. Can you look up a passenger that flew in from Seattle last Tuesday for me?"

"As long as you don't tell anyone, and buy me dinner."

"Deal."

"OK, who are you looking for?"

"Erica Hunt, and if it's possible, anyone she is traveling with."

"Well, Erica will be easy. The others, if any, will take more time. And it will cost more than dinner."

"Whatever you want, Marlene." Brad knew she was smiling. "I'll be at home waiting for your call," he said and hung up.

Brad realized he was hungry, so he found some cold pizza, put it in the microwave and had started to make a bloody Mary when the phone rang.

"Wow! That was fast," he said, ID-ing the incoming number.

"Like I said, Erica was easy, and once I saw that she booked through SATO, I called a friend. And she looked it up while I was on the phone," Marlene said.

"Is this going to get either of you in trouble?" Brad asked.

"Not if no one finds out. But I did say you'd buy her a dinner too, next time you're in Portland."

"I can do that. Email her information to me when you get a chance. What did you find out?"

"Erica did fly into Juneau on Tuesday morning, and according to Sara, it appears she was with six others. They have no return flight scheduled."

"Thanks, Marlene. I do owe you a big dinner," he said and hung up.

Brad looked up a number in the phone book. Finding he had two possibilities, he picked one and dialed it.

"Steve's Air Services," was the answer.

"Hey Steve, Brad Michaels."

"Hey Brad, long time. What can I do for you?"

"I was wondering if you took some of my co-workers from Seattle on a charter this past Tuesday."

"Well, it was Wednesday, not Tuesday, I dropped off five souls at William Henry Bay, and I was told that I would be running another three out there today, in a couple of hours or so."

"One of them a cute redhead?"

"Yep, looked like she could be a handful."

"Thanks, Steve," he said, hanging up.

Brad hit the dedicated button on the microwave, giving the pizza thirty seconds and then he finished making the bloody Mary.

Standing at the kitchen counter, he looked out the window at another nice day in Tee Harbor, but he wasn't seeing it. His mind was trying to put the pieces together.

Spike lay on the damp, soft moss looking through the scope, the rifle securely resting on its bipod; he adjusted the scopes parallax, not that it would make any difference at this range. This was a chip shot, one hundred and sixty yards. He was shooting through a glass window at a slight angle, but he'd done it before, and didn't think it would be a problem now.

His spotter, Dave, was at his right looking through his spotting scope and Tom was ten yards back, watching their six. Spike thought, "Way too much overkill for this target." But orders were orders, and the money was paid.

Dave touched Spikes arm, re-focusing him to the task at hand. They both could see a man walk into the kitchen; he was on the phone. Two taps, "Target confirmed".

Spike waited for the target to finish his call. You don't want to announce the hit any sooner than necessary. Dave's hand on his arm also told him to wait.

The target hung-up the phone and looked out the window, facing slightly away and frozen in thought. Dave tapped once and removed his hand. "Go"

Spike placed the crosshairs just behind the target's ear, aiming at the base of the scull and pressed the trigger. The shot broke clean, the suppressor minimizing the muzzle's report. But the rifle shot went off at the same time the target started to move, but it didn't matter, the results were obvious. The window shattered, sending glass flying, its reflections of the outside light partially obscured the view for a second, but the spray of blood and gore all over the wall and refrigerator conformed a good hit.

Three taps. "Good hit," came from Dave.

"Clear," came from Tom.

They got up and at a low run, hurried back to the waiting rental car.

"Better call the maid," said Dave, and they laughed as they drove away.

CHAPTER 41

ERICA WAS AWAKE IN her tent. She had spent most of the night going over what happened in the last few days. This was even worse than Admiralty Island, and Erica never thought that could happen, much less this soon. When the CEO called her in and assigned her to another field operation in Alaska, she jumped at the chance to work with Brad again, without asking for the details.

She had been so excited that she didn't think to ask about all of the secrecy. She was told, "No calls or emails about the mission to anyone, including team members," of which she didn't even have a list of names. When she arrived in Juneau and Brad wasn't there to greet them at the airport or meet them after they checked into the hotel, she started to wonder. So she went to the room of the team leader, Brian Robbins, and asked about him. Brian told her that Brad wasn't part of the crew. She couldn't believe it and protested, demanding to talk to the CEO. Without any argument, as if her protest was expected, Brian called the CEO and handed her the phone.

That's when she should have known she was in trouble. The CEO advised her that she was to follow orders and keep her mouth shut, and to turn the phone back over to Brian. But Erica hung it up, then handed it back. The cell phone rang back less than ten seconds later. Erica removed her own cell phone and texted Brad while Brian was on his cell phone getting directions from the CEO.

She met some of the other team members when Brian made

another call on his cell phone. Within seconds, two men showed up at the door. When the first one came in the door Erica almost lost her breath. It was Jack Spelling. She almost didn't recognize him—he'd lost a lot of weight—but that wasn't it. His jaw was misshaped and the scar on Jack's face was horrible. She could see the hate in his eyes. "But I saved his life," not understanding his reaction.

Jack reached down and took her phone. He nodded at the second one and they both escorted her to her room. Once in the room, Jack picked up her laptop bag and left. The other one stood by the door, watching her. Jack hadn't said a word. She wondered if he could.

She thought, "What could be so secret to treat me this way?"

Surprisingly, they didn't search her duffel bag, not that she had another phone, but she did have her .357 magnum revolver.

The next morning, the unknown big man came and got Erica, and Brian, Jack, and Matt Barnes, someone she actually knew, joined them. They took a short floatplane flight to a remote bay, unloaded and took most of the day setting up camp near an old mine. That was yesterday.

She started to hear others roaming around outside, so she got dressed and followed the smell to the coffee pot, dug a blue metal cup from a plastic tote and poured herself a cup. Matt was sitting by the fire, holding a cup of coffee in both hands, looking like he was having a hard time waking up, while the others were moving about, busy with starting the day.

"Sleep OK?" Matt asked.

"No. What's going on?" she asked quietly.

"I'm here to evaluate the status of this colony, and see if anything can be salvaged from the training program." Matt then added, "I have no idea why you're here."

The door to the mine opened and Brian stepped out, stopping her from voicing her next question.

He had cut the lock off the mine door and made the empty room his sleeping quarters, which was okay with Matt. That let him have a tent to himself. Two other larger tents were setup at the edge of the camp near the trail leading to the bay. The big guy she didn't know who was obviously ex-military, along with Jack were in one tent and the other had been set up for three more. Erica could only surmise that more were coming. "Why am I here?" she asked, looking at Brian.

"I was told you are the most experienced field biologist we have, and you have firsthand experience in dealing with Tacks, so to speak. As a matter of fact, your after-action reports were very useful. Matt here has different experiences with Tacks. He was part of a program that attempted to train them. And last but not least, your friend Jack has graciously agreed to join us. His experience with the Tacks will be most useful."

Brian could see the disbelief in her eyes. "The key word is 'attempted.' All attempts have failed so far, except for this one, maybe. Some of the reports from this site hinted at some success. We hope to find more documentation on site, like you did on Admiralty Island."

"Whose bullshit idea was that?" Erica said.

Matt cut in, "It was before both your time. A group of agencies EPA, DHS, WCC, and maybe others that I don't know about, got together, and the idea to try to train Rhunken to be useful was hatched, maybe get back some of the money we spent on them. No one knew for sure if it could be done, so a few of the more senior PCO's were assigned to the project and off they went. They discovered right away that the Rhunken were not trainable, they were much too independent. But someone in Russia had some good results with a Tack."

Erica shook her head. "You guys are nuts."

Matt nodded, "That's what Bob said. He wanted nothing to do with the project, but in the end he was forced to deal with some of the aftermath. Although I don't think he minded studying the Tacks that killed their trainer on Admiralty, and the rumor was he was going to cull those Tacks before he retired, but he died first. I guess you had to deal with that."

Erica stood up with her fist clinched, staring at Brian. "Am I supposed to do that again?"

"No. You're here for your experience only," Brian said calmly, then added, "and as insurance, if needed."

"Insurance against what?" Erica asked.

"Hopefully, nothing. Anyway, we'll find out today," Brian said, standing up and walking over to Jack and the ex-military guy. They talked in hushed tones that Erica couldn't make out.

Erica asked, "Matt, I've heard your name and seen you around, but don't know anything about you. Where are you from?"

"Canada. I've been around a long time, and I knew Bob well, but I never worked with him. Now, I've heard a great deal about you, and I must say, it's a pleasure to finally meet you."

"You worked on this training program?"

Matt nodded. "Briefly, mostly on the failed Rhunken part. I only had one Tack, and it went bad fast and I had to terminate it."

He got up and started breakfast. Erica roused herself in order to help.

Brian, Jack and the big guy came over when the food was done, helping themselves to the skillet full of scrambled eggs, sausage and potatoes.

The big guy looked at his watch. "When are they supposed to get here?"

Jack said in a forced gravelly voice, "Noon-ish.

Brian looked at his watch. "We'll wait until they get here before going in."

Matt looked at Brian, and then at Erica. She met his gaze, realizing that Matt had a problem with that plan, but wasn't going to say anything.

CHAPTER 42

THE WINDOW OVER THE sink shattered as the bloody Mary exploded in his hand. The thick red fluid sprayed all over the right side of his head, the white kitchen walls and the refrigerator. At the same time Brad whirled and dropped to the floor. Before he hit the deck he heard the supersonic crack of the rifle bullet, but no report from the gun, telling him what just happened.

Belly crawling through the red mess and broken glass to the back door, he opened it slightly and scanned the ridge just north and west of his property. He knew he'd be able to see a vehicle in the small clearing as it drove out to the main road.

The bloody Mary started to burn the cuts in his hands and face, but he stayed down, hiding and watching the road. Time passed slowly, but soon a dark gray cross-over calmly drove by. Brad could see that it held three people. He couldn't make out the two in the front seat, but the guy in the back seat was looking out his window, his face lit by the sun. He had short hair, like someone in the military, and he was laughing.

Brad crawled back through the kitchen and living room to the guest bathroom. He stood up and checked himself in the mirror. He looked like hell; he was covered in bloody Mary mix and blood from multiple small cuts on his face. It was bad enough that he stripped off his clothes and climbed in the shower. The water didn't help with the stinging at first— it made it worse. Once he rinsed off, he went back to the mirror and removed the glass shards that were imbedded in his face. Like all typical head wounds, they bled a lot, but nothing looked like it needed stitches.

While he dressed, he thought about calling the cops. But Erica was with them, and now he was sure that they had taken her for insurance in case this hit went wrong. And they were right. The fact that they had her did make his choice of response more difficult. But he was sure that they thought he was dead, or they would have come after him to finish it. That gave him some time, but he didn't know how much. So he picked up the phone and dialed.

"Steve's Air Service."

"Steve, Brad again."

"Wow, twice in one day."

"Hey, have your clients for the charter to William Henry Bay showed up yet?"

"No, not yet."

"I need you to delay the flight for two hours."

"Must be important, or you wouldn't ask. I can do that," Steve said, hearing something in Brad's voice.

"Thanks," Brad said and hung up.

He had the S&W 500 and twelve-gauge in the boat already, but the rules had changed, so he went to the back room, opened the safe and pulled out an AR-15, six magazines and a can of 5.56. Brad also pulled the cell phone out of the nightstand and turned it on. After a few seconds it made a twirly sound. He picked it up and flipped it open; it read, "One new message." He hit view. It came from Erica's phone; it read "In Juneau, weird. Will call tonight." It was sent Tuesday morning. There were no missed calls.

Brad put on his rain jacket, put the magazines in his pockets, picked up the AR and ammo and headed to the C-Dory at a trot.

Brad ran down the dock, untied the bowline and jumped in the boat, storing the rifle and ammo before starting the motor. Then he went aft, untied the stern line and made his way to the helm. The C-Dory was under way in less than a minute.

Brad ignored the no wake zone and pushed the throttle all the way forward, swinging the boat around and heading for Favorite Channel at full speed. Clearing the mouth of Tee Harbor, the semi-protected channel sported a windblown three-foot chop. Brad kept the bow higher than he normally would for the speed and took the pounding. Low lenticular clouds hugged the mountains, defying the winds.

The C-Dory made good time until it reached the north end of Lincoln Island and the open Lynn Canal with its five-plus feet of confused seas, forcing Brad to slow down and fight each wave. Every wave that hit the bow exploded, the wind driving it into the windshield and making the windshield wipers unable to keep up. Brad could see the blurry shape of the Chilkat Range but was unable to make out the entrance to the harbor. The GPS chart plotter showed him he was on course, but his speed was less than half of what he wanted.

A large rogue wave rose on the C-Dory's starboard bow, pushing her into the trough, then dropped away. The next wave hit broadside, threatening to capsize the boat. Brad pushed the throttle forward and spun the helm hard left, righting her and bringing her downwind and driving into the face of the next wave. When she started to climb, Brad went hard right on the wheel, whipping her around and back on course. He could see the shore was close and angled nearer to the rocks, hoping for some calmer seas. That came to pass and the waves lay down nearer the shore, allowing Brad to breathe easier. He hit the throttle again, getting the boat on step, once again beating the hull in the choppy sea.

Brad looked at the GPS and saw he was almost past the entrance to the harbor. He peered up through the wet windshield and could just make it out, so he came hard left and shot through the opening in the rocks at high speed.

The protected waters of Boat Harbor lay unbelievably calm, with almost no wind. Brad throttled back slightly and headed to the north end. Once the depth hit thirty feet, he killed the motor and released the anchor. By the time he got to the bow, seventy feet of rode had played out. He deemed it good enough and he tied it off. The raft was unsecured and tied to the side. Quickly grabbing his holster with the big revolver, the AR-15 and two magazines, he took three boxes of 5.56mm out of the ammo can and put his day pack on. He jumped into the raft and rowed to shore.

Climbing out of the raft, he tried to stand, but his legs gave out and he collapsed to his knees, dropping the AR in the wet sand. Forcing himself back to his feet, using the AR as support, he felt his thighs shaking uncontrollably. After a few seconds, the shaking slowed and he slung the rifle over his shoulder. Picking up the raft's bow rope, he dragged it up the shore to the trees.

By the time he tied off the raft, his legs started to calm down. Brad took out a bottle of water from a side pouch of the pack and downed the whole thing, then threw the empty in the raft. He looked at his watch, 12:01. Brad eyed the ridge in front of him, realizing he had to climb and run the length of it to get to Erica. Brad told himself sarcastically, "Hell, it's only five miles," and he took off.

The first half mile was the worst. The slope rose from the bay and Brad had to force his way through the heavy grass and ferns, a thicket of devil's club and young pines to scale the thousand feet. From there the trek became a little easier.

Brad stayed just above the tree line and headed along the ridge, following it northwest. After an hour he stopped and took a break. He ate a power bar and drank another bottle of water, his last. Now he had just the 100 ounces left in the bladder of the pack. Assessing the terrain before him, he saw a large open saddle that held a grassy meadow. He knew it would be too marshy to cross, so he took off at a trot, skirting it to the west on the uphill side, staying clear of the water.

Once past the saddle, he headed around the last peak to the east and came to the ridge above the mine. Looking down, he could see the clearing that held the mine about a mile away. As he came off the ridge, the brush got thick again and the slope was steeper, so he slowed down.

No point announcing his presence to the crew down there.

CHAPTER 43

AT 2:30 THE SOUND of the floatplane caught everyone's attention, and they walked to the edge of the campsite to watch it land on the bay and motor to the shore. Jack and big guy took off down the trail to meet it.

The plane's engine shut off and the hush of the day returned, reminding them of their remoteness. But twenty minutes later, the raised voices of the returning men cut the silence, and then the floatplane's engine sputtered, caught, and then roared as it took off down the bay and headed back to Juneau.

Within minutes, the five men made their way into camp, each carrying a gun case, duffle or a box of food. All of them were laughing and smiling.

Erica saw they all knew Jack; it was obvious they were some sort of team. These men looked like ex-military, or mercenaries. Each one of them was Brad's size, or slightly bigger, and except for Jack, they were all younger. She guessed that the professional hunters and scientists the CEO used last time weren't effective enough. Suddenly, she was afraid. Not just for herself, but for Brad as well.

Brian met them at the campfire and shook the hands of the three new arrivals.

"You're late," Brian said.

"The plane had some kind of mechanical problem," said one of the new guys.

Brian nodded, and then asked, "How'd it go?"

The smallest of the new men put his fingers to his head and then spread them out and said, "Poof."

The others laughed.

Jack glanced at Erica and said to Brian, "Looks like you won't need that insurance policy anymore."

Erica looked at Matt, but before she could ask, he said, "I think your friend is dead."

Erica turned around and looked at the ground, her mind reeling. She heard the men laughing. She headed for her tent, even though she knew her gun only held five shots. She didn't care. She bent over and unzipped the door. But before she entered, something caught her eye in the trees just beyond. A man materialized out of the trees; he was dressed in woodland camouflage, and he had gray hair. She knew him. It was Bob Strom. He shook his head, telling her no.

Erica looked back at the others behind her, but none of them saw him. When she turned back, Bob was gone.

Her head started to spin and she thought she was going to pass out, but she didn't. Instead she bent over and threw up.

CHAPTER 44

WHEN SHE WOKE UP, she could hear them laughing. Erica didn't know when she fell asleep or for how long. She remembered crawling into her tent and digging out her revolver, checking to make sure it was loaded, then lying down and waiting for whatever was going to happen next.

Brian's voice came through the tent. "I don't want to have to worry about her. She needs to go."

"I'll do it," came the voice of one of the guys she didn't know.

They all laughed again. "All right Ted. She's all yours," came Jack's gravelly voice.

"Thanks, Lieutenant," said Ted.

Erica shoved the revolver into her waistband at the small of her back and pulled her blouse over it.

She heard his footsteps in the gravel as he approached the tent. He stopped in front and unzipped it. The first thing she saw was a black pistol pointing at her.

"Come on out, honey," Ted said. The others laughed again.

Not saying a word, she crawled out of the tent, stood up straight and defiant, and put on her jacket. This made the men laugh again. But not all of them. She could see Matt was looking at his feet; she could also see he was shaking. Looking over at Jack, she saw his malevolent smile distorting his ruined face. She couldn't understand his hatred, but all it did was make her mad.

"This way," Ted said, pointing to the trees behind her tent.

She walked ahead, wanting to get away from the others, if she could get him one on one; she'd be able to do something. What, she didn't know yet.

Not more than thirty yards into the woods, she came to a small clearing. A blanket was already spread on the ground and her heart sank. She turned around to see him smiling.

A large gray rock next to Ted stood up and grew arms. Ted caught the movement and spun toward it, bringing the 9mm pistol around with amazing speed, and fired three times in rapid succession. The rounds hit the Rhunken in the chest. It flinched, but it didn't go down, or even stop moving forward. It grabbed Ted's right arm and jerked hard. The mercenary was pulled to the ground at the Rhunken's feet. Erica had her .357 in her hands—she didn't remember pulling it out—and she put the front sight on Ted's chest and pulled the trigger, then twice more as fast as she could.

The first shot was good, hitting Ted in the right lung, but the other two missed because the Rhunken pulled Ted out of the way—not to keep him safe but to step on his chest and then rip his arm off.

The large Rhunken walked casually into the trees, carrying the arm with the gun still grasped in its fist.

Ted got up, his face white. He looked at the blood-soaked sleeve and coughed up some blood. He turned around and headed shakily back to camp. Erica ran after the massive Rhunken, but collided with Bob instead as he was heading toward her.

Brad heard the shots, stopping him in his tracks. "Two guns, three shots each," he said aloud. Then he thought, "Not even a half-mile away."

He took off his pack, dug out the two boxes of 5.56, and loaded thirty rounds in each magazine. Then he inserted one into the AR-15 and pulled back the bolt and let it go, carrying the round home, loading it. He put the second magazine in his jacket pocket and started again, this time paying more attention to any noise he was making.

With the first three shots they laughed, Tom saying, "That was fast." But with the second set of shots followed by Ted's scream, they all scrambled for their weapons and ran to help. But Ted came out before they made it to the woods. Their feeling of relief only lasted for a second. When Ted tried to speak, only blood came out of his mouth. He stopped short and fell on his face. Dead.

Matt turned him over, opened his shirt, and said, "She shot him."

Tom pointed at Ted's arm. "Did she do that?"

Matt smiled. "No. Looks like he found one of the Rhunken."

Tom looked at Matt. "The Rhunken shot him?"

Jack shook his head. "You fucking idiot, she shot him and the damn Rhunken ripped his arm off."

Tom asked, "What about the girl?"

Matt said, "Odds are, she's dead too."

Jack looked at Tom. "You can go check if you want."

Tom looked at Jack, then at Dave. "Fuck that."

Jack stood up and looked around, then at his watch. "Take care of him. We'll bunk in the mine room tonight, and clear the mine in the morning."

CHAPTER 45

BRAD WATCHED FROM HIS hide, eighty yards out. Just after 7:00 AM the men came out, one at a time, none of them in any hurry. They made coffee and ate breakfast. Erica had not made an appearance yet.

Finally, the man someone called Lieutenant, said in a raspy voice, "Get the net guns ready and let's move out."

The others got up and got busy filling daypacks, checking weapons and headlamps, and the two strange-looking rifles that must be the net-guns the Lieutenant mentioned. After twenty minutes, they all entered the door leading to the mine, except one.

"Stay away from the beer, Dave," someone yelled from the mine door.

Brad recognized Dave; he was the one in the back seat of the car he saw just after the attempt on his life. He must be serving as their sentry. Dave walked back to the fire and poured himself a cup of coffee. The sky was overcast, but it didn't look like rain. The Lynn Canal looked rough with whitecaps building, telling of the winds coming from the north. He looked like a man without a care in the world. An AR-15 was lying on top of an ice chest not far away, and he had a 1911 in a Kydex holster on his side.

Once the door to the mine closed, Brad waited fifteen minutes to make sure the men were far enough into the mine to minimize the chance that they'd hear anything outside.

Dave put another chunk of wood on the fire, leaned back and stretched out his legs, enjoying the heat.

Brad centered the front post in the rear aperture of his AR-15 and placed the front sight on Dave's chest. With his thumb he moved the safety from "Safe" to "Fire" and squeezed the trigger.

The AR rocked back with the recoil and then quickly settled back on target. Dave was still sitting in the chair, but he had dropped the coffee cup and his chin was resting on his chest. He would have looked like he was asleep if it wasn't for the blood soaking the front of his gray sweatshirt. Brad stayed in position and surveyed the camp for movement. Nothing.

Getting to his feet, he double-timed it to the campsite, rifle at the ready, scanning left and right. "All clear," he thought, and he allowed the rifle to fall into the three-point sling and slid it around to his back. He pulled out the S&W 500 and searched the tents. The second one was Erica's, but she wasn't there. It was trashed: her backpack had been searched, its contents scattered and her wallet lay open in the middle of the sleeping bag on the cot.

Brad walked over to the mine door, then changing his mind, turned to head back to the first tent, but was stopped by the shape of a body wrapped in a military poncho near the entrance. A knot started to develop in his gut, but stopped when he noticed the size of the body. Much too big for hers. He unwrapped it, saw that it was a man with a .357 hole in his chest, and smiled. "Good girl," he said. He noticed the missing arm—she'd had help—and nodded his head.

Brad stood up and dug the pine air fresheners out of his pack. Opening a package, he put it in the breast pocket of his vest.

Going to the first tent, he dumped the clothes out of a duffel bag with the name "Matt Barnes" on the tag, and took the duffel outside. He put Dave's AR and 1911 in it. Then he moved to the last two tents and found what he was looking for, weapons and ammunition, including a suppressed M-24 sniper's rifle with five rounds in its magazine. All the weapons and ammo went into the duffel and he slung the load on his back, except the M-24, which he carried as he headed back up the hill to his hide. "Two down, five to go," he told himself.

Bob had led Erica up the ridge and behind the mine. A rifle shot startled them. It came from the camp below. They both stopped and looked down the valley, but paused only for a few seconds. On top, a cairn marked a hole in the ground; it was surrounded by an old barbed-wire fence with an equally dilapidated warning sign.

"Vent shaft," he said, then handed her a small paper pine tree.

"Do I smell?" she said, smiling.

"No, it's for protection."

Without asking, she tied the attached string to her jacket zipper pull.

Bob pulled out a whistle and blew multiple short bursts, waited a few seconds, and repeated the sequence.

Erica jumped back when the first Tack climbed out of the hole, followed closely by a second. Bob grabbed her arm to steady her. "It's OK. Old Anthony has them trained pretty good."

"Anthony who? Anthony Morris? Is he alive too?" she asked.

Bob smiled. "Yep that's the one, but I don't think he pulled the same Houdini trick I did."

The third Tack climbed out of the shaft and fidgeted next to the other two, sniffing the air.

Erica looked on in amazement as Bob pointed down to the valley where the mine entrance was and blew two short blasts on the whistle. The Tacks spread their wings, hooked their hands in the bend in the ulnas, locking them together, took two large steps and lifted off. Once they cleared the edge, they dove down the valley and out of sight.

Erica inhaled, realizing she had been holding her breath. "Wow," was all she said.

"Exactly. That's why I refused to do it."

"Do what?"

"Train them. They're way too deadly and unpredictable," he said. After a pause he added, "Anthony named them."

Erica looked at Bob. "Names?"

"Yeah. Buck, Rush and Nugget," Bob said, shaking his head, but smiling at the same time.

He checked the sky to the south, then the north. "We need to get back to civilization. A friend of mine has a cabin with a dirt airstrip about fifteen miles north of here. I'm sure he'll come and get us, if we can get there."

"Fifteen miles?" Erica said.

"The hike won't be bad once we get to the shore. Plus, he lives in Haines. So we'll hop a bush plane to Gustavus from there and take a jet back to Seattle." Then Bob added, "It's the first two to three miles that will be the problem; the terrain is the toughest there and we'll be passing just north of the camp."

Erica looked at Bob. "Great."

CHAPTER 46

BRAD HID THE CAPTURED weapons, with the exception of the sniper rifle, and then moved farther down the valley but higher on the hillside, to a location that gave him a better view of the campsite and mine door opening. It was a tough call. Judging by the gear and the sniper tactics they'd used on him, he knew they were well-trained mercenaries. If he used the AR, it would give him more firepower, but he'd have to be closer and his position would be easier to locate. So he decided on the suppressed sniper rifle, slower, but it would be all but impossible to locate him and he might get two of them before they all got out of the mine.

Movement on the hill behind the mine caught his attention. Brad smiled as the Tacks landed at the campsite. One landed in the open at the end of camp farthest from the mine door, and the other two split and flanked the door on either side. Ambush. Just like Admiralty Island.

"Well, this changes everything. I guess I'll watch and see what happens," Brad thought.

An hour later, the mine door opened. One of the mercenaries came out and scanned the area with his weapon at the ready, while the others stayed inside. He was the one they called "Lieutenant" and as Brad watched, there was something familiar about him, but he couldn't place him and he couldn't make out his face through the scope. Brad watched him spot the guy he'd killed, still sitting in the camp chair. Then he saw the Tack at the far end of the camp. As soon as he made eye contact, the Tack started to change colors. But the mercenary didn't freeze. He quickly backed into the mine room while scanning left and right, but he left the door open.

The decoy Tack stopped flashing and took a few paces toward the mine, then sat on its haunches, waiting. Brad could just make out the other two, blending in with the rocks. If he hadn't watched them settle, he would never have known they were there.

Five men came out of the mine in tight formation. The man in the lead, the Lieutenant, had his AR-10 ready and pointed at the decoy Tack. Two others covered their flanks and the last two had odd-looking weapons at the ready. It took a few seconds to recognize that they were loaded net-guns. They moved out about thirty feet, then stopped and kneeled. The Lieutenant shot the decoy Tack as they stopped, killing it. The Tack on the south side launched and dove at the group. Two seconds later the other Tack launched as well. But the men were ready and one of the men with a net-gun rose and fired. The net shot up and opened to meet the southern Tack, but it saw it and veered. It wasn't fast enough, though, and the net caught its left wing and arm. Yet its momentum kept it headed for the group of men.

The second man with a net-gun stood up and aimed at the third Tack, but the entangled Tack hit the group, taking everyone down. The third Tack hit the second net-gunner, knocking him back into the group with blood spraying from a ripped-open jugular. Then it flew into the trees.

The netted Tack rolled and became even more entangled in the net when it hit the tight formation, but its head was free and a leg was within reach, so it elongated its face and bit a chunk out of the right thigh of one of the mercenaries. The bitten man screamed, kicked the Tack away and pulled out his M-9. The Tack snapped back and bit the man's AR-15 and shook its head. The wounded man stuck the pistol in the Tack's eye and pulled the trigger, blowing the back of its head off.

The Lieutenant stood up and moved toward the dead decoy with his rifle at the ready. The blow from Brad's shot struck him in the chest, knocking him off his feet and back on the pile of men behind him. But he rolled off the squirming mob and grabbed the breast plate of his bulletproof Kevlar vest and cursed. "Fuck. Incoming, make for cover."

Jack's chest burned and he struggled to catch his breath, but he helped Tom to his feet. Tom's leg was bleeding badly, and he'd lost his rifle. Brian and Spike were right with them as they headed for cover.

"Fuck, they're wearing vests," Brad said, working the bolt and sending a new round home. But they were moving now, low and fast.

Spike looked at Jack and said, "Does that bitch have my rifle?"

Jack took a sharp painful breath. "That'd be my guess."

Spike looked up at the tree line and spotted two people moving on the north ridge. He pointed, "There, on the ridge, two of them, one klick out, heading to the channel." Then they were out of sight again.

None of them had binoculars on them. They weren't any good in the mine, so Spike belly-crawled to his tent. Staying in the tent with the binoculars, he scanned the ridge but didn't see anyone.

Spike yelled loud enough to let the others hear, "I don't see them, but they were headed east. And those bastards took our guns and ammo."

Jack said, "Bring me the first aid kit. And keep down—one of them assholes can shoot."

Brad saw one of the mercenaries point north and up the hill, so he brought up his binoculars and scanned the ridge. Two people— one was Erica, she was wearing the jacket he'd bought her, and a man wearing camouflage and moving like he knew what he was doing. Brad smiled, "Welcome back, Bob."

Brad shifted his binoculars back to the camp and saw one man run low back to the group with what must be a first-aid kit. He dropped it, picked up the wounded guys AR-15 and ran down the trail toward the bay.

"Must be trying to head off Bob and Erica," Brad thought.

"Bad idea," he said, picking up the sniper rifle and shifting position slightly for a better shooting lane.

The Tack slammed into Brad, landing on his back, pinning him facedown to the ground. He could feel its claws digging into his flesh. In one quick movement Brad brought his right knee up, left arm under his chest, and turned on his left side, swinging his right elbow with all his force at the Tack's midsection. But the Tack caught his arm just above the elbow and pinned it to his side.

Brad could now see the Tack, its face stretched, bearing its teeth, mouth opening. Brad saw the scar on its face running from the left eye to its lip and remembered its name from Anthony's notes.

"Buck, no," Brad said sternly but quietly.

The Tack stopped and flattened its face, both eyes focusing on Brad. It moved its head lower to his chest and inhaled, sniffing his pocket. It relaxed his grip and stepped off, sitting on his haunches like nothing had happened.

Brad sat up, eyeing the Tack carefully. Then he remembered the mercenary. Picking up his binoculars, he looked down at the trail. He wasn't in sight. Brad knew Bob and Erica both had weapons, but they didn't know someone was on their trail. So Brad low-crawled deeper into the brush until he figured he could stand without being seen from the camp. Then he stood up and ran along the hillside toward the bay.

CHAPTER 47

THE TREE TRUNK EXPLODED from the warning shot, sending pieces of bark and wood splinters through the air, hitting both of them. The report was loud and the time between the hit and the report was almost nil, telling Bob the shooter was close. He stopped and held his rifle in the air. Erica stopped right behind him and slowly raised her hands.

"Drop the weapons," came a voice from just behind and off to the right of them. Erica recognized the voice. It was one of the military guys, the one they called Spike.

Bob dropped the rifle and Erica pulled the revolver from her vest pocket and tossed it near the rifle.

"All right, turn around and make your way to the mine trail. We're heading back to camp," said Spike, still out of sight.

Brad heard the shot and shifted in its direction, but could not see anything for a few minutes, until he saw Bob and Erica coming down the side of the ridge on the other side of the valley, their hands in the air. Scanning with his binoculars, he couldn't see who was covering them.

Keeping to the deep brush, he angled back toward camp, working closer to the trail, but staying higher in elevation. Twice he stopped and searched for the mercenary covering his two friends, but the guy was good, real good. Bob and Erica kept heading up the trail back to the mine.

Brad looked behind him. The Tack was there, following him like a dog. It stayed back about ten yards and stopped when he did, changing its color, blending into the background. The entire way it was completely silent.

The sound of voices stopped Brad short. Still unable to see anyone, he started to crawl. He came to an uprooted spruce tree, following it to its upturned root ball. He slowly eased around the lower side until he could see the campsite. The voice he heard came from the wounded mercenary, cussing up a storm. Off to his right, Brad could hear Bob and Erica coming up the trail. Bob was scuffing his feet, making a lot more noise than he should. Brad smiled.

Brad turned to the Tack. Not sure of the proper commands, he made a sweeping horizontal hook with his hand and said "Buck, go." The Tack changed color to a dull gray-green and silently disappeared uphill, hopefully heading to the flank of the camp. Brad worked his way back to the root ball hide and settled into position, his AR still slung on his back.

Everyone at the camp, except for the wounded man, got to their feet and met the two prisoners, followed by their unseen captor, their weapons at ease. Brad removed the dust covers from the scope and waited. The shot would be easy, eighty yards; the suppressor would reduce the muzzle noise enough for the supersonic crack to cover the direction of his shot.

Erica came into view first, her hands down, looking defiant. Bob almost had a smile, as if he knew something. Then their captor walked into view. Brad could see his short hair and he was holding his AR at port arms, smiling. Brad put the crosshairs behind his left ear, at the base of the skull and applied pressure to the trigger. The shot broke and resettled for a complete follow through, fast enough to see the mist where the head used to be. The body stood for a long second before falling without another twitch.

Bob pounced on Erica, covering her, while the others went diving for cover. Brad got up, leaving the sniper rifle and bringing his slung

AR-15 to bear, and ran straight down the hill, not trying to be quiet at all. He broke cover and ran across the trail in full view and into the brush on the other side. A bullet whizzed by, well behind him, not even close, and the rifle shot was followed by a useless shotgun blast.

Jack got up on one knee, with his AR-10 ready and pointed at the spot where the man was last seen. "Don't waste the ammo. That fucking shotgun is useless at this range," he said to Brian.

Jack looked over to Tom and saw that he had his M-9 out and ready. He was using a dead Tack as cover. "Can you cover me?"

"I don't know how much use I can be, but sure, I'll scare the hell out of him," he replied.

Jack got up and ran to cover on the same side as the man, moving deeper into the woods next to a dead tree. He stopped, searching the trees ahead for movement.

The Tack dove out of the sun without a sound, hitting Tom in the back of the head with its knee, knocking him out cold. It unhooked its arms from its wings, folded its wings as it grabbed his body with its clawed hand, turned him over, elongating its face, baring the black, plated teeth, and then bit his throat out, all in one easy motion.

Brian saw what the Tack had done and froze in place for the count of three, long enough for Bob and Erica to get up and cover the short distance. Bob kicked Brian in the side of the head, knocking him out, while Erica picked up his gun.

Jack saw Bob and Erica get up and run toward Brian. So he started to swing his AR around, but it wouldn't move. It was stuck on a branch. But the branch was a large hand. The old tree spun around and a large arm struck Jack across the left side, sending him into the open trail without his rifle.

Jack got to his feet, shaky at first, but his head cleared fast. He looked back at what hit him, but didn't see anything except trees. He felt him before he saw him—fifteen feet away was a man standing in the trail, with an AR pointed at his chest. Jack smiled. "Hello, Brad, I guess it shouldn't surprise me that you're still alive."

Brad finally recognized Jack. "I should have let Scout kill you on Admiralty."

Jack's eyes were wild. His lips distorted by the scars, curled in a sinister grin.

"It's fate."

Brad realized that the sick son-of-a-bitch finally had the duel he'd always craved.

Both knew that only one of them would walk away.

Brad also knew his AR's 5.56 wouldn't go through the vest Jack had on, and that Jack knew it also. They both also knew the SIG 226's 9mm round that Jack had in his holster would have no problem going through Brad's jacket and shirt.

So Brad threw the AR at Jack's feet, catching him off guard for a split second. Jack wasn't fooled and he went for his pistol. But that slight delay was all that Brad was hoping for. He was already grabbing the big revolver from his bandoleer holster and bringing it up with two hands just as Jack's pistol was coming level. The big .50 caliber revolver roared first. The 440-grain bullet traveled the distance in less than a hundredth of a second and hit the ceramic plate of the vest. The plate had stopped the sniper rifle round earlier, slightly weakening its integrity, but it still stopped the massive slug from going through. But the bullet transferred its 2,500 foot-pounds of energy to Jack's chest, destroying the sternum, bursting capillaries, rupturing arteries and veins in his chest and turning the lungs to jelly. His heart stopped before he hit the ground.

Brad walked over to Jack, lying on his back with his arms out wide, the SIG still in his right hand. Jack was looking at the sky, blinking, trying to breathe. Blood bubbles coming from his mouth popped, sending small splatters of blood across his face. Within seconds the bubbles stopped and Jack's eyes glazed over.

Brad put the 500 away and turned to Erica. He could see the question in her eyes. But she ran over and jumped in his arms, giving him a hard kiss. Then she pulled out Brad's S&W 500, moving it out of the way, "Ow, that hurt." Brad smiled, took the 500 in his hand, and picking her up, continued the kiss.

Bob smiled. "It's about time," he said, turning his attention to the man he'd kicked in the head. Erica had told him his name was Brian, and that he was the leader of this disaster. But Brian wasn't moving, and his color wasn't good. So Bob bent down and checked his pulse, confirming what he thought. His kick to stop him worked better than expected.

Bob looked over at Brad and Erica. They had come up for air, but Erica was examining the cuts on Brad's face.

"They said you were dead," Erica said to Brad.

"They missed me, but I still won't forgive them for killing my bloody Mary," Brad said, and then looked at Bob.

Bob smiled, "I missed my flight."

Erica looked at Bob, then back to Brad. "Fuck both of you. You could have called or something."

Brad said, "I promise, next time I'm dead, I'll call you." They all laughed, and started to look around at the carnage. The Tack was sitting at the edge of a rock cliff, the color of the stones. The stone Rhunken wasn't in sight.

"What do you want to do with all these bodies?" Bob asked.

Brad replied, "I'm a big believer in the three S's."

Erica asked the question with her eyes.

Bob laughed, and then answered her, "Shoot, shovel and shut up."

CHAPTER 48

BRAD, ERICA AND BOB SPENT the rest of the day retrieving the firearms scattered over the valley. When they got back, they noticed the dead Tacks were gone, to no one's surprise. Erica was a little disappointed she didn't get samples, but she let it go. They packed up the unnecessary camp equipment and moved it down to the bay shoreline, leaving one tent up and the cot in the mine room. Then they buried the bodies in shallow graves in a muskeg near the mine, covering the graves with rocks, logs and moss, blending them in with the landscape as much as possible. Before dumping Spike's body, Brad wiped his prints off the sniper rifle, and ammo, and then pressed Spike's fingers to the rifle to apply his prints to it. He did the same to the remaining ammunition. Brad then put the rifle and ammunition in its hard case using gloves. Bob found Brian's cell phone and put it in the case with the rifle. Brad nodded at Bob.

"What's with the fingerprints? The guy's dead already," Erica asked Brad.

"It may come in handy sometime," was Brad's answer.

It was nearly ten o-clock when they were done with their task, and they were all wiped out. Bob got three beers out of the cooler. They weren't Alaskan, but they were cold, and he handed Erica and Brad one each and raised his beer in a toast. "Here's to luck." Brad and Erica raised their beers, and then all three took a long drink.

The stone Rhunken came out of the woods. It slowly walked over to the mine entrance and gave out a low rumble. Then he moseyed over to a salmonberry patch at the edge of the campsite and started eating some of the extremely ripe berries. Within minutes two old female Rhunken came out and joined him. The last one out of the mine was the oldest Rhunken Bob had ever seen. She was light gray and her skin sagged heavily as she moved slowly and stiffly to the berry patch. The stone male and other female brought her branches from the plants and she slowly picked off and ate the red and yellow berries. The Tack hadn't moved. It was just looking at Brad.

Bob saw the Tack watching Brad and said, "I think you've got a friend."

When Brad made eye contact, the Tack changed color to a lighter gray. "I was wondering about that. Any ideas on how to handle him?"

Bob shook his head. "Nope, you're the only PCO I've ever heard of that's had a pet Tack. But I think you'd have better luck with a rattlesnake."

Brad smiled and said, "Hey, thanks for your help."

"I'm hungry, and I need some hot water so I can clean up. Will one of you start a fire?" Erica asked, getting up and digging through the plastic food tote. Brad restarted the fire, while Bob dug out a big aluminum pot and filled it with water from a blue five-gallon jug, and set it on the fire.

Erica found a big can of stew and some sourdough bread, and handed them to Bob. Going to the tent, she grabbed a change of clothes, soap and the like. After a few minutes she picked up the hot water and set up her wash site just behind the old rusted boiler.

Bob opened the stew can with a P-38, and Brad got up to retrieve two more beers. Handing one to Bob, he asked, "How did you miss your flight?"

Erica yelled out from behind the boiler, "I want to hear too, so speak loud."

Bob dumped the stew in a pot and placed it on the fire, then sat back in his chair and opened the beer. "We were already checked in, if you want to call it that, for the WCC–chartered flight. And as they called for us to start boarding, I received a call on my cell from a friend I used to work with in the DOD. He said he needed to talk to me, and told me it was urgent. He said that he had just landed, and would give me a ride to Jackson Hole in his private jet. Well, who could pass that up? So I let the WCC plane take off without me. But my friend and his jet never showed up."

"Did he ever call back?" Brad asked.

Bob shook his head. "Nope. So I cussed a bit and arranged to take a scheduled flight, but canceled it when I heard about the crash."

"Wow, that was lucky," Erica yelled.

Bob stirred the stew and then continued. "Lucky. I thought so too at the time. Oh, Erica, just so you know, I did try to call, but I wasn't going to call your office and I didn't have your personal number and Brad doesn't have a cell phone. I did call Brad's home phone, a couple of times, but he never answered it, and I wasn't going to leave a message. But anyway, it's amazing how quickly life gets locked up when people think you're dead. So it took a great deal of time to unfreeze my assets before I could get up to Alaska. And I didn't want to go to the WCC office, especially after I heard who the new boss was. Something I really didn't want to deal with. Remember, I was retiring."

Bob stirred the steaming stew again, and the scent made Brad's mouth water. Now he felt famished. Brad said, "You must have known something was wrong. You stayed out of sight for a while and then wrote the note leading me here."

"I guess I did have a bad feeling about something. I found out about the Admiralty lair. Good job with that, by the way. And it wasn't too long after that, someone must have found out I was still alive, because I discovered someone was following me. At first I figured it was the IRS trying to catch me is some sort of scam. I even called them to double-check that they knew I was still kicking."

Bob dished out some stew, handed it to Brad, got some for

himself, and continued between bites. "That's when I received a text on my phone. All it said was "Anthony Morris," and that's when my conspiracy theory alarms went off. I think they wanted to know the location of this place. I had already sent you a package with some notes on the two colonies—this one and the one on Admiralty, including cryptic directions to both places before the crash. I figured I'd give you the problem of dealing with these problems however you wanted. You know, I am retired, after all. Then I lost my tail and came up here to check out Anthony's lair. After looking at it, I could see that you probably never got the package because I sent it to the WCC address. So, I had to have a second key made, and then I sent that to your Juneau office along with the directions again. In retrospect, I probably should have done that with the first package. Well, anyway, the second time worked, and you showed up. That's about it."

Erica came out from behind the boiler. Her hair was wet, and she had clean clothes on; they looked new. She threw Brad a towel. "Your turn. If you want hot water, you'll have to heat some more."

Then she asked Bob, "Brad said the second letter was postmarked Seattle?"

"That's easy. I went to Haines, had the key made and then sent the letter from there, in another envelope to my landlady in Seattle, and asked her to put it in the mail for me."

"I guess I'm not as good as you when it comes to losing tails. I was also being followed and I thought I lost him before heading up here," Brad said.

Bob nodded, "They probably got more serious with you, went high tech. Odds are, you have a tracking device on your boat.

Brad grabbed another five-gallon water jug and went behind the boiler tank.

Erica sat down with her stew. "Brian said this was about some Tack training program."

Bob nodded. "As with most ideas, it started off innocently enough. The Rhunken have a sense of smell about twice as keen as a dog's and they're more intelligent, but the biggest factor was the ability to scent change and get past guard dogs. The DHS asked if they could be trained for anti-drug work. I didn't think it would work, but I wasn't dead set against it at first. Then the Russians had the idea of using the scent change abilities as well as the manipulation of their heat signature to bypass multiple layers of security, for sabotage or assassinations. That idea scared the U.S. and NATO, so instead of outlawing the program, everyone wanted trained Rhunken. By then I was fighting it tooth and nail, and therefore handed my hat and got removed from the project.

"That's a fucking stupid idea," Brad said.

Both Bob and Erica smiled and said at the same time, "That's what I said."

"If I remember right, it was the Department of Homeland Security's idea. As a matter of fact, your Dr. Clark was one of the nuts that started it. Thank God it didn't work. So, Jim Starkey finally put an end to it about six months ago," Bob added.

Erica said, "But it kind of worked. Anthony was able to train them."

Bob nodded, "Yeah, he did. But he was the only one out of dozens. We found out that even the reported Russian success was bullshit, so all of us senior PCOs, including Anthony, agreed to terminate the program, and Jim agreed."

"My guess is that someone at the DHS didn't like that," Brad said, still behind the boiler.

"I guess it also explains Dr. Clark's appointment, but why all the cloak and dagger, following you and Brad around? Aren't these lairs locations documented?" Erica asked.

Bob shook his head. "No, not these. It was actually my idea to keep them secret. I knew there would be way too much temptation for management to come and visit the sites. You know, to check on progress. I only knew the locations of the two training colonies, and that was only because they were in my area. And I didn't even learn those until after Jeff Moore was killed and I had to clean up that mess. That's when I met Brad."

Erica looked at Bob. "So, now what?"

But Brad answered, "Nothing. We just go back to work, just like nothing happened. You just tell them, nothing was found and Brian sent you back early."

Bob agreed. "Yep, exactly. But you may want to add something about an internal squabble to give them something to think about."

Brad came from around the boiler still drying his hair with the towel. He had pants on, but the top button was undone and he had no shirt on.

Erica gave him a long look, put what was left of her stew on the ground and got up. "Ok, it's time for bed. Good night, Bob." She grabbed Brad's hand and turned him, pulling him along.

They could hear Bob laughing softly as they made their way to the tent.

Brad woke and looked at his watch: 2:31. He could feel Erica's warmth and hear her steady breathing, telling him she was asleep. It had been a long time, and this was the first time since his wife passed that he felt—well, he didn't really know how he felt, almost like he was cheating. Feeling uneasy, he got up carefully, grabbed his pants, went outside, and put them on. It was dark, but the sky was clear and the stars were brilliant. He looked south in the direction of the island with a rocky hilltop, not knowing what to think. The light caught his attention, not from the ground, but from the sky. To the north, the aurora borealis danced. Not the slow beautiful shifting of light greens and pinks, but a vibrant, shooting dance with greens and brilliant reds covering the whole northern hemisphere.

Erica came out of the tent and saw Brad standing in his bare feet. She had one of the sleeping bags wrapped around her. "What are you doing?"

Brad just smiled and tilted his head up, and she followed his gaze.

Erica gasped, but didn't say anything. He put his arm around her shoulders and they watched in silence.

Erica finally asked, "You looked sad when I came out. Everything OK?"

Brad turned slightly and said, "Yeah, I think everything is just fine."

CHAPTER 49

"WELCOME BACK. WOW, YOU look great! You must have had a great time," Kathy, the WCC receptionist, said when Erica came in through the glass doors of the main entrance.

Erica blushed slightly and replied, "Better than I expected."

"I was told to call up to the CEO's office and let him know when you came in," Kathy added.

"I would expect nothing else," was all Erica said as she made her way to the stairs.

An hour later the call came that summoned her to the CEO's office. Erica took a deep breath, turned on the recorder on her phone and put it in her pocket, then headed up the stairs. She decided to take the stairs instead of the elevator, mostly to give her more time to collect herself. When she got to the CEO's lobby, the blond secretary coolly said, "Go right in, they're expecting you."

"They?" Erica thought.

She opened the door and walked in. The CEO was sitting behind his big desk with his hands folded and resting on top of it. His bodyguard was standing behind him, just off to the left from her view with his hands behind his back. She had never seen him in the office, since normally he waited outside. And the chairs facing the desk were occupied with two men she didn't recognize. Both were in their fifties with short gray hair and nice suits.

"Good morning, Miss Hunt. I didn't expect you back so soon, or returning alone," said the CEO.

Erica just gave him a small smile and waited. He hadn't asked a question.

Slightly annoyed, the CEO asked, "Well, can you explain that?"

"I'm surprised Brian didn't call. We didn't find any sign of Rhunken at the site, so he sent me back early. He just said the rest would stay a day or so, and then head back," Erica said.

The CEO asked, "Why?"

"He didn't give me much of an explanation, just that some of the mercenaries you hired were upset with you and he wanted time to cool them down. So I caught a ride with Brad Michaels back to Juneau," she said.

All the men snapped their heads toward her. She kept a small smile as she looked back at each of them. Then the two men facing the CEO shifted in their seats. The bodyguard dipped his head slightly, but otherwise didn't move. The CEO sat forward and glared at Erica.

"When was this?" he asked.

"Yesterday morning."

The men traded glances again, but said nothing to each other.

"I don't believe we've been introduced," Erica said to the two unknown men.

But the CEO broke in. His face was now red, "That's not necessary. Thank you, Miss Hunt. You may go."

Erica gave them one more pleasant smile and left the office. Other than the presence of the two unknown men, it went just as Brad said it would.

The liberated cellphone buzzed, but Brad let it go to voice mail. After a few seconds the phone gave a short buzz and he checked the message. Dr. Clark's voice said, "What the fuck is going on? Call me now."

Brad smiled and waited. Ten minutes passed and a black limousine pulled up to the front of the WCC building. Brad opened the phone, selected the recently received phone number, but didn't hit send. He just set it next to the dead mercenary's sniper rifle with his gloved hands and looked through the scope.

The front door of the WCC building opened and the bodyguard came out, looked around and waved for the CEO to come out. Brad pushed the send button in the phone, then speaker. The phone's speaker started to ring.

Dr. Clark and two other men came out the door, but the CEO stopped, opened his coat and pulled out his cell phone. Brad could tell he recognized the number before he answered it.

"What the fuck is going on?" came the CEO's voice over the cell phone speaker.

"I told you I would come for payment. It's due."

Dr. Clark knew the voice and it froze him in place. He heard the line go dead.

He never heard the shot.